I0763274

THE RESONANCE FRACTURE

Victoria E. Charles

GODDESS
& GLYPHS
PRESS

THE RESONANCE FRACTURE

First edition: 2026
Printed in the United States of America
ISBN: 979-8-9945109-1-9

For those who were held when they could not hold themselves.
And for those who did the holding without being asked.

What is fractured does not ask to be made whole.
It asks to be handled correctly.

Content Note

This novel explores themes of violence, coercion, and violation, as well as the psychological impact of trauma. These elements are integral to the story's examination of power, consent, and survival, and are presented without sensationalism. However, some readers may find portions of the book distressing.

Please read with care and at your own pace.

I

THE WORK OF LIVING

Nearly a year after the last machine screamed and fell silent, the valley learned how to make ordinary sounds again.

Hammers struck wood. Pots clinked. Someone whistled tunelessly while hauling water up from the stream. Smoke rose in lazy columns instead of urgent signals. Gardens had taken root where there had once been only trampled moss and ash—rows of greens, stubborn squash vines, herbs tucked close to stone walls like secrets being kept warm.

Shelters had become structures.

Structures had become homes.

Solar panels scavenged from old facilities angled along the southern ridge, catching the sun without ceremony. Cables ran neatly into battery banks housed in stone sheds that once held emergency supplies. The pumps still worked when needed, but people preferred the old ways now—less noise, fewer dependencies.

Not perfect.

Not permanent.

But chosen.

Rowan watched it all from the edge of the ridge path, Bramble stretched at his feet, tail thumping against the earth with slow satisfaction. The dog had grown broader in the chest, calmer in the way animals did when they decided a place was theirs. He barely lifted his head when people passed now.

That alone told Rowan more than any scanner ever could.

Isorae was below him near the stream, sleeves rolled to her elbows, hands submerged in cold water as she rinsed dirt from freshly pulled roots. Sunlight caught in her hair, turning it warm and almost human-looking—if you didn't know how closely to watch her breath, or how the air bent just slightly when she moved.

She looked… settled.

The word still startled him when it surfaced.

She straightened, glancing up the slope as if she felt his attention before she saw him. Her mouth curved—not surprised, not searching. Just knowing.

Rowan felt the familiar pull low in his ribs, quiet and constant. No surge. No alarm. Just alignment.

Behind him, voices drifted up from the nearest cluster of cabins.

Dax's laughter—sharp, unmistakable—followed by Erin's voice, dry and amused. Something crashed. Someone swore. A moment later, the crash resolved into shared laughter and the sound of footsteps retreating toward one of the newer cabins with an actual door and a window someone had bothered to glass.

Rowan shook his head faintly, a corner of his mouth lifting.

Across the clearing, Evan sat on the steps of a low stone structure beside Ryan, their shoulders pressed together, heads bent close in quiet conversation. Ryan gestured animatedly, hands moving too fast, and Evan laughed—open, unguarded. The sound still caught Rowan off balance sometimes. It was easy to forget how new that laughter was.

Silas moved along the perimeter without being obvious about it. He never stopped doing that. Even now—gardens in place, doors on hinges, smoke rising peacefully—Silas still checked sightlines and listened for things no one else noticed.

Old habits.

Necessary ones.

The valley did not object.

Rowan felt that too.

Not approval.

Not command.

Accommodation.

He descended the path toward Isorae, boots finding the right places without conscious thought. The ground felt solid beneath him—

no tightening, no warning hum. When he reached her, she didn't turn immediately. She finished rinsing the last root, set it carefully into a woven basket, and only then leaned back against the stone at the stream's edge.

"You're staring again," she said softly.

"You keep doing interesting things," he replied.

She smiled, eyes still on the water. "I am washing vegetables."

"Dangerous work."

She glanced up at him then, expression warming. "You settled?"

"For now."

Her gaze lingered on his face—not searching, not afraid. Something steadier. Something chosen. She reached for him without hurry, fingers brushing his wrist, then his forearm, grounding herself there as if the contact no longer needed negotiation.

"I can feel the land when you're close," she said. "It's… quieter."

Rowan crouched beside her, resting his forearms on his knees. "Good quiet?"

"Yes." A pause. "The kind that doesn't mean hiding."

They sat like that for a while, listening to the stream talk to itself and the valley go about the business of being inhabited. Rowan became aware—again—of how different this quiet felt from the one that had preceded violence. This quiet had weight. History. Memory.

Something earned.

From farther up the slope, voices drifted again—people arguing gently about whether the new western shelter needed reinforcing before winter, whether the path down to the stream should be widened, whether the place deserved a name yet or if naming it would invite maps, signals, and the wrong kind of curiosity.

Rowan caught the thread of the conversation and felt Isorae's fingers tighten slightly on his arm.

"They keep circling it," she murmured.

"A name?"

"Yes." Her lips curved faintly. "They want to know what to call what kept them alive."

Rowan exhaled slowly. "Names change things."

"They don't summon," she said. "They recognize."

He studied the way the water moved around stone. The way roots gripped the banks without strangling them. The way the valley seemed to lean—not inward, not outward—but around the people inside it.

"Let them talk," he said finally. "The land will tell us when it's ready."

Isorae rested her forehead briefly against his shoulder, a quiet, private touch. "It already has."

Rowan didn't answer. He didn't need to.

Above them, the sky remained empty. No hum. No fracture. No distant pressure testing the edges of reality.

But far beyond the ridgelines—far beyond where anyone here could feel it—systems still turned, models still recalculated, and someone, somewhere, was still thinking about what had gone wrong.

For now, though, the valley allowed itself to exist.

And Rowan allowed himself—just this once—to believe that might be enough.

By late afternoon, the light softened into something amber and forgiving.

Someone had strung dried herbs along a line between two cabins. Children—no longer kept close to the center out of fear—ran the length of the clearing chasing Bramble, who allowed the indignity with patient tolerance before trotting back to Rowan's side. Smoke from cooking fires layered the air with rosemary, onion, and something sweet Rowan couldn't quite place.

Isorae moved through it all easily now.

Not floating.

Not shimmering.

Walking.

She carried the basket of vegetables toward one of the communal tables, nodding to Nora as she passed. Nora smiled back—tired, real, human—and went back to coaxing dough into shape with flour-dusted hands. Parker leaned against a post nearby, one hand resting absently where her ribs had once been broken, watching the children with an expression that mixed relief and something like grief she hadn't finished processing yet.

Rowan tracked Isorae instinctively, even as he joined Silas near the perimeter where the trees thickened and the land sloped into deeper shadow.

"You feel it," Silas said quietly, not looking at him.

Rowan nodded. "I do."

"Not wrong," Silas added. "Just… different."

The ground beneath them felt steady, but not inert. It responded the way muscle did when it knew how to move now—no longer flinching, no longer guessing.

Silas glanced toward the heart of the settlement. "They're getting comfortable."

"They earned it."

Silas's mouth twitched. "That doesn't stop the world from noticing."

Rowan's gaze followed a hawk circling high above the ridge—too high to mean anything. Probably. "It hasn't forgotten us."

"No," Silas agreed. "But neither have we."

They stood in companionable silence for a moment, listening to the land breathe around them. When Rowan turned back toward the clearing, Isorae had finished unloading the basket and was wiping her hands on a cloth, laughter tugging at her voice as Erin said something dry and sharp enough to earn a shove from Dax.

Dax grinned like he enjoyed the shove entirely too much.

Rowan felt the familiar pull again—low, grounded, unurgent. He crossed the clearing without hurrying, stopping behind Isorae as she turned, surprised only for a heartbeat before her shoulders relaxed.

"You smell like smoke," she murmured.

"So do you."

She tilted her head, studying him. "I like it on you."

His hand settled at her waist without ceremony. Not claiming. Not guarding. Simply there. The land did not tighten around them. It did not lean.

It allowed.

"You done pacing for the night?" she asked.

He nodded. "Trying to be."

"Good." A pause, her thumb tracing the seam of his sleeve. "I don't like it when you circle until dawn."

Rowan's expression softened. "Neither do I."

As evening deepened, lanterns were lit—not in haste, not all at once. People gathered where they pleased. Conversations braided and loosened. Evan and Ryan disappeared toward one of the western cabins, hands brushing, shoulders bumping with the casual intimacy of something no longer hidden or fragile.

The valley watched.

Not possessively.

Witnessing.

Rowan felt it settle into its deeper rhythms as night came on—not bracing, not scanning, but attentive in the way old things were attentive. A presence that remembered danger without letting it dictate every breath.

Isorae leaned into him, her head resting against his chest. "They're starting to believe this can last," she said quietly.

"Can it?"

She considered. "Nothing lasts forever." Then, softer: "But this can endure."

Rowan pressed his lips briefly to her hair, a wordless answer.

Above them, the sky remained empty and dark, stars sharp and indifferent and ancient. Somewhere far beyond that, systems continued to turn, minds continued to model outcomes that refused to resolve.

But here—here—the land held what it had claimed.

And Rowan, for the first time in a long while, did not feel like a boundary under siege.

He felt like part of something learning how to live.

2
THE NAMING

The idea does not arrive all at once.

It surfaces the way things do here now—slowly, from different mouths, at different moments, until it can no longer be ignored.

It begins with Nora.

She's the one who says it first, not as a declaration, but as an inconvenience.

"We need to call this place something," she mutters, adjusting the strap of a water bucket on her shoulder as she passes Erin near the eastern gardens. "I'm tired of saying the valley like we're afraid it'll hear us and leave."

Erin snorts. "You say that like it hasn't already decided it owns us."

"Exactly," Nora replies. "You name things you plan to stay with."

The words linger longer than either of them expects.

Later, Parker brings it up again while helping Silas reinforce one of the new cabins along the slope. She pauses mid-hammer, looking out over the widening spread of structures—cottages and cabins now; paths worn smooth by feet that no longer move like they're fleeing.

"I keep thinking about maps," she says.

Silas glances at her. "You planning to make one?"

"Maybe. But maps need labels."

Silas considers the land—the way the stone rises beneath the trees, the way the ground remembers weight, remembers footsteps. "Whatever we call it," he says slowly, "it'll need to fit. The land won't tolerate something wrong."

Parker smiles faintly. "I think it already knows its name. We're just late to it."

By midday, the conversation has spread.

Not formally. No one gathers everyone together. It happens in fragments—over meals, during repairs, while children chase each other between cabins and gardens that didn't exist a year ago.

Evan mentions it while stirring a pot over the fire. Ryan perks up immediately, enthusiasm bright and unguarded.

"Yeah," Ryan says. "I hate telling people back home I live in a valley somewhere west. It sounds like I joined a cult."

Evan smirks. "You kind of did."

"Still. Cults have names."

Dax overhears and offers three terrible suggestions just to see Erin roll her eyes.

Rowan listens.

He doesn't participate yet. He feels the land respond every time the conversation circles closer—not tightening, not warning, but shifting, like something turning its face toward a sound it recognizes.

Isorae feels it too.

She stands near the stream, watching the water curl around stones smoothed by centuries of insistence. When Rowan joins her, she doesn't look up.

"They're still circling it," she says quietly.

He nods. "They are."

"It won't accept a name chosen lightly."

"No."

She finally turns to him. Her expression is thoughtful—grounded. Present. "Names are agreements," she says. "This place has already agreed to us. Now it wants to know what we'll call it when we're not afraid it will vanish."

Rowan looks across the settlement—the gardens, the cabins, the people moving without flinching when shadows shift.

"What if they get it wrong?"

Isorae smiles. "Then the name won't stick."

That evening, someone finally says it out loud.

Not as a suggestion. As an observation.

Ryan again—sitting on a log near the fire, hands wrapped around a chipped mug, eyes tracking the way the ground seems to subtly rise and fall beneath the light like something breathing.

"This place wakes when things try to hurt it," he says.

A few heads turn.

Silence gathers—not heavy, not tense.

Ryan shrugs, suddenly self-conscious. "I mean… you feel it, right? Like the stone itself stirs. Like it remembers how to stand up."

Rowan feels the valley shift—not dramatically. Just enough.

Erin's brow furrows. "Stone that wakes…"

Dax tilts his head. "Stonewake."

The word lands.

Not with thunder.

With recognition.

The fire pops softly. The wind threads through the trees without resistance. Somewhere beneath them, stone settles—not bracing, not withdrawing.

Accepting.

No one speaks for a moment.

Then Nora exhales. "Yeah," she says. "That's it."

Isorae's breath catches—not in surprise, but in relief.

Rowan feels it seal—not like a lock, but like a door finally knowing which way it opens.

Stonewake.

The valley does not answer.

It already knows who it is.

No one votes.

There is no raised hand, no formal agreement.

The name simply begins to be used.

"Meet me by the western rise," Erin says later, distracted, already walking. She pauses, frowns slightly, then corrects herself without thinking. "The western rise in Stonewake."

The word feels strange for half a breath.

Then right.

Dax grins at her back. "See? You said it like it's always been that."

She flips him off without turning around.

By morning, it's everywhere.

"Stonewake's water runs colder at dawn," Evan tells Ryan as they haul baskets from the stream.

Ryan hums. "That's because it's awake earlier than we are."

Silas uses it when assigning watches. Nora mutters it while mending torn fabric. Parker says it softly to herself while walking the perimeter paths, testing the sound of it in her mouth like a prayer she doesn't quite believe in yet.

Each time it's spoken, the valley responds—not dramatically, not performatively.

Paths settle where feet expect them.

Stone firms under load.

Roots ease back instead of catching ankles.

The land doesn't change its nature.

It clarifies it.

Rowan notices it most when he's alone.

He walks the upper slope near dusk, following no path in particular, letting the quiet press against him the way it always has. When he speaks the name aloud—just once, low and steady—the ground beneath his boots warms faintly, like acknowledgment traveling up through stone.

Stonewake.

Not owned.

Not claimed.

Recognized.

Isorae finds him there later, barefoot despite the cooling air. She doesn't ask why he's smiling.

"It accepted it," she says.

He nods. "It already had."

She steps closer, resting her palm flat against his chest, then lowers it slowly to the earth between them. Her shimmer is calm now—no defensive edge, no flicker of pain. Just presence.

"Names anchor," she murmurs. "But they also invite."

Rowan exhales. "Invite what?"

Her gaze lifts to the darkening canopy, thoughtful—not fearful. "Witness."

That night, the fire burns longer without tending.

Mist drifts low but loose, uncoiled.

Stonewake does not brace.

It does not listen for threat.

It listens for itself.

And somewhere deep beneath the village—beneath the cottages and gardens and the bones of things that have chosen to stay—the valley settles more fully into its shape.

Not as refuge.

But as a place that has remembered how to stand up.

3
What Names Make Visible

The next morning settles warm and slow over Stonewake, sunlight threading through the newer cabins and half-finished roofs, catching on the pale green of planted rows. Smoke rises from hearths instead of emergency fires. The sound of hammer on wood is steady, unhurried. Life has stopped bracing.

That is how Rowan knows something is coming.

He feels it as space—too much room in the air, the way stillness sometimes swells before it breaks into motion.

Isorae is already awake when he returns to their cabin. She stands at the open doorway, hair loose, bare shoulders warm with sun, watching the valley the way one watches a living thing breathe. When she turns, her smile is unguarded.

"You're thinking too loudly," she says.

"Am I?" He steps behind her, arms sliding around her waist without urgency, just contact. Just confirmation.

"Yes," she murmurs, leaning back into him. "You always do when things feel good."

He exhales against her hair. "I don't trust it."

She tilts her head, amused. "You trust the land."

"I trust what it does," he corrects. "Not what it promises."

Her fingers lace with his where they rest against her stomach. "Stonewake didn't promise anything."

"No," he agrees. "It answered."

That word still does something to her. He feels it in the way her breath changes, the faint pulse of shimmer beneath her skin—not defensive now, not flaring. Responsive.

Alive.

She turns in his arms slowly, deliberately, presses her palm flat to his chest. "You feel different since the name."

"So do you."

Her smile softens. "I feel… here."

The word lands between them heavier than it should.

Rowan tightens his grip, just slightly. Protective. Anchoring. "You are."

She studies his face, then nods, as if deciding something. "Come with me."

She doesn't wait for agreement.

They walk the long way down through the village, past Evan and Ryan arguing cheerfully over whether a roof beam is level ("It is absolutely level." "It's lying to you."), past Nora stringing herbs to dry, past Parker laughing with a child whose name Rowan still hasn't learned but recognizes by the sound of his footsteps.

Isorae leads him beyond the last cabin, past the gardens, to where the land rises gently and stone shows through soil like memory breaking the surface.

She steps onto it barefoot.

"This," she says quietly, "is where it shifted."

Rowan feels it the moment his boots touch stone.

Stonewake hums—not loudly—but in a way that feels like being seen without being watched.

Isorae kneels, palms to the ground, eyes closed. Her shimmer threads outward, not as signal, not as beacon, but as conversation. The land answers in pressure and warmth, stone firming, wind easing.

Rowan drops beside her, one hand braced in the dirt, the other at her back. The connection slides into place like a joint resetting.

She gasps softly in recognition.

"It knows me differently now," she whispers.

Rowan's jaw tightens. "How?"

"Not as a breach." She opens her eyes, luminous, steady. "As someone who stayed."

That should be comforting.

It isn't.

Rowan pulls her closer, forehead to forehead, grounding both of them. "That makes you visible."

She smiles, feral and fond. "I've always been visible. I just wasn't claimed by place."

The word *claimed* sparks something low and dark in him. A responsibility.

Below them, Stonewake goes on living. Laughter. Work. Breath. A village settling into its bones.

Above them, the sky remains empty.

For now.

And far beyond the ridgelines—too far to be felt yet, too precise to be accidental—something recalibrates.

Not in response to threat.

In response to stability.

Because names don't just anchor places.

They make them locatable.

4

THE PATTERN THEY KEEP

The light changes first.

It thins along the cabin walls, shifts angle through the open doorway, warms the wood where shadows had held overnight. Birdsong filters in—uneven, persistent—threading through the quiet the way breath returns after sleep.

Somewhere downhill, the smell of bread drifts upward, yeast and warmth carried on air that hasn't learned to hurry yet.

Ryan wakes to it.

Not with a jolt. Not with the old reflexive inventory of exits and threats. Just waking — the quiet, ordinary act of opening his eyes and staying where he is.

Beside him, Evan shifts, muttering something incoherent, an arm settling across Ryan's ribs with familiar weight. Ryan stays still, adjusting his breath to match Evan's without thinking about it. Evan sleeps deeply now, the way people do when their bodies are no longer bracing for interruption.

Ryan learned that pattern the hard way.

He watches Evan for a moment — not studying, not searching — just registering. The scar at his temple. The faint crease between his brows that never quite disappears. Proof of a life that didn't soften him, but didn't break him either.

Ryan slips free of the bed carefully, easing boots on before the cold floor can fully bite. Outside, the valley is already moving.

Stonewake doesn't wake all at once. It stirs in pockets.

A hammer strikes wood somewhere uphill. Voices drift from the fire circle. Smoke curls lazily from chimneys, not signals, not warnings — just the byproduct of people feeding themselves.

Ryan grabs a basket on his way past the door. He doesn't remember when it became his habit to carry one. It just… happened.

He moves through the morning without fanfare.

Helps Nora rehang a door that's caught on warped wood. Carries water to Silas, who accepts it with a grunt and no commentary. Laughs when Parker loses a brief, undignified battle with a chicken that clearly has its own priorities.

"Unbelievable," Parker mutters, brushing straw from her sleeves.

Ryan grins, breathless. "I was rooting for you."

By midmorning, Ryan is dusted in flour and sawdust, hands smelling faintly of something green and sharp he never bothered to ask about. No one thanks him. No one needs to.

Stonewake doesn't work that way.

At the edge of the gardens, movement catches his attention.

Isorae sits on a low stone wall, sleeves rolled, braid slipping loose down her back. Erin stands in front of her, chalk smudged across one hand, gesturing at a board balanced between crates — diagrams half-drawn, half-erased. Rowan lingers nearby, not hovering, not disengaged, listening the way he always does, attention split between voices and the land beneath them.

They look like people solving a problem that matters only because they expect to be here tomorrow.

Isorae laughs — bright, unguarded — and Rowan's mouth curves in response, brief and unselfconscious. Erin says something sharp and efficient, taps the board once, already moving on. Dax leans against a post a few steps away, watching Erin with the kind of focus that pretends to be casual and isn't.

Ryan slows.

Not to stare.

Just long enough to register the shape of it.

This — whatever this is — holds.

He turns back toward the cabins instead, adjusting the basket against his hip, already thinking about dinner. About whether Evan will eat if he adds too much spice. About whether bread counts as a vegetable if it's warm enough.

Behind him, Stonewake continues its quiet work.

Footpaths settle. Wind threads cleanly through leaves. The land makes room where people expect it to.

Not for any single person.

For the pattern they're all choosing to keep.

And somewhere between the gardens and the worktable — between laughter and planning — Erin steps away from the chalkboard, already reaching for something else that needs doing.

Erin closes the door behind them.

Not carefully. Not forcefully.

Just enough.

The latch settles with a muted click that means privacy, not performance.

Dax hears it anyway.

The corner of his mouth lifts as he turns. "You finished yelling at geometry?"

"I finished tolerating it," she says, shrugging her satchel off her shoulder. Glass shifts inside. Tools knock softly against each other. She sets it down where it won't tip, already moving past him.

Three strides.

That's all it takes.

She grabs the front of his shirt and shoves him back against the worktable hard enough to make it creak — not because she needs leverage, but because she knows exactly how much force it takes to make him still.

Dax laughs — low, pleased, unmistakably aware.

"Good," he murmurs. "I was worried you'd start explaining."

She doesn't.

She kisses him like she's already decided what happens next.

No hesitation. No warmth yet. Teeth graze, mouths collide, breath sharp and intentional. Erin doesn't soften when she wants something — she sharpens, and Dax has always known better than to mistake that for anger.

His hands come to her hips instinctively, lifting her onto the table in one smooth motion, stepping in close enough that the space between them disappears entirely. Her thighs lock around him without thinking.

"You're wound tight," he says against her jaw, voice dark with amusement. "What happened?"

"Nothing," she snaps — then exhales sharply, the truth cutting through. "Which is the problem."

That earns him a slow smile.

He hooks two fingers beneath her chin, forcing her to look at him. His eyes are bright now — not playful, not casual. Focused.

"You want me to fix it," he says quietly, "or make it worse?"

Erin grins — feral, unapologetic. "Surprise me."

He doesn't rush her clothes.

That's the cruelty of it.

He takes his time stripping away her patience — kisses drawn out just long enough to make her breath hitch, mouth lingering where she's already too sensitive, hands claiming space inch by deliberate inch. He touches her like he's inventorying reaction, like he's memorizing exactly how much restraint it takes to make her shake.

Every pause is intentional.

Every moment he doesn't give her what she wants is a reminder that he could — and is choosing not to.

Her breath stutters despite herself, a sharp inhale she tries and fails to control as he finally thrusts into her.

He pins her wrists to the table—just long enough to feel the power of it. Just long enough to watch her eyes flash, to feel the immediate, feral pushback in her body.

Her pulse jumps under his grip.

That's what does it.

She snarls and bites his shoulder hard enough to mark him, teeth scraping skin with intent, not play.

Dax groans like it's a gift.

"Fuck," he breathes, tightening his hold at her waist, grounding her there, unyielding, each thrust harder than the last.

They move like a controlled detonation — not tender. Precision instead of chaos. Pressure traded knowingly, limits tested. Erin's laughter turns rough and breathless against his throat as he crowds her space, as she arches into him without hesitation, without apology.

She wants this.

He wants that she wants it.

The table creaks beneath them. Heat builds — not just between bodies, but in the air itself — skin slick, breath ragged, control narrowing down to sensation and instinct and the mutual understanding that neither of them is going to let this stop too soon.

The room heats.

The world narrows.

Outside, Stonewake continues its afternoon.

Wood splits. Water is hauled. Someone swears, someone laughs. Life goes on without ceremony.

Inside, the air fills with low sounds — rough breath, the scrape of skin, the quiet violence of want — and the unmistakable energy of two people who are not pretending this is new or fragile. They've survived too much to treat this like something delicate.

When it finally breaks — when the tension snaps instead of frays — it's not sudden.

It's earned.

Dax leans his forehead against hers, both of them breathing hard now, hands still firm at her hips, still certain, still holding.

The room smells like heat and iron and familiarity — like bodies that know each other well enough to fight and still choose closeness.

Dax exhales first, a shaky huff of a laugh. "You know," he says, voice rough and unguarded now, "one of these days that's going to get us killed."

Erin snorts softly, still catching her breath. "If it does," she says, fingers curling into his shirt again, unapologetic, "I'll make sure it was worth it."

He kisses her again — slower this time, deeper — not gentler, just anchored. The kind of kiss that says *I'm here, I'm not leaving, and I still know exactly what you are.*

Only after that do they separate.

Only after that does Erin straighten her clothes, roll her shoulders, reclaim her composure piece by piece — like armor settling back into place. Dax watches her do it with something that borders on reverence and doesn't try to hide it.

When they finally step outside minutes later, the valley doesn't react.

No tightening. No hum. No attention paid.

Stonewake accepts it.

Because this is what peace looks like, too.

And because the most dangerous thing about a place that finally feels safe—

is how easy it becomes to forget how much pressure it took to get there.

5
ORIENTATION

The afternoon stretches on.

Not lazily — productively. The kind of time that follows intimacy without interrupting it, where people return to their hands and tools still warm, still grounded. Stonewake exhales and keeps moving.

Rowan notices the first sign while splitting wood at the edge of the eastern terraces.

The axe lands clean, familiar, the rhythm steady — until the echo comes back a fraction of a second late.

Not enough to startle.

Enough to itch.

He pauses with the axe head resting in the stump, breath slow, listening.

The valley breathes.

But the breath doesn't land where it should.

Stonewake has developed habits over the past year — subtle ones, only noticeable if you've lived inside them long enough. Wind curling a certain way through the upper canopy. Birds lifting just before dusk in lazy arcs. The land answering effort with a quiet kind of cooperation.

This is… off-beat.

Rowan straightens slowly.

The hum beneath his ribs — the one he's learned not to chase or command — hasn't changed in strength.

It's changed in direction.

Halfway down the slope, Isorae feels it without knowing why.

She's walking with a basket tucked against her hip, bare feet dusted with soil, hair loose against her shoulders. She stops mid-step, almost frowning, and turns toward Rowan instinctively — not searching him out, just orienting.

"You felt that," she says when they're close enough to speak.

Rowan nods once. "Yeah."

Her expression tightens as she listens inward — not reaching for the land, not probing — simply allowing it space to answer if it wants to.

"It's not a threat," she murmurs. "Not yet."

That makes his jaw set.

They meet near the old stone line where the first shelters once stood — now replaced with cabins, gardens, smoke curling gently from chimneys. A village. A real one.

Too real to lose quietly.

Rowan sets the axe aside and takes her hand, grounding himself through the contact.

"What is it?"

Isorae hesitates.

The pause is small — but deliberate.

"Something brushed the outer resonance," she says finally. "Not probing. Not cutting."

"Then what?"

She swallows. "Listening without asking."

The hum beneath Rowan's sternum shifts again — not pain, not warning — but orientation, like a compass correcting itself without permission.

On the far side of the lower terraces, Erin straightens abruptly from where she's been recalibrating a handheld scanner.

Her brow furrows as the screen flickers — not spiking, not alarming — just… wrong.

"That's new," she mutters.

She runs the diagnostic again. Then a third time.

"I'm not getting a signal," she says slowly to no one in particular. "I'm getting an absence where one shouldn't be."

Further upslope, Dax pauses mid-stride where he's been reinforcing a footpath, sensing the change not through instruments but through Erin's voice carrying across the terraces.

"Define 'absence,'" he calls.

Erin doesn't answer immediately. She turns the device in her hands, frustration sharpening.

"Like something is present but refusing coherence," she replies. "Not masking. Not hiding. Just… not participating."

That's when Silas moves.

Not instinctively. Not prematurely.

He moves after Erin's words ripple outward and don't settle.

He heads for the ridge without comment, boots sure, posture already adjusting. From the highest point above Stonewake, he scans the tree line, the horizon, the sky.

Everything looks the same.

That's the problem.

No drones. No distortion. No weather anomalies.

Nothing that would justify the quiet tightening in his shoulders.

He exhales sharply and taps his comm.

"Rowan."

Rowan answers immediately. "Yeah."

"Something's standing just outside the valley's attention," Silas says. "I don't know how else to put it."

Isorae closes her eyes.

Not to reach outward — but to check herself.

For the briefest moment, her shimmer tightens, pulling inward instead of expanding, like light folding back toward its source. It isn't alarm. It isn't defense.

It's recognition brushing up against uncertainty.

She inhales slowly.

When she opens her eyes again, they're focused — not distant, not altered — just clear in a way that makes Rowan's spine go still.

"There's attention on the perimeter," she says carefully. "Not pressure. Not intrusion."

Rowan watches her face. "From where?"

She hesitates — not because she's afraid to answer, but because she's confirming it as she speaks.

"Outside the valley's awareness," she says. "Close enough to feel the outline. Far enough not to register as threat."

That's when Dax's voice carries from upslope, sharp with instinct rather than certainty.

"ARIS?"

Isorae shakes her head immediately. "No. Not like before."

She exhales, grounding herself before continuing.

"This isn't a system," she says. "It's not scanning. It's not mapping."

Rowan tightens his grip on her hand.

"Then what is it doing?"

Isorae's jaw sets.

"Orienting," she says.

"Like it's figured out where I am — and is deciding what that means."

Rowan's jaw tightens. "They're not taking you."

Her gaze softens for a heartbeat.

Then hardens.

"I don't think they're asking."

The valley shifts.

Not recoiling. Not bracing.

Adjusting its stance — the way a body does before a blow that hasn't landed yet.

Stonewake does not panic.

But it remembers how to prepare.

Rowan and Isorae remain where they are a while longer, listening as the land resettles into its altered rhythm before turning back toward the distant sounds of the village — laughter, movement, the ordinary music of people who do not yet know they are being observed.

Far beyond the trees — far enough that no sensor should reach — someone is already watching the place where the land wakes when it's touched.

Not to destroy it.

Not yet.
But to decide which piece of it to take first.

6

STILLNESS WITH TEETH

Stonewake does not relax all at once.

After the disturbance, there is a stretch of time where nothing visibly changes — where people keep moving because stopping would mean naming what just brushed past them. Tools are set down deliberately. Conversations resume, but softer. A few more eyes track the tree line than usual, then look away on purpose.

No alarm is raised.

No one calls a meeting.

The valley holds its posture.

It's only later — when no further wrongness arrives — that the air begins to loosen.

That is when the smell of bread drifts up from the communal oven near the lower gardens, where someone has decided — quietly — that tonight deserves something warm.

Warm, slow bread. The kind that takes time. Yeast and grain carried on late-afternoon air, tangled with woodsmoke and herbs crushed underfoot. Not the sharp, desperate baking of scarcity — but something made because Ryan trusted there would be an evening to eat it.

A long table has been set near the garden edge. Boards scavenged and sanded smooth, legs braced into the earth like they expect to stay awhile. People gather in ones and twos, bringing bowls, cups, whatever they were holding when the decision quietly formed.

Rowan arrives with Isorae at his side.

Not late. Not early.

Bramble trots ahead of them, tail high, then circles back to brush against Rowan's leg before flopping down near the end of the table with a satisfied huff. He stays there, chin on his paws, eyes open — relaxed but attentive in the way only a dog who knows this land can be.

Rowan stops a few paces back from the table at first.

Old habit.

He scans — not for threats, but for placement.

Silas is still upslope, exactly where he was earlier, seated on a low rise with a clear view of the clearing and the tree line beyond. He hasn't joined the table, and no one expects him to. Parker sits partway down the slope from him on a stone, close enough to talk without raising her voice, far enough not to crowd his sightlines. She's laughing at something he murmurs, her posture easy, healed ribs no longer guarded.

Down below, Erin and Dax emerge from between two cabins at the edge of the clearing — not together-together, but close enough that anyone paying attention would know. Erin's jacket is back on. Dax rolls his shoulders like he's working off excess energy. They split naturally: Erin veers toward the table to drop off a bowl, Dax grabs a cup and leans against the table's far side.

No one comments.

That, too, is peace.

Isorae steps forward without hesitation. She takes a seat on the bench along the long side of the table, posture upright, grounded. Rowan sits beside her after a beat, their shoulders nearly touching but not pressed — proximity without clinging. Her glow stays low and warm, steady as breath.

The hum beneath Rowan's ribs is present tonight. Not loud. Not demanding. Just… aware.

Across the table, Ryan is mid-argument with Nora.

Not loud. Not performing.

Just stubborn.

"This is balanced," he insists, gesturing with a knife still dusted in flour. "You people just don't appreciate restraint."

Nora snorts. "That's not restraint. That's fear of salt."

A few people laugh.

Ryan grins and relents, tearing off another piece of bread and handing it to a child who has already eaten at least three. Evan stands nearby, elbow resting on the table, watching with a fondness he still doesn't quite trust. Ryan drifts rather than anchors — moving where he's useful, refilling cups, listening more than he talks.

Rowan notices.

So does Isorae.

"They've settled," she murmurs.

Rowan nods. "For now."

As the meal takes shape, Dax finally drops into a chair at the end of the table, stretching his legs out. Erin claims the seat beside him a moment later, tablet set aside, attention fully here.

For a while, no one is measuring outcomes.

They eat.

They talk.

They let the day finish becoming evening.

It's Ryan who lifts his cup — not dramatically, just when he realizes the table has quieted enough to hear him.

"Okay," he says. "I know we don't really do speeches."

Groans ripple.

He lifts a brow. "But you're all eating my bread, so you're trapped."

That earns a little laughter.

He clears his throat, glances briefly toward Evan, then back at the group — not centering himself, just speaking.

"I just wanted to say… this place?" He gestures vaguely — the table, the gardens, the people. "It works. Not perfectly. But it lets you wake up without flinching."

The silence that follows isn't heavy.

It's listening.

"So," Ryan finishes, softer, "whatever this is — whatever we're building — I'm glad I'm here for it."

He raises his cup.

"To Stonewake."

"To Stonewake," the table echoes.

The valley hums.

Isorae closes her eyes briefly — not in fear, not in awe — but in something close enough to gratitude that it tightens her throat. Bramble lifts his head at the shift in energy, tail thumping once against the dirt.

Rowan rests his hand on the bench behind her — not touching, just there.

"Still here," he murmurs.

She nods. "For now."

Fireflies begin stitching pale light between the garden rows as dusk deepens. Someone hums while clearing dishes — off-key and unapologetic. Someone else joins in to make it worse.

Upslope, Silas scans the horizon once more.

Not because he expects danger.

Because peace doesn't erase vigilance.

Nothing is there.

That is what unsettles him.

Far beyond Stonewake — far enough that no one here feels it — attention lingers.

Not landing.

Not acting.

Just noting the way a place that should not exist keeps insisting on itself.

The watching does not interrupt.

It waits.

And the night settles over Stonewake — not ignorant, not naïve — but choosing warmth anyway, unaware that this exact arrangement of bodies, breath, and ground has already been memorized.

Not as a target.

Not yet.

But as something worth returning to.

Night settles over Stonewake like a held breath finally released.

Fires burn low. Laughter thins into murmurs. The valley eases into itself, satisfied, unwatchful — the kind of quiet that invites rather than warns.

Rowan and Isorae leave the table together without a word.

No one tracks them.

That feels deliberate.

Their cabin waits upslope, moonlight threading through the trees to spill pale across the threshold. Rowan feels the shift as they cross it — not power, not vigilance — but allowance. Stone. Root. Heat. All of it aligning as if to say *yes, this too belongs.*

Inside, the fire glows steady and low.

Isorae slips out of her cardigan and hangs it with care she doesn't quite feel, movements slower than necessary, like she's savoring the space between moments. Her fingers trail the table edge. The wall. The chair. As if grounding herself in the fact that these things stay where she leaves them.

Rowan watches from the doorway.

His control tightens — not because he's restraining himself, but because the sight of her moving like this makes him want to stop pretending he's composed.

She turns when she feels his attention.

"You're staring," she says softly.

"Yeah," he answers. Honest.

She steps closer, closing the distance until her warmth bleeds into his space. Her glow is subtle tonight — not defensive, not flaring — just present, like heat under skin.

"You're wound tight," she murmurs.

Her hand settles against his chest.

Not tentative.

Intent.

Rowan inhales sharply before he can stop himself.

She rises onto her toes and kisses him.

Not gentle.

Hard enough to steal his breath.

Rowan growls into her mouth, sound low and involuntary, and his hand comes up fast—fingers burying in her hair, grip firm, possessive. He pulls her closer, mouth opening, teeth grazing just enough to make her shudder.

Her breath breaks.

That's it.

He moves her without thinking.

The bed catches her knees and she grabs his shirt, hauling him down with her. Her back hits the mattress and his weight follows immediately — decisive, claiming, knocking the air from her lungs. Somewhere between the fall and the heat of him over her, fabric gives way—shirt dragged loose, pants off, dress pushed aside, skin finding skin without pause.

Her body answers before thought.

One wrist is pinned above her head—just enough pressure to make her pulse jump. Her hips lift instinctively, searching, needy, unguarded, heat gathering between her thighs as he pushes in.

His weight settles heavier, deliberate, crowding her open with intent.

Closer.

Harder.

"Like this," she breathes, already breathless. "Don't stop."

Rowan's breath stutters. He swears under it, jaw tight, body burning with the effort of staying present inside the heat roaring through him. He slows—not to be gentle, but because he wants to feel her react to it.

The pause is torture.

She whimpers, frustration and want tangling sharp and sweet. Her body trembles under his, every nerve screaming for friction, for pressure, for more.

"Fuck—," he rasps, voice wrecked.

His hand moves — claiming ground, grip firm enough to leave no doubt. No hesitation. No softness. Just possession carried out with intent.

Her head tips back, throat exposed, breath coming apart. "Rowan—"

That sound—his name pulled raw from her chest—snaps the last thread.

He thrusts harder now. Faster. The bed creaks under the force of it. Breath turns ragged, bodies colliding, heat building sharp and relentless. Every sound she makes feeds him—every gasp, every broken noise dragging him deeper.

"Mine," he growls, low and feral.

"Yes," she breathes, clinging to him, nails biting into muscle. "Yours."

Awareness narrows to motion and heat and the weight of him holding her exactly where he wants her.

There's no room left for anything else — no past, no future, no control—just this.

When it breaks, it breaks hard.

Bodies tighten.

Breath tears loose.

The moment consumes everything.

Rowan stays over her through it, teeth clenched, muscles shaking, refusing to pull away as the force of it leaves him unsteady.

His forehead drops to her shoulder, breath hot and uneven, heart hammering like it might crack his ribs.

After, he doesn't move much.

Just enough to pull her against him.

She presses her face into his shoulder, lungs burning, grounding in the solid fact of him—warm, heavy, real. His hand settles firm at her hip.

Not gentle.

Holding.

They stay there while the world slowly crawls back into shape around them—sweat cooling, pulses easing, the air thick with heat and spent want.

Outside, Stonewake breathes on—steady, unremarkable, unaware.

And somewhere beyond its borders, something adjusts its attention—not because what they share is fragile…

…but because it is embodied, chosen, and fiercely claimed.

7
Layers of Wakefulness

Stonewake wakes in layers. Rowan feels it as steadiness rather than relief — the land holding its shape without effort, the hum beneath his ribs even and uninsistent.

Isorae stands beside him near the central path, arms folded loosely, gaze following the morning's quiet choreography. Her glow is calm today — threaded, contained, responsive instead of reactive.

"It's holding," she murmurs.

Rowan nods.

Near the eastern gardens, Ryan works a stubborn hinge on one of the water barrels, coaxing it until it finally settles into place with a dull click. Evan appears with a mug of tea and a yawn, squinting against the light.

"You know," Evan mutters, "there's a point where being useful becomes suspicious."

Ryan grins. "That's a dangerous accusation."

Evan presses a brief kiss to his temple before handing him the mug.

As the morning stretches, Stonewake fills itself in. Repairs continue without being assigned. Baskets are carried where they're needed. Someone laughs sharply near the storage sheds, the sound echoing once before dissolving into work again.

Later, Isorae slows near the stream, her steps faltering just enough to matter. Not fear — awareness. The valley leans inward, almost imperceptibly.

She exhales. "The quiet isn't empty."

Rowan studies the tree line. "No."

"It's deliberate."

From the ridge, Silas stands watch, eyes scanning not for movement but for absence. Dax pauses near him, following his gaze.

"You look offended by the weather," Dax says.

Silas doesn't smile. "I don't trust silence that feels curated."

Below them, Erin frowns at her tablet, turning it once in her hands before checking the display again.

"My baselines are smoothing," she says.

Dax sighs. "Of course they are."

No alarm sounds.

By midday, Stonewake moves the way lived-in places do — meals shared, tools passed, small disagreements sparked and resolved without edge. Children run between cabins. Laughter carries without people turning to track it.

Ryan drifts through the work without urgency — helping Nora with a coil of rope, teaching Parker a card trick that earns a sharp laugh, steadying Evan when a ladder wobbles. Nothing lingers long enough to become a moment.

The light shifts. Shadows stretch longer across the paths. The heat eases out of the air.

As evening approaches, Rowan notices Ryan standing near the outer paths, gaze resting on the trees without tension.

Old habits.

Rowan doesn't comment.

Ryan glances back, catches the look, and lifts a shoulder. "Hard to shake."

Rowan answers evenly. "You don't have to."

Ryan nods once.

Dusk settles without ceremony. Fires are fed. Conversations soften. The valley exhales into itself, warm and contained.

That night, as flames burn low and the last voices drift toward quiet, Isorae rests her palm against Rowan's arm.

"Something is paying attention," she says quietly.

Rowan doesn't ask where.

"Not us," she adds. "Not yet."

The land hums — steady, unalarmed, aware.

Above Stonewake, stars emerge one by one. Cabins darken. Footsteps fade.

Far beyond the valley — too distant to be felt, too precise to be accidental — a system logs a harmonic return it did not expect.

No alert triggers.

No response is deployed.

Only time is marked.

And patience — old, practiced, inhuman — waits.

8

THE QUIET THAT LEARNED

Rowan wakes before Stonewake does.

Not abruptly — not to danger — but to the sensation of being slightly out of step with himself. His breath comes easily, his body rested, yet something beneath his ribs refuses to settle back into alignment.

The land is there.

Steady. Familiar.

But it is not answering him the way it usually does.

He lies still for a moment, listening — not outward, but inward — tracking the absence as carefully as he would track pressure or threat. Nothing spikes. Nothing resists.

Nothing responds.

That should not be possible.

Carefully, Rowan shifts, easing himself upright on the edge of the bed so he doesn't wake Isorae too quickly. She stirs anyway, breath changing before her eyes open.

"You're awake early," she murmurs, voice still rough with sleep.

"Didn't sleep badly," Rowan says quietly. "Didn't sleep right."

She pushes herself up beside him, blanket slipping from one shoulder, hair loose down her back. For a moment she just watches him, reading the tension he hasn't named yet.

Then she feels it.

Her posture stills.

"Something's off," she says.

Rowan nods once. He pulls on his boots and crosses the short distance to the open doorway, the cool predawn air brushing his skin.

He crouches and presses his palm flat to the packed earth just outside the threshold.

Nothing flinches.

Nothing leans.

Nothing hums back.

Isorae joins him, kneeling at his side. She doesn't touch the ground at first — her fingers hover just above it, shimmer threading outward with deliberate restraint.

Her brow furrows.

"It isn't braced," she says quietly. "But it's… paused."

Rowan exhales through his nose. "Like it's waiting to see if it needs to move."

"Yes." She looks up at him. "That's exactly it."

They remain there, side by side, listening to a quiet that feels almost rehearsed — not empty, not peaceful.

Prepared.

Later, Erin notices it in the numbers.

She's standing at the worktable in the cabin she shares with Dax, tablet propped against a crate, hair half tied back in the way it gets when she hasn't decided whether the day is going to behave yet. Dax is behind her, pulling on his shirt, the room still warm and disordered in a way that says they didn't leave it long ago.

She frowns.

Re-runs the scan.

Adjusts a parameter she hasn't touched in months.

The tablet chirps softly, obliging.

The output is clean.

Too clean.

"That's irritating," Erin mutters.

Dax, now leaning against the doorframe with his boots in hand, arches an eyebrow. "You say that like it's a threat."

"It is," she replies. "Noise doesn't vanish. It gets filtered. And I didn't filter this."

She pulls up a comparison overlay — six months ago, three months ago, last week.

The baseline hasn't drifted.

It has flattened.

"That's not decay," Erin says slowly. "That's suppression."

Dax straightens. "By what?"

She doesn't answer immediately. Her fingers move faster now, isolating a thread she hasn't seen since before the valley closed itself the first time.

A faint pattern flickers at the edge of the screen.

Her stomach drops.

"No," she breathes. "That's not possible."

Dax steps closer. "Erin."

She swallows. "Someone's pinging around Stonewake."

"Inside?"

"No." She shakes her head. "Not probing. Not testing."

She turns the tablet so he can see.

"Circling."

Erin exhales once, sharp and controlled.

"I need eyes," she says — not asking.

She palms the tablet dark and pushes out of the cabin, the door closing behind her with a soft, unfinished sound.

Rowan feels it the moment Erin steps into the clearing.

He looks up before she speaks.

"You found something," he says.

She nods once. "I found a ghost."

Silas appears from the ridge path without being called, expression already set. Dax follows Erin out, tension replacing his earlier ease.

Erin holds the tablet out between them. "It's not ARIS proper. There's no command lattice attached. No escalation tree."

"Then what is it?" Dax asks.

"A residue," Erin replies. "A behavioral echo. Like someone kept a fragment alive long enough to teach it how to listen without reporting."

Rowan's jaw tightens.

Beside him, Isorae's shimmer draws inward, compact and sharp.

"They are not meant to do that," she says. "Listening without containment breaks their rules."

Erin meets her gaze. "Then someone broke ranks."

Silence stretches.

Ryan approaches at a jog from the lower path, breath a little fast, expression open — until he registers the stillness.

"What's wrong?"

Rowan studies him for a beat too long before answering. "Nothing yet."

Ryan nods, accepting it — but his eyes flick toward the trees again, instinctive as a flinch.

Silas folds his arms. "If it isn't acting, what's it waiting for?"

Isorae answers softly, her voice steady but cold.

"For us to forget it exists."

The valley hums faintly beneath their feet.

Not warning.

Not threat.

Just acknowledgment.

And far from Stonewake — not in orbit, not in command chambers — a single human consciousness watches a quiet data feed with obsessive patience.

He smiles.

Because the land is no longer screaming.

And silence, he has learned, is where things are easiest to take.

9
HALF A SECOND LATE

The first mistake is small enough that no one calls it danger.

A little girl wanders too far downslope while chasing a frog — laughing, barefoot, unafraid — and the valley does not immediately lean to guide her back. No root curls into a subtle barrier. No soft rise in ground redirects small feet toward home.

She keeps going.

Ryan notices because he's looking where no one else is.

He's carrying a bundle of split wood toward the communal fire when he catches the flicker of movement beyond the fern line — a flash of yellow ribbon, too far past the cottages, too close to the stone ravine where the land drops steep and sharp.

"Hey," he calls lightly. "Hey—"

She doesn't hear him.

Ryan drops the wood.

He runs.

Rowan feels it at the same moment — a lag — like the land inhaling half a second too late. He's already moving when Isorae's breath catches beside him.

"No," she whispers. "That shouldn't be—"

The ground gives way.

Not dramatically.

Just enough.

The girl's foot slips on loose gravel at the ravine edge, laughter snapping into a startled cry as her body tips sideways toward stone that has no memory of catching falls.

Ryan launches.

He doesn't think.

He doesn't shout.

He throws himself forward, arm locking around her middle as momentum yanks them both toward the drop. His boots skid. His shoulder slams into rock. Pain detonates down his side — bright, immediate, breath-stealing.

For a heartbeat, gravity wins.

Then the valley remembers itself.

Stone shifts — not smoothly, but urgently.

A rib of rock thrusts upward beneath Ryan's knee, halting the slide just long enough for Rowan to grab his collar and haul both of them backward into moss and shaking breath.

Silence slams into the clearing.

The girl is crying — loud, terrified, whole.

Parker reaches her first.

She scoops the girl up without asking, one arm firm around her middle, the other cradling the back of her head as the child clings to her shirt, sobbing hard enough to hiccup.

"I slipped," the girl gasps into Parker's shoulder. "The ground— it moved wrong."

Parker presses her cheek briefly to the girl's hair, murmuring nonsense meant only to slow her breathing. "You're okay. You're safe. I've got you."

The girl twists just enough to look back.

Her eyes land on Ryan.

"He caught me," she says, voice thin but certain. "I didn't fall because he caught me."

Something tightens across the clearing.

Parker nods once — acknowledgment — and carries the girl away toward the cabins, already calling softly for the girl's mom.

The sound of crying fades.

The silence left behind does not.

Ryan lies on his back, chest heaving, eyes squeezed shut as pain ripples through him in sharp waves.

Evan is there instantly.

Not frantic — precise.

Hands check ribs, shoulder, spine. Fingers steady Ryan's jaw when he sucks in air too fast.

"Easy," Evan says, voice tight but controlled. "Don't sit up yet."

Ryan exhales through clenched teeth, then huffs a breath that might almost be a laugh. "Guess I—guess I forgot I'm not built for flying."

Evan presses his palm flat against Ryan's chest, grounding pressure, eyes scanning instead of pleading. "You hit hard. That's all I need you to tell me right now."

Rowan stands frozen from recognition.

The land is humming now — louder than it should be — a low, uneven reverberation beneath bone that feels uncomfortably like self-correction.

Isorae steps closer, breath shallow. Her shimmer is wrong — not bright, not dim — but stretched thin, like light pulled past its tolerance.

"That should not have happened," she says.

Erin arrives last, scanner already screaming.

She ignores it.

Her gaze goes to the ravine.

The stone.

The way the land patched instead of prevented.

"This wasn't an accident," Erin says quietly.

Silas's jaw hardens. "Then what was it?"

Erin finally looks down at the display.

"Interference," she answers. "Not inside Stonewake."

She swallows.

"Around it."

Rowan exhales slowly, fists clenched at his sides.

Isorae turns to him, eyes dark with a truth she does not want to speak.

"They didn't touch the land," she whispers. "They touched the timing."

Ryan groans softly as Evan helps him shift — careful, deliberate — into a sitting position. Pain still rides him, but he's solid. Present.

"Can someone explain," Ryan mutters, "why everyone looks like I just insulted the valley's mother?"

Rowan crouches in front of him, steady, eye-level.

"You didn't," he says.

Then — quieter —

"But you got close enough to hear it hesitate."

The land settles slowly — unevenly — like something forcing itself back into calm.

But the damage is already done.

Stonewake hesitated.

And somewhere far from the ravine, far from the people who call the valley home, a human hand pauses over a control that is not officially supposed to exist.

The rogue smiles.

Because now he knows:

He doesn't have to break the land.

He only has to make it late.

10

Assesment

Ryan insists he's fine. He says it once to Rowan, once to Erin, and once to Evan—each time with a little less conviction than the last. By the fourth attempt, Evan has already stopped responding to the words and started responding to the body.

"You hit stone," Evan says, kneeling beside him, hands steady, voice controlled. "Stone that moved, but still stone."

"I've hit worse," Ryan replies, aiming for levity. "Remember the oak by the creek? Fell right out of it. Landed on my ass in front of half the valley."

Evan presses two fingers along Ryan's ribs.

Ryan hisses despite himself.

"That wasn't worse," Evan says flatly.

Evan walks Ryan home.

They're quiet once the door shuts.

The cabin holds them the way it always does — hearth cold, rugs bunched where they never quite get straightened, the air still carrying the ghost of tea and smoke and something Ryan once burned and promised not to attempt again.

Evan exhales only once they're inside.

He eases Ryan onto the bed with practiced care.

"You don't have to hover," Ryan murmurs.

"I'm not hovering," Evan replies. "I'm assessing."

Ryan smiles faintly. "You're hovering."

Evan exhales through his nose and reaches for the basin of water anyway.

When he turns back, Ryan is watching him—not teasing now, not deflecting. Just looking. Choosing to be seen.

"You scared me," Evan says quietly.

Ryan's smile fades.

"Yeah," he admits. "I scared myself, too."

Evan cleans the scrape along Ryan's brow with gentle efficiency. His hands don't shake much—but enough. Ryan notices. He lifts his own hand slowly and cups Evan's wrist.

"Hey," he says softly. "I'm still here."

Evan closes his eyes.

For a moment, the room holds only breath.

"I don't like who I am when I think I'm about to lose you," Evan says. His voice is low, stripped of humor, stripped of defense. He swallows. "The world gets very small."

Ryan's thumb traces the inside of Evan's wrist, grounding.

"I like that you care," Ryan says. "But I don't want to be the thing that breaks you."

"You're not," Evan replies immediately. "You're the thing that keeps me intact."

Ryan lets out a quiet, disbelieving laugh.

"God," he murmurs. "If you'd told me a year ago I'd be living in a sentient valley, building gardens, and falling in love with a man who can set a rib and still somehow make tea that tastes like regret…"

"My tea does not taste like regret," Evan mutters.

"It absolutely does."

Evan presses his forehead briefly to Ryan's.

"You ran without thinking," Evan says after a moment.

Ryan shrugs, careful this time. "Kid was going to fall."

"That's not what I mean," Evan says. "You didn't calculate. You didn't wait. You didn't ask if the land would catch her."

Ryan's voice is quieter now. "No."

"Why?"

Ryan thinks about it.

Then: "Because sometimes you don't trust systems. You trust people."

Evan's breath catches.

Outside, the valley hums—steadier now, quieter—listening without intruding.

Ryan adds, lighter but not flippant, "If I end up permanently wrecked doing something stupidly heroic, I'd prefer a bench somewhere. Not a plaque."

Evan lifts his head instantly. "Don't."

Ryan sobers. "Okay. Too soon."

Evan cups Ryan's face, thumb brushing gently beneath his eye.

"Don't joke about losing yourself," he says. "Not with me."

Ryan nods. "I won't."

They sit like that for a long time—Evan's hand steady on Ryan's chest, Ryan's fingers loosely laced with his—until the tension finally bleeds out of Evan's shoulders.

When Rowan checks in quietly at the door, Evan looks up.

"He's going to be sore," Evan says. "I'll keep an eye on him."

Rowan nods. "I know."

There's nothing else to say. Rowan leaves them to their space, to the quiet rituals of care.

When the door closes again, Ryan exhales.

"You know," he says, "for a medic, you're very bad at emotional detachment."

Evan leans in, pressing a careful kiss to Ryan's temple.

"Good," he replies. "I don't want to be detached from you."

Outside the cabin, Stonewake settles into evening—fires lit, voices low, the land breathing slow and deep.

But beneath the calm, something has shifted.

Because now there are people in the valley who are no longer just protected.

They are chosen.

They are anchored.

They are loved.

And that—more than any signal or structure—is what makes a place visible to the wrong kind of attention.

II
THE LONG LOOK

Stonewake sleeps differently now. Not shallow. Not braced. But not careless, either.

Fires burn down into coals that don't throw far light—only heat that settles into hearthstones and the undersides of blankets. Doors are latched. Curtains are drawn. Even the dogs have learned when the night is only night.

Bramble sleeps with one ear half-raised anyway.

Because trust is a kind of softness.

And softness has a sound.

High above the valley, where the ridgelines fracture into long shelves of stone no one uses unless they mean to disappear, a man kneels in the dark and does not move.

He has been there since before the last voices faded.

He is dressed for cold that wants to get into bone—layers that don't whisper when he shifts, gloves that can press against rock without leaving skin behind. His hair is pulled back tight. His face is still in the way disciplined men learn to make it still, as if expression is a leak that can be tracked.

He watches without binoculars.

He doesn't need magnification.

The valley is the lens.

Below him, the settlement is a constellation of dim squares and soft orange throbs—windows, coals, a single late lantern flickering near the hub as someone forgets to blow it out. The paths are barely visible. The gardens are only shadowed geometry.

And yet he can tell where the center is.

Not by light.

By difference.

He adjusts the device at his wrist.

Not a scanner. Not a beacon. Nothing that screams into the world and asks it to answer.

This is quieter.

A listening bone.

He turns the dial a fraction and holds his breath as if breath itself might contaminate what he's trying to hear.

The valley does not reject him.

That is the first thing he notes.

Not welcome—no. Stonewake does not welcome strangers. But it does not bristle. It does not rise. It does not shove him out with roots and sudden turns of terrain.

Tolerance.

Like a hand hovering over a blade that hasn't decided whether it needs to close.

He waits for the land to notice him.

It doesn't.

Or worse— it notices, and decides he isn't worth the effort.

His mouth twitches, almost pleased.

"Good," he whispers into the dark, voice so low it's more vibration than sound.

He changes the setting.

Not louder.

Narrower.

He isn't looking for the whole valley.

He's looking for one aberration inside it.

One thread that doesn't belong to the weave.

He closes his eyes.

Listens with his wrist, with his teeth, with the thin, trained part of his nervous system that can read a pattern the way other men read weather.

At first there's nothing but the ordinary hush of a living place—the faint hum of Stonewake's agreement, the soft pulse of sleeping bodies, the mineral patience of stone.

Then—

a frequency that does not fit.

Not wrong the way a siren is wrong.

Wrong the way a doorway is wrong when it pretends to be a wall.

It slides up his spine in a slow, private shiver.

His hand tightens on nothing.

His throat works once.

And there it is.

A signature that doesn't belong to any human record.

A resonance that feels like light trying to remember how to be flesh.

An anomaly.

He opens his eyes again and looks down at the valley like a man looking through glass at something he has wanted for so long he has learned to want it silently.

"So you're real," he murmurs.

He doesn't say her name at first.

Names are for possession.

Names are for later.

He says what she is.

Softly. Reverently. Almost tender.

"Interdimensional," he breathes.

The word settles into him like confirmation.

"Fae," he adds—not as folklore, but classification.

His lips part, as if the pairing tastes like power.

"A threshold species, he continues. "Embodied."

He exhales the last word like a prayer that makes his ribs ache.

The device at his wrist gives a faint, obedient pulse—barely a tick.

Not enough for anyone else to notice.

Enough for him.

He lowers his gloved hand, presses his fingertips to the stone beside him, and feels the valley's patience through mineral.

"You've been hiding her," he whispers.

Not an accusation.

An admiration.

A devotion with teeth behind it.

He watches one cabin longer than the rest.

Not because it's grand.

Because it's weighted.

Like the air around it knows a boundary and respects it.

His wrist pulses again—subtle, intimate.

The anomaly is there.

Inside.

Warm.

Sleeping.

Unaware.

Something in him softens the way men soften when they look at something they've decided belongs in their world.

Voyeur isn't a word he would use.

He would say witness.

He would say study.

He would say reverence.

But the way he watches is the way a hand lingers at the edge of someone's throat without touching.

Learning.

Planning.

Inside that cabin, Rowan wakes without knowing why.

Not abruptly. Not alarmed.

Just… out of step.

As if his body has heard a sound his mind refuses to translate.

He lies still for a moment, letting the silence settle.

Isorae is curled against him, warm along his side, hair spilled across his chest. Her glow is quiet tonight—contained, smooth—no jagged flicker, no defensive flare. She breathes like someone who has begun to believe in mornings again.

Bramble sleeps at the foot of the bed, chin on paws, tail twitching once in a dream.

Rowan brings a hand up to his sternum.

The bridge hums.

Steady.

But crowded.

Like another awareness brushed past it and didn't ask permission to be near.

He frowns, slow.

In the dark, Bramble's head lifts.

One ear cocks.

A low sound gathers in his throat and dies before it becomes a growl—as if even the dog is unsure whether the night has earned teeth.

Rowan's fingers press more firmly against his chest.

Outside the window, wind moves.

Not toward the ridge.

Not away.

Sideways—slipping between cabins like a body passing through a room without touching anything.

Rowan sits up carefully.

Isorae makes a small sound—half-asleep—then settles again, the curve of her spine easing back into warmth.

Rowan doesn't wake her.

He swings his feet to the floor and pulls on his boots as silently as a man can. Bramble stands immediately, stretches, and pads after him without being invited.

The door opens.

Cold threads in.

Stonewake greets him with familiarity—the creak of settling wood, the faint murmur of the stream, the soft, layered breath of sleeping bodies.

The land hums beneath his feet.

Steady.

Untroubled.

Too untroubled.

Rowan walks the perimeter anyway.

Not searching.

Confirming.

Bramble ranges a little ahead, nose low, moving like a creature who knows where the safe edges are and wants to confirm the world still agrees.

They reach the western slope.

Rowan stops.

The ferns there are bent—not broken, not crushed—just… parted.

Recently.

Bramble's hackles rise in a thin line. He sniffs once, twice, then huffs softly and circles, as if the scent is there and not there. As if it's been wiped and the wiping missed a seam.

Rowan crouches, presses his palm to the soil.

Stonewake responds.

Late.

Not much.

A fraction.

A hesitation in something that never hesitates for him.

Rowan's jaw tightens.

"Who came through here," he murmurs.

The valley does not answer.

Or worse— it answers by not answering, the way a loyal thing goes silent when it has done something it didn't want its person to see.

Rowan stands slowly, scanning the darkness.

The ridgeline stares back at him—silent stone, indifferent sky. Nothing moves. No eyeshine. No shape.

And yet the feeling doesn't leave.

The echo of being watched after the watcher has gone.

Bramble gives a low, dissatisfied growl—finally committing to the truth of his body.

Rowan rests a hand on the dog's neck.

"Easy," he breathes.

Not because it's fine.

Because the sound of fear would travel.

Rowan turns back toward the cabins.

Stonewake hums beneath him again—steady, almost innocent.

As if it is trying very hard to be what they believe it is.

High above, the man smiles faintly.

Because he felt it—the moment the land hesitated.

Not enough to alarm. Not enough to wake the whole system.

Just enough to confirm:

Stonewake can be entered.

Carefully.

Lovingly.

With the right patience.

He rises at last, joints stiff from stillness, and dusts his glove against his coat as if wiping away the night.

His wrist device dims.

Not off.

Waiting.

He looks down at the cabin again—at the place where the anomaly sleeps beside the boundary-man who thinks he's the only one who can hold the line.

The man's mouth parts.

He speaks to the valley like it's a collaborator.

Like it's a door that just needs the right hand.

"I won't rush you," he whispers.

A pause.

And then, softer—almost tender, as if speaking to her skin through miles of dark—

"Little threshold creature."

He says it like a pet name.

Like an ownership that hasn't been negotiated.

"You deserve patience."

He steps back into the higher shadows and begins to move along the ridge with the quiet ease of someone who knows exactly where the blind spots are.

No pursuit.

No consequence.

For now.

Because the most dangerous hunters do not chase.

They curate.

They observe until observation becomes a kind of touch.

And Stonewake—settled, named, beloved—does not yet know it has been chosen.

Not as a target.

As a collection.

And at the center of that collection:

a bright anomaly pretending she is only a woman—

sleeping unguarded in a place that believes it is alone, while the man who would burn the world to protect her stands outside in the dark, unaware of what it means to be watched with reverence.

12

THE COST OF PREDICTABILITY

Peace makes patterns. That is what unsettles Rowan.

Not the calm itself — Stonewake has earned that — but the way the valley has begun to move on instinct instead of attention. Fires are fed at the same hours. Paths are walked without looking down. People stop listening for the land's answer because it has answered the same way for weeks.

Reliably.

Predictably.

Isorae fits into that rhythm now.

She no longer moves like someone translating herself into a place. She belongs to it — weight settled, breath deep, shimmer quiet enough that Rowan sometimes has to remind himself it's there at all. She laughs without checking the tree line. Sleeps without anchoring herself to him first.

It should feel like relief.

Instead, it sharpens his awareness of what's at stake.

They are by the stream in the late afternoon when Rowan feels it — a pressure shift beneath his sternum, like the bridge has reached the end of a familiar phrase and found silence where the next word should be.

Isorae hums softly, bare feet skimming the water. Her back rests easily against his chest, warm, present, unguarded.

Too unguarded.

Rowan stills.

The bridge doesn't flare.

It… adjusts.

As if accommodating an observer who knows not to touch.

Rowan's gaze lifts, slow and deliberate, scanning the opposite bank.

Nothing.

No distortion. No sound mismatch. No land-level response.

Which is the problem.

Because the bridge is no longer reacting to intrusion.

It's reacting to attention.

Someone is close enough to matter.

And careful enough not to register as threat.

Rowan's hand tightens at Isorae's waist.

She glances back at him, smiling faintly. "You just went somewhere."

"Did I?" he says.

She nods. "Briefly."

He angles his body without thinking — turning so the slope is at his back, Isorae shielded by posture alone. Not because she needs it.

Because he does.

That night, the awareness returns.

Rowan wakes with his heart already racing, the bridge vibrating beneath his ribs. Isorae sleeps deeply beside him, her shimmer smooth, unbroken — a signal left unencrypted because it has never needed to be.

Rowan sits up slowly.

The valley is quiet.

He steps outside barefoot, letting the cold bite into his skin, grounding himself through sensation instead of command.

"Show me," he murmurs.

The land hesitates.

Not refusal.

Confusion.

He walks farther than the night before, following the bridge's lateral pull instead of its depth — not toward danger, but toward context. The northern slope feels wrong in the way a room does after someone has left without opening a door.

Someone stood here.

Not long.

Not clumsily.

Long enough to learn the angle of the valley's breath.

Rowan crouches and presses his palm to the soil.

The response is delayed.

That has never happened.

"What did you let through?" he asks quietly.

The land answers — uncertain, defensive, embarrassed — like something that followed a rule it didn't realize had changed.

Rowan straightens slowly.

It isn't Isorae they're studying.

Not her body.

Not her power.

Her function.

The crossing.

The way she exists between states without tearing them.

The way the valley reorganizes itself around her presence.

The way Rowan anchors her without diminishing her.

This isn't reconnaissance.

It's rehearsal.

Rowan turns back toward Stonewake with something cold settling behind his ribs.

Because the valley hasn't been breached.

It's been learned.

And peace — warm, earned, beloved peace — has made them easy to predict.

Not an attack.

Not yet.

A timing.

13

Unobserved No Longer

Isorae feels it while doing something ordinary.

That is what unsettles her most.

She is kneeling near the stream, sleeves rolled, hands submerged in cold water as she rinses soil from freshly pulled roots. The sun sits low behind her, warm on her shoulders. Stonewake breathes around her in its familiar, unguarded way — not braced, not listening.

Just living.

And then—

Attention.

Her hands still in the water.

The stream keeps moving.

Birdsong does not falter.

Nothing happens.

And yet her spine tightens, instinct sharp and immediate, like the moment before someone speaks her name from behind.

Isorae lifts her head slowly.

Nothing is there.

No movement in the trees. No distortion in the air. No shift in the valley's hum. If anything, the land feels too calm — like rest held a second too long.

She rises to her feet.

The sensation does not fade.

It adjusts.

As if whatever is watching has changed its angle.

Her glow responds before thought — not flaring, not dimming — drawing inward, tightening close to skin like a veil pulled shut. She presses one hand to her ribs, grounding herself in the undeniable truth of her body.

I am here, she tells herself.

I am not being taken.

She turns in a slow, deliberate circle.

Still nothing.

Rowan's presence brushes the edge of her awareness — distant, steady — somewhere near the ridge. Erin and Dax's laughter carries faintly from the east. Evan's voice drifts from the gardens.

Life. Sound. Continuity.

And yet—

Eyes.

Not many.

Singular. Focused.

It does not feel like ARIS.

That is the wrongness.

ARIS listens like an ocean listens — vast, distributed, impersonal. It catalogs without caring. Measures without wanting.

This feels narrow.

Intent.

Isorae's breath catches.

She steps onto stone. The valley responds immediately — not alarmed, but attentive. Moss tightens. The hum beneath her feet deepens by a fraction, like a quiet question asked without words. *Do you want me to see this?*

"No," she whispers.

Not yet.

The attention does not retreat.

It does not advance.

It simply remains — patient, unblinking.

She closes her eyes.

Not to hide.

To feel.

There — a thread. Thin. Artificial. Human-shaped in its desire. It skims the outermost edge of her resonance and recoils slightly, like something surprised to discover she can feel it back.

Her pulse stutters.

That's new.

Isorae opens her eyes.

The valley looks unchanged.

But she knows — with the certainty of something recognized too late to deny — that someone, somewhere, has learned how to look at her without triggering the alarms.

Not a system.

A person.

Her stomach turns.

She steps backward toward the heart of Stonewake, glow drawn tight, posture composed. She does not run. She does not signal. She does not give the watcher the satisfaction of reaction.

The attention loosens — withdrawing by degrees. Like a hand pulling back from flame, already memorizing the heat.

When Rowan reaches her moments later, concern already set in his face, she is calm on the surface.

Only on the surface.

"Something wrong?" he asks quietly.

She meets his eyes.

Chooses precision over comfort.

"Something is looking at me," she says. "And it knows how not to be seen."

Rowan's jaw tightens — slow, lethal.

"When?"

"Just now."

"Where?"

She shakes her head. "Not where. From."

The valley hums lower around them.

Rowan does not ask if she's sure.

He never does.

His hand settles at the small of her back — protective without possession — and he turns them subtly toward the inner paths of Stonewake.

"We'll figure it out," he says. "Together."

Isorae nods.

But as they walk away, she feels it once more.

That singular attention.

Satisfied.

As if whatever is watching has learned exactly what it came to learn.

And far beyond the ridges, someone smiles — not with triumph, not yet —

—but with classification complete, and ownership beginning to take its first, dangerous shape.

14
DELIBERATE ABSENCE

Erin knows something is wrong before the numbers tell her.

That, more than anything, makes her stop.

She's recalibrating the perimeter lattice out of habit more than concern — the quiet has stretched long enough to itch, and ARIS never stopped listening. It only learned new ways to pretend it wasn't.

Still, the data scrolls clean.

Too clean.

No harmonics bleeding in from high altitude. No residual echo patterns skimming the valley's outer skin. No machine signatures brushing Stonewake's boundaries. The land hums steady beneath her boots — resting, unbraced.

And yet—

There is a shadow where no shadow should be.

Not a spike.

Not a dip.

A gap.

Erin frowns and drags two fingers across the display, isolating the band. The readout refuses to settle — not scrambling, not resisting — just… sliding sideways every time she tries to pin it down.

"That's not right," she murmurs.

Dax looks up from the solar rig he's been coaxing back into alignment. "What's not right?"

"This," Erin says, angling the screen toward him. "See how it won't anchor?"

He squints. "Looks like interference."

"That's the problem," Erin replies. "It isn't interfering."

She widens the range.

The anomaly tightens.

Subtly.

Like it noticed.

Erin's stomach drops.

"That's not ARIS," she says slowly.

Dax straightens. "You sure?"

"ARIS is loud even when it's quiet," she answers. "It leaves residue. Structure. This is deliberate absence. Someone masking presence without using system-level cloaking."

She pulls historical overlays — old ARIS incursions, orbital triangulation attempts, severance vectors.

None of them match.

The signal doesn't resonate like code.

It resonates like intent.

Rowan is beside her before she registers movement.

"What did you find?" he asks.

Erin swallows. "Someone is observing the valley without ARIS infrastructure."

The land hums lower.

Isorae feels it immediately.

Her glow tightens — condensing into something alert and contained. "That's who I felt," she says quietly. "Not the system."

"Human?" Dax asks.

Erin hesitates.

"Yes," she says. "But not just human."

She applies one last filter — something she hasn't used since before the valley sealed itself.

For a breath, the signal locks.

Just long enough.

Her hands still.

"Oh," she whispers. "Oh no."

Rowan's spine goes rigid. "What?"

"They aren't tracking Stonewake," Erin says. "They're riding a resonance already inside it."

The words take a moment to land.

Isorae closes her eyes.

The sensation sharpens — no longer just attention, but familiarity. Pattern recognition. Expectation.

"He knows my shape," she says softly. "Not the way ARIS knew me. The way people learn things they aren't supposed to touch."

Dax exhales through his teeth. "He's piggybacking on her."

Erin nods, pale. "He's listening through her without crossing the thresholds."

Silence presses in.

Ryan steps closer — not rushing, not posturing. Just present. "Okay," he says evenly. "Then we plan."

Rowan turns, surprised.

Ryan holds his gaze. "He hasn't acted. Which means he thinks he has time."

Erin's fingers resume their motion, slower now. Careful. "He's not hunting yet. He's building confidence."

Isorae opens her eyes.

"And watchers always believe they're entitled to what they're watching."

The valley tightens in warning.

Rowan's hand settles at her back — steady, grounding, immovable.

"No one takes you," he says. Not a promise. A boundary. "Not system. Not man."

Far beyond the ridges, a lone observer adjusts his instruments — not military-grade, not corporate — custom-built. Intimate. Personal.

He exhales slowly.

Satisfied.

Because the anomaly has confirmed awareness.

She feels him.

And soon—

She will learn his name.

15
Negative Space

He arrives the way people always do when they believe they are invisible.

Not at the rim.

Not during daylight's obvious hours.

Not with desperation loud enough for the valley to recoil.

He comes late in the morning, when Stonewake is already moving—when hands are busy and attention is diluted into ordinary things. Bread cooling on windowsills. Water buckets carried in pairs. Laughter drifting without anyone stopping to listen for echoes.

Nora notices him first.

She's hanging laundry between two young maples near the southern gardens, humming under her breath, when she becomes aware of a shape where the path bends—just far enough back that it's unclear whether he has just arrived or has been standing there a while.

He doesn't wave.

He doesn't step forward.

He waits.

That's what makes her pause.

Most people who come here cross the threshold like they're afraid it might vanish behind them. They hurry. They speak too quickly. They look around like they're bracing for refusal.

This man stands still, posture loose, hands relaxed at his sides. As if he's letting the place decide what it thinks of him before he decides anything at all.

Nora adjusts the last cloth on the line and approaches.

"Hey," she says easily. "You lost?"

He smiles—not wide, not charming. Measured.

"No," he says. "Just didn't want to intrude."

That word settles strangely.

Intrude.

The valley tightens by a hair—not enough to startle, not enough to signal danger. Leaves still. Wind hesitates.

Nora doesn't notice.

She smiles back. "You're fine. Are you hurt?"

"No," he replies. "Just… tired."

It's the right answer.

People arrive here tired.

"I heard this place helps," he adds after a beat. "Or maybe I hoped it would."

The land does not refuse him.

Not immediately.

That, in itself, is not unusual.

Stonewake has learned patience. It allows space for intent to declare itself. It lets people sit at its edges before deciding whether they are staying or passing through.

The man remains where he is.

Minutes pass.

Not awkward ones.

The kind that gather permission by not demanding it.

Nora finishes with the laundry and returns with an empty basket tucked against her hip. She hesitates, then gestures lightly toward the fire circle with her chin.

"You can sit, if you want," she says. "No pressure."

He inclines his head — not grateful, not relieved. Simply acknowledging an option offered.

"Thank you," he says. "I won't be in the way."

Another right answer.

He does not move immediately.

That, too, matters.

Only when someone else — Jalen, passing with an armful of tools — drops a spare mug onto the bench near the outer ring without comment does the man step forward. He takes the seat closest to the edge, the one people use when they're undecided about staying long. He wraps his hands around the mug, letting the warmth do its work.

Conversation does not stop.

No one makes space for him.

No one asks his name.

The fire crackles. Someone laughs too loudly. Someone else complains about the bread crust. Life absorbs him without ceremony.

Stonewake notices.

It does not tighten.

It does not lean away.

It allows.

By the time Evan looks up, the man has already been folded into the negative space of the gathering — not centered, not isolated. Accounted for without being claimed.

Evan pauses near the outer fire ring, scanning faces out of habit — the quiet inventory he does whenever the hollow feels full.

The man sits at the edge of the circle, posture loose, mug warming his hands. He isn't talking much. Mostly listening. When someone jokes, he smiles.

Not late.

Not eager.

Exactly on time.

When someone complains, he nods like he understands the weight of small frustrations.

"You eaten?" Evan asks, almost absentmindedly.

The man looks up, mildly surprised — as if he hadn't expected to be addressed yet.

"Not today," he says.

Evan hands him the mug without thinking.

Only later does it occur to him that he can't remember when he decided the stranger belonged to the afternoon.

Conversation drifts. Someone mentions a collapsed fence near the west path. Someone else complains about the goats. The man contributes a comment here and there — nothing clever, nothing memorable — just enough to keep the thread moving.

Time passes.

Ryan wanders over at some point, dust on his hands, hair tied back badly. He listens for a while without speaking, then adds something about how paths always look shorter until you start walking them.

It's not funny.

Not really.

But Ryan laughs anyway — a soft, surprised sound, like he didn't realize he was going to.

The sound lands wrong.

Not alarming.

Just… misplaced.

Rowan looks up from where he's been splitting wood.

The man is seated comfortably now, posture loose, hands warm around the mug. Listening more than speaking. Smiling at the right moments. Saying very little.

Too little.

Rowan approaches—not fast, not slow.

Up close, the man's eyes are unsettling—not bright, not dark—focused in a way that feels practiced. He stands when Rowan reaches him, polite without being deferential.

"Rowan," Evan says, belatedly aware of the shift. "This is—"

"Graham," the man supplies easily. "Just Graham."

He offers his hand.

Rowan does not take it.

He studies the man for a long moment before speaking.

"Where did you come from?"

The man doesn't hesitate. "North."

Rowan waits.

The pause is deliberate.

"And before that?"

Graham's mouth tilts, thoughtful rather than evasive — like someone choosing the version of the truth that won't invite follow-up.

"Systems analysis," he says. "Predictive infrastructure. Pattern response."

A beat — not hesitation, but selection.

"Contract-side work. ARIS-adjacent. Modeling only — never command, never enforcement."

His shoulders lift slightly, almost apologetic.

"At first it felt… necessary. You tell yourself you're helping people by making the system more efficient. Less reactive. Cleaner."

He exhales, quiet.

"Then you start seeing what gets categorized as acceptable loss."

He meets Rowan's eyes — steady, earnest.

"I didn't leave because I was afraid of ARIS," he says. "I left because I didn't agree with what it considers order."

A pause.

"And because once you understand how it thinks… you realize you don't want to stay long enough for it to understand you back."

It's specific enough to sound real.

Too neat to be comforting.

Across the hollow, Erin's tablet goes dead in her hands.

Not powered down. Not errored.

Just… empty.

She blinks, frowns, taps the screen once. Nothing. No baseline. No background noise. No passive read.

Like someone shut a door she didn't know was open.

Her stomach tightens.

She looks up.

Isorae is already on her feet.

No flare. No surge.

Her glow has pulled inward, compressed tight against her skin — not defensive or panicked — but braced. Her attention is locked on Graham with a precision that has nothing to do with curiosity.

Recognition sharpened to a point.

Graham's eyes flick to her.

A fraction of a second.

Enough.

The mask slips.

Not surprise.

Relief.

There you are.

The thought does not arrive as sound. Not resonance. Not language.

It arrives as placement — like a pin dropped into a map.

Isorae inhales sharply and takes one involuntary step back.

Rowan is there instantly.

Not just protective — alert.

His hand comes firm at her spine, body angling between her and the fire ring without ceremony. His gaze never leaves Graham.

Not accusation.

Assessment.

"Isorae?" Rowan says quietly. A check.

She doesn't answer right away.

Her eyes never leave Graham.

"Later," she murmurs. Just for him. "Not here."

That's all Rowan needs.

Graham smooths his expression, warmth returning like a practiced habit.

"Your valley is beautiful," he says lightly. "You take care of it."

Rowan doesn't respond.

The valley doesn't either.

No welcome.

No refusal either.

It holds him the way flesh holds a needle — still, alert, waiting to see if it will pierce.

Erin lowers her tablet slowly.

Ryan notices her face and straightens. "Erin?"

She shakes her head once. "Nothing. Just… tired."

It's the fastest lie she's told in months.

Rowan finally speaks.

Not to reassure.

To control the board.

"You can stay the night," he says.

Not inviting.

Measured.

Graham's eyes brighten — not with gratitude.

With confirmation.

"Thank you," he says. "I won't be any trouble."

Rowan meets his gaze.

Flat.

Unmoved.

"People who say that usually are," Rowan replies. "We'll talk in the morning."

Isorae feels the lie settle into the earth like a fracture you don't feel until weight is applied.

That night, Isorae wakes with certainty. She lies still, breath even, glow quiet beneath her skin.

Across the hollow, Graham is awake too. Staring up through the branches. Hands folded over his chest like a man in prayer.

He doesn't reach for instruments.

He doesn't need to.

He exhales slowly.

Reverently.

Closer than you think.

The valley shifts in its sleep.

And for the first time in almost a year, Stonewake does not rest.

16
REARRANGED

The dream is wrong from the start.

Not violent or loud.

Just… rearranged.

Isorae knows the valley in her sleep the way you know your own pulse — without effort, without vision. It usually meets her as sensation: soil warm beneath bare feet, breath moving through leaves, the quiet gravity of stone holding everything in place.

Tonight, the ground feels farther away.

She stands at the edge of the stream, but the water does not curve. It runs straight — narrow and disciplined — its surface smooth as glass. No fish break it. No insects touch it.

The trees lean inward.

Not protectively.

Curiously.

She turns, expecting Rowan.

Instead, there is a corridor.

Not built.

Implied.

The space between two stands of pine has been widened, stripped of undergrowth, shaped by repetition rather than feet — a passage that suggests itself without ever admitting to being there. Pale light spills along it. Not moonlight. Not firelight.

Something cooler.

Something instructional.

Her glow tightens beneath her skin.

"No," she whispers.

The corridor waits.

She steps back.

The valley does not follow.

That's when she feels it — the pressure behind her eyes, the faint tug low in her sternum, as if someone has found the edge of a thread and is testing whether it will move.

Her breath stutters.

A shape forms at the far end of the path.

A presence.

She does not see his face.

She doesn't need to.

Graham's attention slides across her like a hand that never touches skin.

There you are.

The thought is not spoken.

It doesn't echo.

It simply exists — confident, patient, already certain she will answer eventually.

Her glow flares — hot, defiant — and the valley tries to respond.

Roots surge toward the corridor.

Stone tightens.

The path narrows.

But something resists.

The corridor holds its shape.

Graham does not step closer.

He doesn't have to.

You don't belong to the land, the thought presses — not cruel, not forceful —*you belong to the space between what it can hold.*

Her pulse slams hard against her ribs.

She screams—

—and wakes.

Isorae jerks upright in bed, breath tearing out of her throat, glow spiking sharp and bright beneath her skin. The cabin answers immediately — wood creaking, the low hum of the hearth shifting as if startled.

Rowan is awake in the same instant.

He's already moving, hand firm at her back, the other bracing her shoulder, anchoring her before she can leave herself.

"Isorae."

His voice is low. Certain.

He presses his forehead to hers without asking.

"Stay in your bones," he murmurs.

She clutches his shirt, fingers digging in, breath coming in uneven pulls.

"He was there," she gasps. "Not touching me. Not speaking. Just—"

Her voice fractures.

"Watching."

Rowan goes very still.

"Graham?"

She nods.

"Yes."

Outside the cabin, the valley shifts — not loudly, not in alarm — but uneasily. A dog barks once, then quiets. The hum beneath the floorboards falters, then resumes at a lower pitch.

Rowan cups her face, forcing her focus back into him. "You're here," he says. "You're awake. You're not alone."

She swallows hard. "He wasn't in the land. He was beside it."

That lands.

Rowan exhales slowly. "That's not how this works."

"It is for him."

They sit like that for a long moment, listening to the valley resettle itself by degrees.

Elsewhere in Stonewake, Erin wakes with a sharp inhale.

Not from fear.

From displacement.

The dream has shifted — not broken, not interrupted — but reorganized. She sits upright in the dark, heart racing, the shape of the valley wrong in her mind. Too clean. Too distant. Like a map stripped of scale.

Beside her, Dax stirs immediately.

"Hey," he murmurs, already half-awake. "What's wrong?"

Erin doesn't answer at first. She reaches for the scanner on the low table by the bed out of habit more than hope. The screen lights. Scrolls.

Nothing.

No baseline. No passive hum. No background noise.

Empty.

Her jaw tightens.

"Erin," Dax says again, sharper now. He pushes himself up on one elbow, eyes on her face. "Talk to me."

She exhales slowly. "My dreams changed."

That's all it takes.

Dax swings his legs over the side of the bed, fully awake now. "Changed how?"

"I wasn't in the valley," she says. "I was… over it. Like I was looking down at something I wasn't supposed to see."

She finally looks at him.

"I need to see Rowan and Isorae. Now."

Dax doesn't argue. Doesn't ask for more explanation. He's already pulling on his shirt, boots shoved on without bothering to lace them properly.

"Okay," he says simply. "I'm coming with you."

They move through the sleeping paths without speaking, the valley quiet around them in a way that feels newly deliberate. By the time they reach Rowan and Isorae's cabin, Erin is fully dressed, pulse steady but wrong — like a compass that's learned a new north.

Inside, the glow beneath Isorae's skin has drawn tight again.

Contained.

Controlled.

Waiting.

"You felt it," Isorae says hoarsely.

Erin nods. "My equipment didn't."

A beat.

"But my dreams did."

Rowan turns to her. "How?"

Erin swallows. "I was mapping the valley in my sleep."

Pause.

"Not with it."

Her voice tightens.

"Over it."

Silence settles heavy.

Isorae presses her palm flat to her sternum.

"He's not just watching me," she whispers. "He's learning how I exist when I'm not awake."

Rowan's jaw flexes — slow, dangerous.

"He doesn't get that access."

Isorae shakes her head, fear threading her voice for the first time in months.

"He already has it."

Far beyond the cabins, far beyond the inner paths, Graham lies awake beneath the trees, hands folded loosely over his chest, eyes open to the canopy above.

He smiles faintly.

Not because the dream reached her.

Because she woke knowing who was there.

That's the first threshold.

And thresholds, once noticed, are easier to cross.

The valley tightens in its sleep.

And somewhere beneath root and stone, something old shifts — not to wake, not to attack — but to prepare.

17

PROVISIONAL

Rowan does not go looking for the man.

He chooses where to be.

The morning unfolds clean and ordinary — the kind of deliberate calm the valley has learned how to generate when it wants people to forget the shape of danger. Smoke lifts from chimneys. Someone hums near the gardens. Two children race each other along the creek path, shrieking with laughter.

Peace, practiced.

Rowan splits wood behind the long shed at the eastern edge, movements steady and economical. Each strike lands true. Each breath remains even. He keeps his awareness wide without sharpening it into expectation.

He knows Graham will find him.

The axe bites deep into the log.

And then—

Presence.

No footstep.

No sound.

Just the subtle shift of space acknowledging that it is no longer unoccupied.

"Rowan."

The voice is familiar now.

That's the problem.

Rowan finishes the swing he's in the middle of, sets the axe down carefully, and turns.

Graham stands several paces back, hands loose at his sides, posture open in that practiced, disarming way — as if yesterday's introduction around the fire ring had been nothing more than coincidence. He looks exactly as he did before: unremarkable, well-contained, dressed like someone who understands how not to stand out.

Nothing about him demands attention.

Everything about him is designed to invite it.

"You chose a quiet spot," Graham says lightly. "I hoped you would."

Rowan regards him without expression. "You shouldn't have hoped."

Graham smiles — not offended. Interested.

The valley hums low beneath them, attentive but restrained. It remembers him now. It has not decided what to do with that memory.

"You didn't sleep," Graham says.

Rowan steps closer.

Not aggressive.

Deliberate.

The air tightens by a fraction — alignment shifting just enough to register. Graham notices. His breath changes. His pupils widen, just slightly.

"You've been in her dreams," Rowan says.

The smile does not falter.

"I wondered how long you'd let that stay unspoken," Graham replies.

Rowan stops an arm's length away.

"I'm saying it now," he says evenly. "So there's no confusion."

Graham studies him with open curiosity. "You're protective."

Rowan's mouth curves, barely.

"I'm territorial."

The valley answers the word.

Not with movement — with presence. Stone settles. Roots hold. The ground beneath Graham's boots firms, not trapping him, simply registering him as something provisional.

Graham glances down.

Then back up.

"You know, ARIS saw both of you," Graham says easily.

"Isorae as the anomaly. You as the bridge."

A faint smile touches his mouth — not amused. Satisfied.

"They understood what you were. They modeled the bond endlessly."

He pauses, eyes sharpening as if adjusting focus.

"What they never accounted for was desire."

His smile thins.

"Systems don't want things," he says softly.

"People do."

A beat.

"And people don't stop just because something is… inconvenient."

Rowan does not blink.

He lifts his hand and places it flat against Graham's chest, directly over his heart.

The contact is not violent.

Not aggressive.

It reads as restraint.

The world destabilizes.

Not visually — but somatically, like a sentence losing its grammar halfway through. Graham's breath stutters as the ground beneath him hesitates, briefly unsure whether it still needs to agree with gravity.

He doesn't fall.

He doesn't sink.

He simply… isn't confirmed.

Rowan leans in just enough that the words belong only to him.

"You've misunderstood the sequence," he says quietly.

"Desire doesn't give you access."

Graham swallows. The thrill hasn't left his eyes — but something else has entered them now.

"I recognize her," he says, softer. Almost reverent.

The valley leans closer.

Birdsong cuts off mid-note, like sound reconsidering itself.

Rowan's voice lowers — not anger, not threat — authority settling into place.

"And because I recognize her," he says,

"I determine what happens to anything that wants her without consent."

For one suspended heartbeat, Graham stands at the edge of something that feels very much like being unmade sideways — not destroyed, not erased — disqualified.

Then Rowan steps back.

The ground remembers how to hold weight.

The world resumes its rules.

Graham inhales sharply, composure snapping back into place with impressive speed. He laughs once — breathless, exhilarated, shaken in a way he mistakes for excitement.

"You could have killed me."

Rowan retrieves the axe and rests both palms on the handle.

"I still can."

Graham's smile tightens — sharp now, calculating.

"You won't," he says. "Not yet."

He turns, already confident in his exit.

As he walks away, he adds lightly, without looking back,

"She's waking earlier every morning."

Rowan does not move.

Does not follow.

Does not answer.

But the valley does.

Not attacking or warning.

Marking.

When Graham disappears into the trees, the air exhales — not relief.

Recognition.

Rowan remains where he is, hands steady on the axe handle.

The valley hums — low, deliberate — settling around the mark it has just made.

Footsteps approach behind him. Unhurried. Familiar.

He knows who it is before she speaks.

Isorae stops a few paces back, her glow drawn tight beneath her skin, posture composed but alert — like someone who felt a door close and wanted to know what passed through it.

"You felt what he did," she says quietly.

Rowan turns.

"Yes."

She studies his face for a beat, then steps closer and presses her palm flat to his chest — not seeking reassurance.

Confirming.

"He's not going to stop."

Rowan covers her hand with his. "No," he agrees. "He's going to escalate."

18

LATENCY

Graham does not return to Stonewake.

That is how Rowan knows the encounter mattered.

Days pass without disturbance. No bent fern. No displaced soil. No sideways hum brushing the valley's skin. Stonewake exhales and resumes its rhythms with the confidence of a place that believes it has already survived the worst of its danger.

That belief is earned.

It is also exploitable.

Rowan allows life to continue — not because he trusts the quiet, but because he understands it. Fear tightens patterns. Normalcy stretches them just enough to reveal their seams.

Watches rotate. Tools are sharpened. Children run the same paths they ran yesterday. The valley hums low and steady beneath it all, deeper than before, like a body that has learned how to hold itself.

Still.

Something has shifted.

Isorae notices it first in moments that should not matter.

Standing alone while rinsing cups after a meal.

Crossing from one cabin's shadow into another's light.

Pausing with her hand on a doorframe, unsure why she hasn't opened it yet.

The sensation never announces itself.

It does not arrive as pressure.

It does not resonate like threat.

It does not echo the way ARIS once did.

It feels like space being held for her.

Not claimed.

Prepared.

She tells herself it is nothing. She has learned not to narrate every internal fluctuation into danger. Healing has taught her restraint.

But her glow disagrees.

It tightens in those moments — not defensively, not brightly — but inward, like silk being drawn close to skin.

She does not mention it to Rowan at first.

She listens instead.

Erin notices the next deviation two nights later.

She has stopped looking for anomalies in the obvious places. Instead, she charts what is no longer present — background noise thinning where it should thicken, harmonics smoothing when they should fray.

Her screens read clean.

Too clean.

"This isn't absence," she murmurs to herself in the dim light of their cabin. Dax shifts beside her, half asleep, an arm heavy across her waist.

"You're doing the thing," he mutters.

She exhales carefully. "It's not masking."

He opens one eye. "Then what is it?"

She doesn't answer right away.

"It's restraint," she finally says. "Like someone choosing not to touch a surface they already know is hot."

Dax sits up fully now. "I really don't like that."

Neither does she.

Ryan experiences it as misalignment.

Not fear. Not pain. Just… drift.

He overshoots where someone should be standing. Misjudges the edge of a path by half a step. Turns his head toward a sound that arrives a fraction of a second later than expected.

He compensates easily. He always has.

Still, one evening, he pauses near the outer paths.

"Does it feel thinner out there?" he asks Rowan casually. "Not weaker. Just… less crowded."

Rowan studies the trees.

"Yes," he says. "Like something stepped back on purpose."

Silas joins them, gaze already narrowed toward the ridge. "That's how hunters stop spooking prey."

That night, Isorae dreams without images.

No corridors. No voices. No presence she can point to.

She dreams of alignment.

Of herself rotated just slightly out of phase with her body, like a door not fully seated in its frame. She wakes before dawn with her glow drawn tight and her heart racing without explanation.

Rowan is awake immediately.

"What?" he asks.

She presses her palm to her sternum, grounding. "Nothing touched me."

He waits.

"But something practiced," she finishes.

That is when she tells him everything.

About the moments between moments.

About attention without pressure.

About the certainty — absolute and cold — that whoever is aware of her now is no longer nearby.

Rowan listens without interruption.

When she finishes, he nods once.

"He's stopped looking from outside," he says. "Which means he's learned how to look from where you already exist."

They tell Erin.

They tell Silas.

They do not tell everyone.

There is no alarm.

Only recalibration.

Watches widen instead of tighten. Erin begins mapping avoidance instead of signal. Rowan adjusts patrols to favor thresholds rather than borders — places where Stonewake meets what it is not.

The valley adapts.

But adaptation assumes rules.

And Graham has already stepped outside them.

Far from Stonewake — far enough that even Isorae cannot feel him directly — Graham stands in a place the land never finished forming.

A dead fold between territories.

No memory. No resistance. No welcome.

Perfect.

He has stripped his equipment down to the bare minimum — not because he lacks resources, but because he no longer needs permission. He has already learned what matters.

Not coordinates or defenses or force.

Intervals.

Latency.

The way Isorae's resonance loosens when she believes herself fully held.

"She's anchored," he murmurs quietly.

Not impressed.

Not afraid.

Certain.

"Just not where they think."

He closes his eyes, fingers still, breath measured — listening not to Stonewake's presence, but to the tension around her. The way the land bends to accommodate something it cannot fully enclose. The way her resonance doesn't root — it passes through.

"There's movement in her," he continues, voice low, almost intimate. "Continuity without containment."

A faint smile touches his mouth.

"They believe the valley holds her because it responds when she's here. Because it steadies around her."

A soft exhale.

"That's correlation, not custody."

His fingers adjust the control — not tuning, not forcing — testing. Mapping the edges of a permission structure that was never meant to exist.

"She isn't of the land," he says gently. "She's of the transition. The seam. The moment where things agree to change."

His pulse quickens — just slightly.

"And seams," he whispers, "are meant to be opened."

He leans closer to the instrument, as if it could hear him.

"I won't take you from what protects you," he says, almost kindly.

"I'll take you from what you trust."

A pause.

"From the certainty that the ground will always answer you first."

His smile is slow. Controlled. Devotional.

"After all," he murmurs, "bridges were never meant to choose who crosses them."

Back in Stonewake, the day unfolds without incident.

Meals are prepared. Repairs are finished. Conversation drifts where it always does when nothing demands attention. The valley hums steady beneath it all — responsive, untroubled, convinced of its own continuity.

Isorae moves through the afternoon easily.

She helps Erin sort salvaged components. Laughs when Dax says something deliberately stupid. Brushes past Rowan once, fingers catching briefly at his wrist — a familiar, grounding touch — before continuing on.

She feels… held.

Not intensely. Not dramatically.

Simply enough that the quiet no longer feels like something to interrogate.

That is the danger.

When she turns toward the stream later, it is not because she feels called. It is because she doesn't.

The path is familiar. The air warm. The valley present in the way it always is when it has nothing to correct.

Rowan registers her direction in the same way he registers everything now — as part of a wider pattern, not a point of concern. Erin's equipment reads clean. Silas's line of sight remains uninterrupted.

Nothing flags.

Nothing resists.

Nothing leans.

Stonewake hums steady.

Normal.

Safe.

And far beyond the ridgelines — in a place without memory or edge — Graham exhales slowly.

Not because the moment itself has arrived.

But because the final condition has.

The land is answering itself.

The watchers are watching outward.

And she is no longer checking whether the ground will answer her first.

His smile is faint. Controlled.

Satisfied.

"Now," he murmurs.

Confirmation.

Because abductions don't begin with force.

They begin when certainty goes quiet.

19

THE INTERVAL

Rowan feels the land answer late mid-stride — not as sound or warning, but as delay.

The hum beneath his ribs lags behind his breath, like an echo that forgot when it was supposed to return.

Late.

He stops.

The valley does not.

Laughter carries from the gardens. A pot clatters. Water moves over stone with its usual patience. Stonewake looks exactly like itself.

That's wrong.

Rowan turns toward the stream.

Isorae is there.

Kneeling at the bank, sleeves rolled, hands in the water, posture loose in a way that twists something sharp in his chest. Her glow is present but quiet, folded close, like she has finally stopped listening for danger.

The land is not leaning toward her.

It is not orienting.

It is… neutral.

Rowan takes a step.

The ground firms too quickly beneath his foot — an overcorrection, clumsy and wrong, like a muscle firing out of sequence.

"Isorae," he calls.

She looks up immediately.

Smiles.

The smile lands like a blow.

"Rowan?" she says. "Did you need—"

The stream straightens.

Not visibly.

Functionally.

The water loses its habit of bending around stone. Its sound thins, smooths, sharpens into something narrow and directional, like flow being instructed instead of allowed.

Isorae's smile fades.

She feels it now.

Not arrival.

Presence.

Her glow snaps tight — instinctive, sharp — and for a heartbeat the valley tries to answer. The hum deepens. Stone tightens. Moss draws close to earth.

But the response stutters.

The land hesitates.

Behind her, the air folds.

Not opening.

Rewriting.

The space between two stones stretches — not widening so much as misaligning, as if distance has been edited without moving the objects themselves. Light thins along the seam, clarifying instead of dimming, until the edge of the stream looks unfinished.

Isorae rises slowly.

Carefully.

The ground accepts her weight.

The valley does not object.

That is the betrayal.

Rowan breaks into a run.

"Isorae!"

Roots surge late — grabbing at his boots, not to stop him but to anchor him — stone lifting in uneven ribs that slow his stride without blocking it. The valley is trying to help.

It is just behind itself.

Isorae turns fully now, breath shallow, eyes dark.

"He's here," she says.

Not to Rowan.

To the space behind her.

The seam answers.

Not with voice.

With certainty.

Her glow flares — brilliant, furious — and for one impossible instant, the valley does respond. Stone locks. The hum roars. The ground remembers how to be a boundary.

Too late.

The seam widens.

Not pulling her.

Making room.

Gravity tilts sideways.

Isorae stumbles — not falling, not standing — caught between directions that can't agree. Rowan lunges.

His fingers close around her wrist.

Contact.

Real.

She gasps — sharp, startled — glow spiking bright enough to hurt his eyes.

Then the ground delays again.

Just a fraction.

Just enough.

Isorae's body jerks — not yanked, not dragged — redirected, folded sideways through a place the valley cannot finish refusing.

Her glow streaks once — a tearing line of light — and then—

Gone.

The seam snaps shut.

The stream resumes its curve.

The sound of water returns.

Normal.

Safe.

Silent.

Rowan hits the bank on his knees.

Hard.

The land slams back into alignment beneath him — furious now, roaring too late, roots tearing free of soil, stone heaving as if it could rewind itself through will alone.

"She was here," Rowan says hoarsely.

The valley answers.

Yes.

Too late.

Erin is running toward him, scanner shrieking now — not reading, not mapping, just screaming static where certainty used to live. Silas appears on the ridge, already moving. Dax shouts something Rowan doesn't hear.

Rowan presses his palm to the ground.

Nothing answers where Isorae should be.

No echo.

No shimmer.

No bridge.

Only absence shaped like precision.

Far away — impossibly far — Graham exhales.

Slow.

Measured.

Satisfied.

The dead fold resolves around him, space knitting itself into coherence where no land has ever agreed to exist. Isorae lies crumpled at his feet, unconscious, her glow pulled tight and erratic beneath her skin — not extinguished, not free.

Breathing.

Alive.

Out of phase.

Graham kneels.

Does not touch her.

Not yet.

"She trusted the ground," he murmurs, reverent. "And the ground trusted me to be patient."

He stands as the seam finishes sealing, the interval collapsing into something stable and wrong.

Stonewake's howl reaches nowhere.

And for the first time since it learned its name—the valley is forced to accept a truth it cannot undo:

Not everything taken is stolen.

Some things are removed with permission the land didn't know it was giving.

20

COUNTERPHASE

The valley reacts. Roots tear free along the stream bank. Stone grinds out of alignment with a sound that rattles teeth. The hum beneath everything spikes — sharp, offended — not panic, not fear.

Violation.

Rowan is already on his knees where Isorae stood moments ago, one hand braced in the mud, the other hovering over nothing. The space is wrong — not torn, not hollow.

Finished.

"She was here," he says.

His voice does not rise.

The land answers anyway — a tremor that runs outward and dies unfinished.

Too late.

Rowan exhales once and stands.

There is no searching in him now. No scanning. No uncertainty. The movement is precise, final — the way a blade settles into its grip.

Erin is at his side, scanner clenched in her hands. "There's no displacement signature," she says. "No residual drag. Like she was—"

"Removed," Rowan says.

The word lands clean.

Silas has already moved upslope, eyes tracking patterns that haven't resolved yet. Dax stands close to Erin, not touching, but ready. Ryan is still near the tree line, very still, watching the place Isorae should be.

The valley surges again — angry this time.

Rowan turns toward it.

"Enough."

The word cuts through the upheaval like a command the land remembers how to obey.

Roots withdraw reluctantly. Stone settles back into place with visible resistance. The stream resumes its curve, pretending nothing has happened.

Rowan's jaw tightens.

"No," he says quietly. "That doesn't get to be finished."

He turns back to the others.

This is not a meeting.

This is definition.

"Graham did not overpower Stonewake," Rowan says. "He didn't breach it. He didn't fight it."

He looks at Erin.

"He made it late."

Erin swallows. "That shouldn't be possible."

"And yet," Rowan replies.

Silas's voice is calm, grim. "Where would he take her?"

Rowan closes his eyes — not to listen to the valley, but to the absence where Isorae should be. The bridge inside him strains outward and finds nothing stable to lock onto.

Not distance.

Misalignment.

"Not a place," Rowan says. "An interval."

Erin stiffens. "That's unstable."

"Yes," Rowan says. "Which means it's survivable."

The valley hums lower — uncertain, listening.

Rowan continues, voice controlled, unyielding. "We are not reacting. We are not panicking. And we are not scattering."

He meets each of their eyes in turn.

"We retrieve her."

Only then does Ryan step forward.

No rush. No bravado.

Just decision.

"I want to help," he says. "However you're doing that — I want in."

Rowan studies him.

"You understand this won't be clean," Rowan says. "And it won't be fast."

Ryan nods once. "She's my family."

Evan moves immediately to Ryan's side.

"And he's mine," Evan says — not challenging, not loud. Just present. "I'm not saying no. I'm saying I don't want him treated like expendable muscle."

Rowan considers that.

Then nods. "He won't be."

Ryan exhales, tension easing just enough to matter.

Rowan turns back to Erin. "Map what's missing. Not what's there. Every hesitation. Every place the land pauses when it shouldn't."

She's already moving. "I can do that."

"Silas," Rowan says. "Widen patrols. Don't tighten them. If the valley feels hunted, he'll feel it too."

Silas nods. "Understood."

Rowan faces the stream again — the ordinary water, the ordinary stones, the place that failed by a fraction of a second.

"He thinks removing her gives him control," Rowan says. "He thinks uncertainty belongs to him."

He places his palm flat against the earth.

His voice lowers — not loud, not pleading.

Certain.

"You did not betray her," he tells the land. "And I will not punish you for hesitating."

The hum shifts — not calm, not obedient.

Aligned.

"But I will not allow him to believe you chose this."

The valley answers — deeper now, slower.

Ready.

Rowan straightens.

"There will be no chase," he says. "No spectacle. No mistakes."

His mouth curves, cold and sharp.

"He wanted her out of phase."

A pause.

"Then we remind him what a bridge is for."

Stonewake breathes.

And somewhere between restraint and violence, Rowan begins preparing to do something the valley has never been forced to do before—

Not defend.

Not contain.

Take something back.

21

THE SHAPE OF ELSEWHERE

Stonewake reorients. Rowan can feel it as soon as they move beyond the inner paths — the valley stretching its awareness instead of tightening it, widening perception like a pupil adjusting to low light.

This is not pursuit. This is recalibration.

Behind them, Erin and Evan stand at the edge of the clearing — the last stable point before the land begins to behave differently.

"I'm not going with you," Erin says, already adjusting the small handheld unit clipped at her belt. Her tone is brisk, certain. "If I leave the baseline, I lose reference. He's working on latency — I need to stay where the delay shows up."

Rowan nods. He never questions her instincts.

Dax pauses mid-step.

Erin looks up at him sharply. "Hey."

He turns back.

"Be careful," she says. Not dramatic. Not soft. Just precise — like everything she offers when it matters.

Dax's mouth twitches. "I always am."

She snorts. "No. You're competent. That's not the same thing."

He steps closer, grips the back of her neck briefly, and kisses her — fast, firm, grounding. Not a goodbye. A reminder.

"Don't let the valley get clever without us," he murmurs.

Erin exhales, one hand fisting briefly in his shirt. "Come back breathing."

He grins faintly and turns away before she can say anything else.

Evan adjusts the strap on his own unit, fingers steady. "I'll stay with her. Medical support. Signal relay." A pause. "And someone needs to keep Stonewake from spiraling."

Rowan meets his eyes. "You're doing more than that."

Evan nods once. "I know."

They don't say Isorae's name.

They don't need to.

Rowan turns toward the ridge.

Silas is already moving upslope, scanning not for tracks but for distortion — places where sound fails to echo correctly, where leaves hang too still, where the land feels… edited.

Dax falls into step beside Rowan, quiet now. No jokes. No commentary. His hand rests near the knife at his belt — not itching to draw. Ready.

They fan out without discussion.

Practice.

Ryan lingers for half a second near Evan, catches his wrist.

"I'll be careful," he says quietly.

Evan doesn't tell him not to go.

He just nods. "You come back."

Ryan squeezes once and jogs to join the others, slotting into the spacing like he's always belonged there.

Stonewake watches them leave.

Then exhales.

The land does not point.

It permits.

Behind them — far enough to be felt but not heard — Erin watches the feed shift from stable to elastic. She doesn't interpret it yet. She just holds it steady, anchoring reference so the others don't lose scale.

Evan stands beside her, one hand resting on the edge of the table, eyes fixed on the tree line.

"They're far enough now," he says.

Erin nods. "Yes."

"Good," Evan replies softly. "That means if it snaps…"

He doesn't finish.

She doesn't ask him to.

Rowan feels the difference immediately — the way the ground no longer guides his steps, only accepts them. The hum beneath his feet has thinned, stretched wider, like a note held too long. Not wrong. Just no longer intimate.

They do not follow the stream.

Rowan knows better the moment they reach the bank and feel nothing pulling forward — no drag, no wake, no residual insistence from the water itself. The stream is calm now, almost studiously so, as if whatever passed through it has already been dismissed.

The stream is where Isorae vanished.

It is not where the land took her.

Rowan angles them upslope instead, away from the water and into the trees, following the faint, wrong pressure that doesn't behave like direction so much as permission deferred.

They move in a shallow arc, climbing gradually. Silas ranges ahead and slightly above, testing elevation where sound should bend and doesn't. Dax keeps close to Rowan's left, gaze flicking not to the trees but to the spaces between them — gaps where the valley's attention seems to slide instead of settle.

Ryan trails half a step behind, alert but unforced. He's not scanning like Silas. He's feeling for rhythm — the way footsteps should land, the way paths should anticipate weight.

"This isn't a trail," Ryan says quietly after a few minutes.

Rowan nods. "No."

"It's not erased either," Dax adds. "It's like… nothing was supposed to mark it in the first place."

They stop where the land subtly misbehaves.

Not dramatically. No broken brush. No displaced stone.

Just a place where the slope should crest and doesn't — where the ground flattens too early, as if it forgot what it was becoming.

Silas crouches and presses his palm to the soil.

"It's thinner here," he says. "Not weak. Indecisive."

Rowan closes his eyes — not to command, not to reach — but to listen the way he's learned to when the land no longer speaks first.

The bridge hums.

Not strained.

But extended.

Like a span holding weight on one end it can't yet see.

"She passed through," Rowan says finally.

Dax exhales slowly. "Not carried."

"No," Rowan agrees. "Allowed."

That lands heavier than any word so far.

The stream wasn't a route.

It has never been meant to carry anything forward.

And whatever took Isorae didn't drag her uphill through stone and root.

It let her go — and the land, uncertain but complicit, made room.

They move again, slower now.

Not searching for Isorae.

Searching around the absence she left behind.

The farther they go, the less Stonewake feels like a place and the more it feels like a decision still being negotiated. Sound behaves oddly. Wind arrives late. Shadows don't quite line up with their sources.

Ryan swallows. "I don't like how quiet it is."

Rowan doesn't answer.

Because neither does the valley.

Out on the slope, Rowan stops again.

This time, the land reacts.

Not pulling or resisting.

Acknowledging.

A low, directional pressure — not a path, not guidance — just a sense of elsewhere beginning to cohere.

Rowan opens his eyes.

"There," he says.

Not certainty.

Orientation.

They turn as one.

And somewhere beyond the next rise — not close, not reachable yet — the shape of the search finally sharpens.

Not into pursuit. Into intent.

22
LEARNED WHILE AWAKE

Isorae wakes into wrongness. Not darkness. Not pain.

A place that cannot decide what it is.

There is no ground beneath her, but there is resistance — as if the air itself has weight. She inhales and the breath returns altered, bent around an invisible geometry that does not agree with lungs. Her glow surges instinctively —

—and rebounds.

Folded inward.

Sensation returns out of order — pressure before gravity, breath before air. Her chest rises too fast, lungs dragging against resistance that doesn't belong to atmosphere. The effort sends a sharp, disorienting pulse through her ribs.

Her glow reacts instinctively.

It surges—

—and rebounds.

Folded inward, reflected back at her like light striking a surface that refuses to absorb it.

Stonewake is gone.

Not severed.

Just muted.

She can still feel it — distant, faint, like a pulse heard through deep water. Present enough to ache. Too far away to answer.

Her heart stutters.

She tries to move.

The space responds immediately — not tightening, not striking — adjusting. Learning the shape of her intent and correcting it before it can complete. Her shoulders lock. Her spine remains upright whether she wants it to or not.

She inhales sharply.

That's when she becomes aware she isn't alone.

Graham stands a few paces away.

Not looming or hidden.

Placed.

As if he chose the exact distance where she would have to acknowledge him without being able to reach him.

He watches her with open interest, but he does not rush.

That is the worst part.

Isorae expects force — expects pressure, pain, the space to punish her resistance the way ARIS did.

Instead, the interval eases.

Not releasing her.

Permitting her.

The alignment loosens just enough to feel dangerous.

"You're awake," Graham says gently.

Her jaw tightens. She grounds hard — bone, breath, memory. Rowan's hands at her back. The weight of the valley answering her name.

Her glow stabilizes, drawing tight and deliberate beneath her skin.

"Where am I," she demands.

Graham smiles faintly. "Between."

She laughs once — sharp, humorless. "That's not an answer."

"It's the only honest one."

He steps closer.

Her body reacts before her mind can stop it — glow recoiling hard beneath her skin, breath hitching as something in her recognizes a predator even when the shape is human.

Graham notices.

Of course he does.

"Good," he murmurs. "You're oriented enough to feel it."

"Feel what," she snaps.

He stops an arm's length away.

Not touching.

Not yet.

"The delay," he says. "The moment between movement and consequence. Most systems can't tolerate it for long."

His gaze tracks her like a living equation.

"But you're still holding."

She curls her fingers into fists. "You took me."

Graham tilts his head. "No."

The word lands softly.

Accurately.

"I stepped aside," he continues. "Long enough for you to take one more step than you realized you were taking."

Her glow spikes — hot, furious. "You redirected me?"

"Yes."

Certain.

Not triumphant.

That is worse.

She strains against the space again — testing, not panicking — and feels the correction immediately.

Not restraint.

Instruction.

"You don't own the paths I walk," she says coldly.

Graham studies her with something like admiration. "No. But I understand how they bend."

That lands colder than threat.

He raises one hand.

Not threatening.

Almost reverent.

"Don't touch me," she says, voice steady by force of will.

He pauses.

For a fraction of a heartbeat, she thinks he might stop.

Then his fingers close around her wrist.

The contact is precise. Controlled.

Isorae gasps — not from pain, but from the way her body reacts before her mind can intervene. Her glow tries to rise again—and finds nowhere to go.

Graham exhales softly. "There it is."

She tries to pull free.

The space resists her instead.

"Let go," she snarls, panic beginning to edge her voice despite her control.

Graham tightens his grip.

"This is the difference between me and ARIS," he says calmly. "They tried to contain you."

His thumb shifts — barely — pressing where her pulse betrays her, fast and unsteady.

"I'm learning you."

Her knees threaten to buckle.

Not because he is overpowering her.

Because he is listening.

Every tremor. Every instinctive withdrawal. Every place her glow folds inward to protect itself.

"You don't get to—" Her voice breaks. She swallows hard. "You don't get to touch me."

Graham's eyes darken with ownership.

"I already have," he says quietly.

That's when she feels it.

A pressure sliding along the inside of her awareness. Cataloging. Mapping. Memorizing.

Her breath goes sharp. "Rowan—"

Graham's grip tightens just enough to interrupt the grounding reflex before it can complete.

"No," he says gently. "You don't call for him."

Her glow flares wild, furious.

The interval shudders.

Far away — impossibly far — Stonewake groans.

Graham feels it and smiles.

"There he is," he murmurs. "Right on time."

He releases her wrist abruptly.

Isorae stumbles back, nearly falling, heart hammering painfully. She clutches her arm to her chest, skin burning where he touched her — not injured, but violated in a way that goes deeper than flesh.

Graham steps back as well.

Satisfied.

"You see," he says, adjusting his cuffs like this was a discussion, not an intrusion. "I don't need to hurt you yet."

She glares at him, shaking with controlled fury. "Rowan will kill you."

Graham considers that.

"Eventually," he agrees. "But not before I finish proving my theory."

He turns to leave, already certain she cannot follow.

"Oh," he adds lightly, without looking back. "You should know — next time, I won't ask your body for permission first."

The interval seals behind him.

Isorae drops to her knees the moment he's gone.

Not in surrender.

In aftermath.

Her breath tears free in harsh, uneven pulls. Her glow flickers beneath her skin — furious, wounded, alive.

She presses her palm to her wrist where his thumb rested.

And she understands with absolute clarity:

He does not need her broken.

He needs her aware.

23
The Allowance

Intent does not hurry.

Rowan knows this as they move.

The valley has shifted from intimacy to allowance — no longer guiding, no longer anticipating — but it hasn't withdrawn. It is present in the way a witness is present: aware, silent, refusing to interfere unless asked correctly.

That refusal is new.

They crest the rise slowly. The ground here feels unfinished beneath their boots — not unstable, but undecided. Pebbles shift without sound. The wind slides past them instead of through them, as if uncertain which side of their bodies it belongs to.

Silas raises a fist.

They stop.

Ahead, the land opens into a shallow basin that should have collected water and didn't. The bowl is dry. Too dry. Grass grows in hesitant patches, as if it forgot the rules halfway through becoming itself.

"This place never resolved," Silas says quietly.

Dax scans the perimeter. "Looks like it tried."

Rowan steps forward alone.

The hum beneath his ribs stretches again — thinner now, longer — like the bridge is being asked to span something wider than it was designed for. He doesn't push. He lets the sensation register fully before responding.

Rowan kneels and presses his palm to the ground.

The land answers — slowly.

Not with memory.

With strain.

This place doesn't resist him. It doesn't yield. It receives the contact the way a surface receives vibration — registering force without claiming authorship.

His breath tightens.

"This is where the stress transferred," he says.

Silas crouches beside him, frowning. "Not the breach."

"No," Rowan agrees. "The extension."

Dax's gaze lifts, scanning the slope. "So whatever took her didn't just pull once."

Rowan's jaw hardens. "It leveraged what was already moving."

The bridge hums — stretched farther than it should be, still holding.

Ryan swallows. "Like grabbing one end of a rope and letting the tension do the rest."

"Yes," Rowan says. "And this is where the rope learned it could keep going."

The land shivers faintly — not alarmed, not resisting.

Acknowledging load.

They don't linger.

They move.

Not because this place is wrong, but because it is no longer neutral.

They move through the basin single-file, spacing instinctive. No one speaks. Even Dax's usual commentary stays locked behind his teeth.

Halfway across, Ryan stumbles. Not hard. Not dangerously.

Just enough to break rhythm.

"I'm good," he says immediately, holding up a hand — but Rowan has already turned.

"What did you feel," Rowan asks.

Ryan frowns, searching for the right language. "Like… I stepped where a step used to be. And it wasn't anymore."

Rowan nods once. "Latency."

Ryan exhales. "Yeah. That."

They clear the basin and the land tightens again — not closing, but refocusing. Trees draw nearer. Sound begins to behave more predictably. The wind remembers how to move.

Dax lets out a breath he didn't realize he was holding. "That was a test."

Rowan doesn't disagree.

Behind them, far downslope, Erin tightens her grip on the handheld and marks the basin with a soft internal tag — not a location, not coordinates, but a behavioral signature. Something the system can recognize without naming.

Evan watches her face instead of the screen.

"That spot mattered," he says.

"Yes," Erin replies. "Not because of where it is."

Evan nods once. "Then they'll try it again."

"Or they already have," Erin says quietly.

Out on the slope, Rowan stops for the third time.

This time, the land reacts immediately.

Not with pressure.

With resistance.

Not refusal — alignment.

The bridge hums deeper, slower, as if something on the far end has shifted weight without warning. Testing.

Rowan straightens.

"She's closer," he says.

Dax's head snaps up. "You sure?"

"No," Rowan answers evenly. "But she's louder."

That doesn't mean safety.

That doesn't mean rescue.

It means contact has not been severed.

They adjust formation without discussion.

Silas ranges wider, scanning for distortion rather than tracks. Dax drifts half a step closer to Rowan, no longer pretending casual readiness. Ryan falls into pace on the right — alert, quiet, jaw set.

They are no longer walking through land.

They are walking through interval.

Behind them, Stonewake holds — stretched now, aware, committed to seeing this through.

Ahead, the terrain begins to misbehave again — subtly at first. Shadows slip out of sync with their sources. Sound arrives early instead of late. Gravity feels just slightly negotiable, like a suggestion rather than a rule.

Rowan's voice is low, ironed flat.

"He knows we're coming."

Silas doesn't look back. "Good."

Dax's hand tightens once at his belt. "Let him."

Ryan swallows, then sets his jaw. "We're not late."

Rowan doesn't answer.

Because the bridge hums with something that feels very much like agreement.

Not promise or victory.

But reach.

And somewhere beyond certainty — not hidden, not fleeing — the space holding Isorae tightens its grip.

Not to crush.

To delay.

Just long enough to see what the bridge is willing to become to bring her back.

The light changes first.

Not dramatically — no sunset blaze, no sudden dark — just the quiet dimming that happens when a day has been spent walking against resistance. Gold thins to copper. Shadows lengthen until they begin overlapping in ways the eye has to double-check.

Ryan notices before anyone says it.

"We've been moving a long time," he says quietly — not complaint, not doubt. Just orientation.

Dax glances up through the canopy. "Sun's dropping faster than it should."

Silas slows, lifts his head, listens — not to sound, but to how sound fails at distance. "Terrain's compressing again," he says. "Night's going to make this sloppy."

Rowan stops.

Not because he wants to.

Because the bridge tells him something important.

The hum beneath his ribs hasn't weakened — but it has stretched to a limit that no longer belongs to daylight. Whatever holds Isorae is still ahead, still reachable — but no longer safely approached at speed.

He exhales once, controlled.

"We don't gain anything by pushing blind," Rowan says. Not permission. Decision. "Not here."

Dax studies him for a beat, then nods. "Yeah. This is where people break ankles and give predators opportunities."

Ryan swallows. "She's still… there?"

Rowan doesn't hesitate. "Yes."

That answer lands heavy — relief braided with dread.

Silas gestures toward a rise off to the east, where the land slopes into something firmer, less misaligned. "There's ground that remembers being ground. Defensible. Wind breaks naturally."

Rowan considers it — not tactically, but relationally. How far the bridge can stay extended without tearing. How much of himself he can hold open overnight without losing precision.

"Take us there," he says.

They move again — slower now, deliberate — not retreating, not advancing. Just choosing where to pause without relinquishing intent.

By the time they reach the rise, the sky has dimmed to bruised violet. Stars begin appearing — not all at once, but in hesitant clusters, as if even the night is unsure whether it's allowed here.

They set camp without ceremony.

Silas marks the perimeter. Dax handles fire, coaxing flame low and disciplined. Ryan gathers water and returns without speaking, eyes scanning the dark like he's memorizing it.

Rowan sits with his back to stone and lets the bridge retract just enough to breathe.

Not release.

Rest.

Dax hands him something warm. Rowan takes it without comment.

"She's not sleeping," Rowan says after a while.

Ryan looks up instantly. "How do you know?"

"Because the pull keeps correcting," Rowan answers. "If she were unconscious, it would go slack."

That earns a grim nod from Silas. "Then he's keeping her awake."

Dax's jaw tightens. "Or she's refusing not to be."

Rowan doesn't respond — because both are true, and neither is comforting.

The fire pops softly.

Night settles fully now, bringing with it a heavier version of quiet — not absence, but expectation. The land doesn't withdraw. It watches.

Rowan closes his eyes briefly — not to sleep, but to hold.

Tomorrow, they will move again.

Closer.

More precisely.

Tonight, the bridge remains extended just enough to remind whatever waits ahead that it is not alone.

And somewhere beyond the reach of firelight — beyond certainty, beyond patience — the space holding Isorae tightens fractionally.

Not in triumph.

In preparation.

Because the night has taught it something important:

The bridge did not break.

24
CONDITIONING

Isorae measures time by strain. Not by light — there is none that behaves honestly here — but by how long she can hold herself upright without shaking, by how often her glow threatens to desynchronize under the constant, low pressure of the interval.

When Graham returns, she knows before she sees him.

The space tightens.

Not abruptly.

Deliberately.

Like a room drawing a breath.

"You didn't sleep," he observes, stepping out of the distortion with quiet confidence.

She doesn't answer.

Her throat is dry. Her muscles ache in places she hasn't moved. The interval has allowed her to stand — but only just — correcting every attempt to lean, to curl inward, to conserve.

Graham circles her slowly.

Not prowling.

Evaluating.

"You should have," he continues mildly. "You'd recover faster if you stopped fighting alignment."

Isorae lifts her chin. "I'm not aligned with you."

His mouth curves faintly. "That's not what I meant."

He stops behind her.

Not touching.

Close enough that she feels the displacement of air — wrong, distorted — brushing the back of her neck.

Her glow tightens reflexively.

Graham notices.

"Still reacting before thought," he murmurs. "Good. That means you're honest."

She turns sharply.

The space corrects her motion halfway through, forcing the movement into a slower arc than she intended. Anger flashes hot through her chest.

"Don't talk like you know me."

Graham meets her gaze without flinching. "I don't," he agrees. "That's the problem."

He reaches out.

This time, he doesn't grab.

He places two fingers against her forearm — light, testing — as if checking temperature.

Isorae jerks instinctively.

The space resists her withdrawal.

Her breath catches.

Graham doesn't increase pressure.

He doesn't chase her movement.

He simply keeps his fingers where they are, letting the interval do the work.

"There," he says softly. "That's new."

Her pulse races beneath his touch.

She hates that he can feel it.

"Take your hand off me," she says, voice tight.

Graham considers this.

Then — deliberately — he slides his fingers a fraction higher, brushing the inside of her wrist where the skin is thinner, more responsive.

Not intimate.

But intimate-adjacent.

Her glow flares sharp and defensive, scraping against containment hard enough to make the space shudder.

Graham inhales slowly.

Not aroused.

Engaged.

"You react before you decide," he says. "That's inefficient."

She bares her teeth. "I don't care."

"No," he agrees. "You don't. That's why this will take longer."

He removes his hand.

The space eases by a hair.

Isorae nearly stumbles from the sudden absence of pressure and hates herself for it.

Graham watches the micro-failure closely.

Files it away.

"You know," he continues conversationally, "ARIS would have restrained you completely by now. Locked you down. Reduced your variables until nothing unexpected could happen."

She says nothing.

"I'm giving you latitude," he goes on. "You should appreciate that."

She laughs — rough, bitter. "You're isolating me in a place that doesn't obey physics."

"And you're still standing," he replies calmly. "Most people wouldn't be."

He steps closer again.

Not touching this time.

Invading space instead.

Her glow recoils so hard it hurts — light collapsing inward, struggling to stay coherent under the constant correction.

Graham tilts his head. "Does it help," he asks, almost kindly, "if I tell you I don't want to hurt you?"

Her laugh cuts off.

Her voice drops low. "That doesn't make this better."

"No," he admits. "But it makes it accurate."

He reaches up — slowly enough that she sees it coming, fast enough that the interval prevents her from stepping away — and brushes his thumb along her jaw.

Barely a touch.

Just enough to feel.

Isorae's breath breaks.

Her glow spikes violently, wild and furious, hammering against the space. The interval tightens in response, forcing the energy inward until her ribs ache with the effort of breathing.

Graham withdraws his hand immediately.

Satisfied.

"That," he says quietly, "is what I needed to confirm."

She glares at him, shaking now — not from weakness, but from rage held too tightly.

"You don't get to experiment on me."

Graham meets her fury without heat.

"I already am."

He steps back, giving her space she can't fully use.

"Rest," he says. "You're going to need the energy."

"For what," she spits.

His eyes linger on her — not her body, not her face — but the way her glow struggles to remain synchronized under stress.

"For when resisting starts to cost you more than cooperating."

He turns away.

The space seals subtly behind him — not locking her in tighter, but making sure she knows exactly how alone she is.

Isorae stands rigid in the aftermath, breath ragged, glow flickering unevenly beneath her skin.

She doesn't cry.

She doesn't collapse.

But something has shifted.

Not broken.

Tested.

And somewhere beyond the interval — far enough to ache — the bridge remains stretched, patient, learning the shape of what it will have to tear through to reach her.

25

THE LONG CORRECTION

Morning returns like a reluctant concession—less light than permission for the world to be legible again.

Rowan comes out of the night in layers, eyes open before the sky fully commits to gray. He didn't sleep so much as fold his awareness inward and hold it there—enough to keep the bridge from tearing, enough to feel what mattered.

The pull is still present.

Not stronger.

Not weaker.

Managed.

That's the first wrong thing.

The second is how it behaves when he shifts his weight—how the bond doesn't drift the way it should after a night stretched too long.

Dax catches it in Rowan's posture before he catches it in the air. "You've been up," he says quietly, crouching near the fire pit where embers still glow dull beneath ash.

Rowan doesn't bother denying it. "It didn't go slack."

Ryan sits up at that, sleep breaking off him in fragments. "So she's conscious."

"Yes," Rowan says. Then, because this is the part that matters: "And whatever's holding her knows we paused."

Silas straightens from the perimeter check, expression tightening. "Nothing changed overnight."

Rowan presses his palm once to the stone beside him—brief, private, purely diagnostic. The bridge hums back.

"Not nothing," he says. "The load redistributed."

Dax's breath eases out slow. "Meaning?"

"Meaning the pocket adjusted," Rowan answers. "Not to move her. To keep pace with us."

That lands heavy in the early cold—an intelligence that isn't chasing, just matching.

Ryan runs a hand through his hair, jaw setting. "So he felt us stop."

"Yes."

"And he didn't take advantage of it," Ryan says—like he hates that the thought had to exist.

Rowan's mouth hardens. "Not yet."

They break camp with practiced efficiency.

No wasted motion. No conversation that doesn't serve orientation. Dax kills the remaining embers cleanly. Silas checks the wind and the ground together, eyes flicking between physical terrain and the places where it subtly fails to agree with itself.

Ryan shoulders his pack and moves closer to Rowan without comment.

"Talk to me," Ryan says quietly once they're clear of the rise. "What does 'held' feel like?"

Rowan considers how to answer.

"Like something bracing against movement instead of pulling away from it," he says finally. "She's being allowed to remain upright — but only just."

Dax's mouth twists. "So he's testing endurance."

"Yes," Rowan says. "And attention."

Silas nods. "If he breaks her focus, the bridge destabilizes."

"If I break mine," Rowan corrects.

They move out.

The land feels different in daylight — not safer, not clearer — just more honest about its fractures. What misaligned last night now shows itself openly: roots growing at wrong angles, stone faces that refuse shadow, paths that almost remember being paths and then don't.

They follow the resistance.

Not the pull.

The distinction matters.

After an hour, Dax breaks the silence. "You notice how everything keeps trying to slow us instead of stopping us?"

"Yes," Rowan says.

"Feels deliberate," Dax mutters.

"It is," Silas replies. "He's shaping the approach."

Ryan swallows. "So we're walking where he wants us."

Rowan shakes his head once. "We're walking where he can't avoid us."

That lands differently.

They stop again — not abruptly, but together — at a place where the ground firms too suddenly, as if the interval has momentarily forgotten to misbehave.

Rowan feels it immediately.

Closer.

Not spatially.

Relationally.

"She's still fighting," Rowan says.

Ryan's voice comes tight. "How can you tell?"

"Because the correction keeps spiking," Rowan answers. "If she yielded, it would smooth out."

Silas crouches, studying the soil. "Then he's escalating pressure."

Dax's hand curls at his side. "Then so are we."

Rowan looks at each of them in turn.

Not command.

Acknowledgment.

"We don't rush," he says. "We don't react. We keep narrowing the interval until he runs out of room to pretend this is theoretical."

Ryan nods, steady. "He's not breaking her."

"No," Rowan agrees. "He's proving something to himself."

Dax bares his teeth. "Let's ruin that."

They move again.

More precisely now.

Not faster — sharper.

And far away—where the interval still can't decide what it is—the pressure around Isorae adjusts again.

Not because she's failing.

Because something in the structure has noticed the bridge moving with daylight behind it—steady, deliberate, and no longer willing to be trained by night.

The correction tightens.

Just a fraction.

26
THE SHAPE OF ENDURANCE

Isorae learns the shape of waiting.

Not patience — patience implies choice.

This is endurance.

The interval does not mark time cleanly. There is no sun to rise or fall, no honest shadow to measure duration. Instead, time announces itself through accumulation: the ache in her calves from standing too long, the dryness at the back of her throat, the way her glow begins to tremble when she lets her focus slip for even a second.

She stays upright because the space prefers it.

When she tries to sit, the correction comes slow and instructive — a subtle torque at the hips, a pressure along her spine that insists on alignment rather than comfort. Not punishment.

Training.

So she stands.

She breathes shallow and steady. She keeps her gaze level. She learns which movements the interval allows to finish and which it interrupts halfway through, redirecting intention before it can become action.

There are rules here.

She does not know all of them yet.

Graham comes and goes without pattern.

Sometimes the space tightens before he appears. Sometimes it doesn't. Sometimes he speaks immediately. Sometimes he simply watches her for long, silent stretches, hands folded behind his back as if he's observing an experiment that hasn't yet decided what it will do.

She refuses to give him reactions he can catalogue.

When he circles her, she doesn't turn to follow him with her eyes.

When he speaks, she lets the words land without answering unless the silence would please him more.

When he reaches for her — not to grab, not to hurt — but to test proximity, pressure, awareness — she does not flinch anymore.

That takes effort.

The effort costs her.

Her glow strains to remain synchronized, light flickering in tight, controlled bands beneath her skin. Every instinct screams to push outward, to resonate, to reach for the valley that no longer answers.

She doesn't.

Not because she can't.

Because she won't give him that data again.

The first time she refuses to react, he notices immediately.

His head tilts. His gaze sharpens.

"You're adjusting," he says mildly.

She doesn't respond.

The interval hums faintly, correcting a micro-shift in her balance before it becomes a stumble.

Graham watches that too.

"You've learned how much movement you're allowed," he continues. "Most people wouldn't bother."

She lifts her chin just enough to meet his eyes.

"I'm still awake," she says evenly. "That seems to irritate you."

A pause.

Then — a smile.

Not pleased.

Assessing.

"It complicates things," he admits. "Yes."

He steps closer than he has before — not touching, not crowding — but close enough that the wrongness of his presence presses against her senses like static. The interval tightens in response, as if accommodating him costs it more effort than it wants to spend.

That, at least, is satisfying.

"You could make this easier," he says. "If you stopped resisting."

She exhales slowly through her nose. "I'm not resisting."

He blinks.

Once.

Then he laughs softly. "Of course you are."

"No," she replies. "I'm enduring."

The word lands between them.

The interval shivers — not violently, not alarmed — but as if something has been named correctly for the first time.

Graham studies her with renewed interest.

"That's a dangerous distinction," he says.

"For you," she answers.

He does not correct her.

Instead, he reaches out — two fingers only — and places them lightly against her forearm again. The contact is brief, almost polite. The space delays her instinctive withdrawal by a fraction of a second longer than before.

She does not jerk away.

She does not look down.

She holds her breath and lets the moment pass without flaring.

Graham withdraws his hand.

Slowly.

Thoughtfully.

"You're trying to starve me of response," he says.

She finally allows herself a small, cold smile. "You said you were learning me."

"Yes."

"Then learn this," she says. "I don't disappear when you stop hurting me."

Something tightens behind his eyes.

Not anger.

Calculation.

He steps back, giving her space she cannot fully use, and the interval eases its correction just enough to let her shoulders drop a fraction of an inch.

"You're mistaken about the goal," he says quietly. "I don't need you compliant."

She doesn't answer.

"I need you precise."

He turns away.

The space seals behind him with a familiar, subtle finality.

Isorae remains standing long after he's gone, breath controlled, glow held tight beneath her skin. Her legs shake. Her vision blurs at the edges.

She doesn't collapse.

She doesn't cry.

She presses her tongue to the roof of her mouth and grounds herself in memory — not reaching outward, not calling — just remembering weight, warmth, the feel of hands steady at her back.

The interval resists that memory.

But it does not erase it.

Somewhere far beyond the distortion, the bridge remains stretched — not straining, not slack — present in the way a held breath is present.

Waiting.

And for the first time since being taken, Isorae understands something Graham has not accounted for yet:

Endurance is not passive.

It is a form of pressure.

And she has learned how to apply it without moving at all.

27

Narrowing the Corridor

They move as soon as the light is usable.

No speeches. No ritual around the fire's corpse. Just packs tightened, straps checked, and the clean decision to keep going.

The terrain doesn't wake with them.

It corrects.

At first it's subtle—the same wrongness as yesterday, but less forgiving. Sound arrives early, then late. Wind slides sideways as if avoiding the shape of their bodies. Shadows refuse to commit to their sources.

Silas ranges ahead and slightly high, scanning for seams instead of tracks. Dax stays left of Rowan, close enough to be felt without looking. Ryan holds the right flank, eyes too sharp for a morning that's supposed to be ordinary.

Rowan keeps his attention on the bridge.

Not the pull—he's learned better than to chase that.

The correction.

The way the bond keeps being asked to re-orient, like something ahead is dragging Isorae through angles that don't want to exist.

When the land finally misbehaves with intention—when the slope pauses mid-curve and the ground holds itself unnaturally flat—Silas throws a fist up.

They stop.

"Same behavior as yesterday," Silas says. "Tighter."

Dax's gaze cuts through the trees. "Like he's narrowing the corridor."

Rowan kneels and puts his palm to the soil.

This time the answer is immediate.

Not welcome.

Not memory.

Resistance—thin, elastic, directional.

Rowan inhales slowly through his nose.

"He's not just holding her," Rowan says. "He's moving her."

Ryan's head snaps up. "You can tell?"

"I can feel correction," Rowan replies. "Like the bond keeps being asked to re-orient."

Dax's mouth hardens. "He's walking her sideways."

Silas crouches, presses his own hand to the ground, and goes still. "Or carrying her through something that doesn't leave tracks."

Rowan stands.

His voice is calm, but it's iron underneath it — the kind of calm that only exists when rage has been disciplined into purpose.

"He's trying to keep us guessing," Rowan says. "So we waste time."

Ryan's hands curl into fists at his sides, then loosen. Controlled. "We're not guessing," Ryan says quietly. "We're learning."

Rowan looks at him once.

A flicker of approval.

Then Rowan reaches for his handheld.

The device is small and ugly and reliable, clipped to his belt, warm from body heat. Erin's work. Evan's maintenance. Stonewake's refusal to rely on anything ARIS ever made.

He presses the transmit.

Static answers first — not interference, but distance translated into noise.

Then Erin's voice cuts through, clipped and steady.

"Rowan."

"We moved," Rowan says. "The interval tightened overnight."

A pause. A faint click as she marks something.

"Say it again," Erin replies. "Tightened how?"

"Same behavior signatures," Rowan says, scanning the terrain while he speaks. "But less drift. More correction."

Silas adds, "He's narrowing whatever he's using."

Erin exhales once, tight. "That means he's spending energy. Or running out of usable folds."

Dax mutters, "Good."

Evan's voice comes in behind Erin's — lower, controlled. "Any injuries?"

Rowan doesn't waste time pretending. "Not yet."

"Don't make that a challenge," Evan says.

Ryan's mouth twitches once — humor that dies before it can live.

Rowan keeps his eyes forward. "Is she—"

He stops. Rephrases.

"Anything on your end?" Rowan asks instead.

Erin's silence lasts a fraction too long.

Then: "Baseline is still holding. Which means you're still tethered."

Rowan closes his eyes briefly. "And her?"

"I don't have her," Erin says. Honest. Firm. "But—" She hesitates, like she hates even admitting this. "The distortions are behaving like a moving pocket. Not random."

Rowan opens his eyes. "Direction?"

Erin speaks carefully. "Not coordinates. Trend. North-east by behavior. Like something is avoiding fully formed terrain."

Silas nods once, already shifting his stance. "Dead folds."

Rowan ends the call with a double-click and returns the handheld to his belt.

He doesn't say thank you.

Erin would hate that.

Instead he turns to the others.

"North-east," Rowan says.

Dax rolls his shoulders like he's about to walk into a fight he's been waiting for since the first night this valley learned fear again. "He picked a place that's unfinished," Dax says. "Because nothing claims authority there."

Silas moves first, leading them toward a line of trees where the air looks normal but feels edited.

By midday the terrain has changed from forest to something harsher — stone shelves, scraggled pines, dead brush that breaks too easily underfoot. The air feels thinner. Not altitude-thin.

Decision-thin.

They hit a place where the world flickers.

Not visually.

Somatically.

A half-second of weightlessness that makes Ryan stumble back into the slope.

Rowan catches his elbow without looking like he did it.

"You good?" Dax asks.

Ryan nods too fast. "Yeah. Yeah."

Rowan's gaze stays forward.

"What did it do?" Rowan asks him.

Ryan closes his eyes for a beat. "It felt like… a door almost opening. And then deciding not to."

Silas's eyes narrow. "He's near."

Rowan feels it too.

The bridge under his ribs tightens into a low, brutal hum — not pulling, not reaching.

Pointing.

And underneath it, something colder:

Graham's awareness.

Not close enough to touch.

Close enough to be offensive.

Rowan stops.

Not because he's hesitating.

Because he refuses to be rushed by someone else's timing.

"This is where we get stupid," Rowan says quietly.

Dax's voice is immediate. "We don't."

Silas nods once. "We don't."

Ryan breathes in through his nose and steadies. "We don't."

Rowan looks between them.

Four men on a seam of land that doesn't want to be land.

Four lives stretched thin by an absence that keeps moving.

Rowan speaks into the air like the air is a throat.

"He's trying to make me come apart," Rowan says. "He thinks anger is a lever."

Dax bares his teeth in something like a grin. "Anger's fine. Panic's the enemy."

Rowan's voice drops lower. "Then we don't panic."

They move again.

Not faster.

Cleaner.

More deliberate.

And as the afternoon begins to tilt toward late, Rowan feels a new thing emerge under the bridge-hum — a faint, wrong pressure, like the land itself is refusing to hold a certain shape for much longer.

A fold under strain.

A pocket that has been dragged too far from where it belongs.

Silas stops and points — not to a place, but to a mismatch in the landscape: a shallow cleft in the rock where shadows pool too dark for the angle of the sun.

"That," Silas says.

Dax's hand tightens at his belt. "That's ugly."

Ryan's voice is quiet. Reverent with fear. "That's him."

Rowan doesn't answer.

He walks toward it.

Not reckless.

Not rage-blind.

A hunter, now — and worse than a hunter:

A bridge that has learned how to become a blade without tearing itself apart.

Behind them, the day continues like nothing is happening.

Ahead of them, the seam waits — patient, loaded, wrong.

And somewhere inside that wrongness, Isorae remains present enough for the bond to ache.

Rowan steps closer.

And the land — unfinished, undecided — begins to decide.

28

PERMISSION TO REMAIN AWAKE

The space doesn't reset between his visits.

That's the first lesson.

Not wrongness—she's learned the texture of wrong. This is continuity: the same angles still holding their breath, the same pressure settled into her bones like a rule that stopped announcing itself because it no longer needs to.

She is still standing.

Or being allowed to stand—upright in a posture the interval keeps correcting as if slouching would be an offense. Her legs tremble faintly with the effort of staying inside a place that insists on alignment. Her glow flickers beneath her skin—muted, constrained, but present.

Always present.

That, she suspects, is the point.

Graham isn't here yet.

She knows because the interval feels incomplete without him—like a sentence missing its verb. She uses the emptiness anyway, pulling breath in the pattern Evan taught her after the last incursion:

In for four. Hold for four. Out for six.

The breath doesn't move right.

But it moves enough.

Time drifts—sideways, uncooperative—until the space tightens.

Not sudden. Not dramatic.

Just the quiet click of attention sharpening.

Graham resolves out of distortion without ceremony.

No sound. No warning. Just the sense of being observed snapping into focus.

"You adjusted," he says.

Isorae doesn't answer.

Her silence isn't compliance. It's rationing.

Graham circles her again, slow, deliberate, like yesterday — but closer this time. Close enough that she feels the pressure of his presence even before the interval reacts.

"You're learning the rules," he continues mildly. "That's faster than I expected."

She lifts her chin. "You're still here."

His mouth curves faintly. "So are you."

He stops directly in front of her.

Not touching.

Never rushing.

His eyes track her face, her posture, the micro-tension in her shoulders she hasn't been able to force out since he last left.

"Your breathing never dropped," he says.

"I don't need you to tell me what my body did," she snaps.

Graham tilts his head. "You're wrong about that."

Her glow tightens reflexively.

Graham notices.

"Still guarding," he murmurs. "Even when there's nothing immediate to guard against."

She laughs under her breath. "That's because you're always immediate."

For a moment, something sharp flashes through his expression.

Not anger.

Recognition.

Then it smooths out again.

He steps closer.

The interval responds instantly, sliding invisible pressure along her spine, keeping her upright, exposed, aligned to his position whether she wants to be or not.

She grits her teeth but does not look away.

"You don't want me asleep," she says.

Graham's brows lift a fraction. "No."

"You don't want me unconscious," she presses.

"No."

"Then stop pretending this is about efficiency."

His gaze sharpens.

"Careful," he says quietly. "You're mapping faster than is comfortable."

She meets his eyes, fury controlled but burning. "You need me aware so you can see what I do under pressure."

A pause.

Then: "Yes."

The honesty lands like a slap.

He reaches out.

Not fast.

Not sudden.

He places his hand flat against the side of her ribcage.

Open palm. No fingers digging in. No grip.

Just contact.

Isorae inhales sharply.

Her glow surges hard, reflexive, scraping against containment with enough force that the interval shudders. Pain flashes bright under her sternum as the space corrects, compressing the energy inward until her lungs burn.

Graham does not remove his hand.

He watches.

Listens.

Feels.

"There," he says softly. "You route it through defense every time. You don't even consider collapse."

"Get your hand off me," she snarls, breath ragged.

"Not yet."

His hand shifts — not downward, not sexual — but inward, pressing closer to her centerline, forcing her awareness into a narrower, more vulnerable column.

Her knees threaten to buckle.

The interval refuses.

She shakes now, anger and effort and the constant, suffocating wrongness of being held in a space that keeps agreeing with him.

"You think this proves something," she says through clenched teeth.

"I know it does," he replies.

He removes his hand abruptly.

The sudden absence of pressure makes her sway.

She catches herself — barely — refusing the humiliation of falling.

Graham watches that too.

Files it away.

"You're remarkable," he says. "Even now."

"Stop saying that," she spits.

"Why?" he asks mildly. "Because it sounds like praise?"

"Because it sounds like ownership."

His smile thins.

"That," he says, "is an understandable confusion."

She lunges at him.

Not far. Not fast.

But enough to make intent undeniable.

The interval slams correction into her mid-motion, locking her joints, forcing her momentum to drain sideways into nothing. The whiplash of it knocks the breath from her lungs.

Graham doesn't move.

He lets the space do the work.

"Don't," he says — not gently now, "make me restrict you further."

Her chest heaves. Her vision spots.

"You don't scare me," she gasps.

His eyes darken.

"No," he agrees. "You scare yourself."

That one hurts.

He steps back.

Gives her space again.

Always after.

"Rest," he says. "You're burning energy you'll need later."

"For what?" she demands.

His gaze lingers — not on her body, not quite — but on the way her glow struggles to stay coherent under sustained pressure.

"For when the bond pulls harder than you can compensate for," he says quietly.

Her heart stutters.

"You feel him," she says.

Graham doesn't deny it. "Yes."

That confirmation sends a cold rush through her veins — not fear.

Hope sharpened into pain.

She lifts her chin again. "He's coming."

Graham studies her for a long moment.

"Good," he says at last. "Then we'll both learn something new."

He turns away.

The interval seals subtly behind him — not locking her down, not escalating — just making sure she understands exactly how far the edges are.

Isorae stands alone again, breath uneven, glow flickering but intact.

Her body aches. Her nerves burn. Her wrists still feel wrong where he touched them.

But underneath it all, something steadier remains.

Not broken.

Not dimmed.

Aware.

And far beyond the interval — closer now, close enough to make the bond thrum painfully under her ribs — Rowan moves through land that has begun to decide it remembers how to become a weapon.

She closes her eyes briefly.

Not to rest.

To hold.

Because whatever Graham thinks he is proving, one truth remains unchanged:

The bridge is still learning.

And so is she.

And somewhere out there, the bridge starts to pull in more than one direction at once.

29
THE SPLIT

Rowan feels it in the bridge before he sees anything change in the terrain.

A soft, wrong redistribution—like tension sliding off a single anchor and spreading across two points at once. Not weakening.

Dividing.

He slows without meaning to. The ground takes his weight too easily, as if the land has stopped arguing.

Allowance.

That's what unsettles him: not resistance, not correction—permission.

Silas notices the change in Rowan's pace and halts them with a raised fist. The group stops without a word.

"What is it?" Dax asks, already tight.

Rowan closes his eyes—not to reach, not to command—just to feel where the pull should narrow.

It doesn't.

It stretches.

Not thinning.

Forking.

Rowan opens his eyes.

Ryan swallows. "That's not right."

Rowan exhales once, controlled. "It's split."

Silas crouches immediately, pressing his palm to the ground between the two directions. His brow furrows.

"I feel it too," he says. "Not a fracture. Not noise."

He lifts his hand, grim. "Two continuities."

Ryan's voice tightens. "Like… echoes?"

"No," Rowan says. "Like choices."

The bridge hums again — deeper now, uneasy. Rowan takes a step toward the leftward slope.

The hum strengthens.

He steps back, angles toward the right.

It strengthens there too.

Equal.

That's the problem.

Behind them, far enough downslope that the land still behaves honestly, Erin's voice crackles through the comm stone — tight, focused.

"I see it," she says. "Don't move yet."

Rowan closes his eyes again, grounding his breath, forcing stillness into the bridge so Erin can read cleanly.

"What do you see," he asks.

A pause. Fingers tapping faintly through the stone.

"It's not duplication," Erin says slowly. "It's load balancing."

Dax lets out a sharp breath. "You're telling me he split her signal?"

"I'm telling you," Erin replies, "that he created two viable continuations that both reference her. Neither one is fake. Neither one is complete."

Silas's jaw tightens. "Fucking bastard."

Ryan's hands curl into fists. "So which one's her?"

Erin doesn't answer immediately.

"That's the point," she finally says. "He's forcing you to choose how much of her you're willing to risk losing."

The words land hard.

Rowan stares ahead, pulse steady, jaw locked.

"He can't actually split her," Ryan says, almost pleading.

"No," Erin agrees. "But he can split you."

Silence stretches.

The land remains permissive — offering both directions without preference, like a witness refusing to intervene.

Rowan feels it then — the subtle cost of delay. Not urgency. Not panic.

Elastic fatigue.

The bridge can hold both directions for now.

Not indefinitely.

"If we hesitate," Silas says quietly, "one of these will collapse."

"Or worse," Erin adds. "He'll reinforce the wrong one."

Dax glances at Rowan. "We can split."

Rowan turns to him sharply. "No."

The word is absolute.

"This isn't terrain," Rowan continues. "It's relationship. If we fracture ourselves, he wins without touching her again."

Ryan swallows hard. "Then what do we do?"

Rowan studies the land again — not the ground, not the slope — but the behavior of the pull.

One continuation feels taut — compressed, efficient.

The other feels stretched — restless, adaptive.

Neither is safe.

But one is familiar.

Rowan exhales slowly.

"We choose the one that costs him more to maintain," he says.

Dax blinks. "How do you know which that is?"

Rowan steps forward — not fully committing — and places his palm against the air where the leftward coherence begins.

The bridge reacts instantly.

Not louder.

Sharper.

Pressure returns — directional now, intolerant of hesitation.

He withdraws his hand and turns to the other.

The hum shifts.

Less force.

More space.

Rowan straightens.

"This one," he says. "He's stretching this side to keep it plausible. That means he's already overextended."

Silas nods once. "So the other path—"

"—is stable because he's anchoring it harder," Rowan finishes. "Which means that's where she is."

Ryan's breath catches. "Then why give us the other one at all?"

Rowan's expression darkens.

"Because if we commit wrong," he says, "he doesn't have to stop us."

Erin's voice comes softer now. "Once you choose, I lose the other signal entirely."

Rowan doesn't hesitate.

"Tag it," he says. "Let it go."

There's a brief pause — then Erin exhales.

"Done."

The rightward coherence thins immediately — not vanishing, but withdrawing, like a thought released mid-sentence.

The land tightens around the remaining path.

Not aggressively.

Decisively.

Rowan feels the cost register instantly — the bridge narrowing, pressure increasing, margin gone.

They move.

Not faster.

More committed.

Behind them, the abandoned continuation collapses quietly — not with drama, not with warning — just a soft loss of possibility.

Ryan flinches despite himself.

"She's still there," Rowan says, firm. "I can feel it."

Dax sets his jaw. "Then let's stop letting him dictate the terms."

They advance into the chosen coherence as the land closes ranks behind them — no longer permissive, no longer neutral.

The search has stopped being hypothetical.

And somewhere ahead — feeling the shift ripple through the interval like a tightened wire — Graham smiles.

Not because they chose wrong.

But because they finally chose.

Somewhere in the interval, the choice registers like a tightened wire—one line pulled taut, the other released.

30
EXPENSIVE

Isorae feels the choice before she understands it.

Not as relief or hope.

As pressure redistributing.

The interval tightens on one side of her awareness and loosens on another, like a body shifting weight after committing to a direction. The geometry around her shudders — not collapsing, not correcting — but recalculating.

She steadies her breathing.

Slow. Controlled. Measured.

If she lets panic spike now, the space will punish her for it.

Graham notices immediately.

He doesn't appear all at once this time.

The distortion thickens first — a subtle skew in the angles behind her, a delay in how sound resolves. Then he steps through as if the space had been waiting for him.

"You felt it," he says mildly.

Isorae doesn't turn.

"Yes," she answers. "They chose."

Graham smiles.

Not wide.

Satisfied.

"So you are still listening," he murmurs. "Good."

She forces herself to pivot slowly, carefully, so the interval can't hijack the movement. Her glow tightens beneath her skin, dimmer than it was yesterday — not weaker, but concentrated.

"You split it," she says. "You made him choose."

"I gave him options," Graham corrects. "What he does with them is his responsibility."

She laughs once, sharp and humorless. "You're lying to yourself."

Graham studies her with renewed interest.

"That tone," he says. "You didn't have that before."

She meets his gaze steadily. "Before what?"

"Before he committed," Graham replies.

The word lands heavier than she expects.

Commitment.

Not pursuit.

Not reaction.

Commitment costs more.

The interval tightens subtly around her ribs as if agreeing.

Graham steps closer — not invading yet, but closing distance enough that she has to account for him.

"You understand something now," he continues. "That this isn't about speed."

She says nothing.

"That it's about load."

He reaches out — not to touch her — but to place his palm against the air beside her shoulder. The space reacts instantly, firming there, creating a boundary she didn't authorize.

She stiffens.

"You're doing it again," she says.

"Yes," he agrees calmly. "Because it works."

He lowers his hand slightly.

The boundary follows.

"Your presence is expensive," Graham continues. "For him. For the land. For the bridge."

Her jaw tightens.

"And yet," he adds, eyes flicking to her glow, "here you are."

She swallows. "You're feeling it too."

His gaze sharpens.

"What?"

"The cost," she says. "You're holding more now. That split wasn't free."

For the first time, Graham does not answer immediately.

The interval hums — low, strained, held too carefully.

Then he smiles again, thinner this time.

"Good," he says. "Then you'll understand why I need you cooperative."

She laughs again — breathy, incredulous. "You think I'll help you."

"No," Graham replies. "I think you'll conserve yourself."

He steps into her space fully now.

Not touching.

Forcing proximity.

The interval corrects her posture, pulling her upright, preventing retreat. Her glow recoils instinctively, scraping against containment hard enough to make the space creak.

Graham watches closely.

"There," he murmurs. "That's the strain point."

She glares at him. "You don't get to decide what I endure."

"I already have," he says, not cruelly. "I'm just refining it."

He lifts his hand again — slow, deliberate — and this time places it against her shoulder.

Flat and firm.

The contact sends a shock through her system anyway, not because of pain, but because of how precise it is. The interval responds instantly, reinforcing the contact, anchoring her there.

Her breath stutters.

Graham doesn't press harder.

He waits.

Feels.

"You're adapting," he says quietly. "That's impressive."

"Get off me," she says, voice steady by sheer discipline.

"In a moment."

His fingers shift slightly, not caressing, not gripping — measuring. Her glow flickers unevenly beneath her skin, struggling to stay synchronized.

"That flicker," he continues. "That's fatigue. You can't hold alignment indefinitely."

She forces herself not to look away. "Neither can you."

That earns her a sharp look.

Then — unexpectedly — Graham removes his hand.

The space loosens a fraction.

Isorae nearly sways from the sudden absence of pressure and locks her knees to stay upright.

Graham steps back.

"Save it," he says. "Not for your comfort. For what I take tomorrow."

Her pulse spikes despite her control.

"You won't break me," she says.

Graham meets her gaze, unblinking.

"I don't need to," he replies. "I just need you expensive enough that he starts making mistakes."

He turns away.

This time, the interval doesn't seal immediately.

It lingers open just long enough for his parting words to land.

"And now that he's chosen a path," Graham adds softly, "he can't afford to stop."

The space closes.

Isorae remains standing, breath tight, glow flickering but intact.

She does not collapse.

She does not cry.

But she feels it now — the subtle drain, the cost accumulating under her skin.

Not pain.

Not fear.

Exertion.

And far away — closer than before, but still unreachable — the bridge holds under increasing load.

Not failing.
Learning.
Tomorrow, something will give.
She just doesn't know yet whether it will be the space…
—or the man trying to control it.

31
DEAD FOLD

They don't reach it all at once.

The land announces the pocket the way a body announces pain—indirectly, through compensations. The wind thins. Sound starts arriving late. Gravity stops feeling vertical and starts feeling conditional.

Rowan slows before anyone else does.

Not because the bridge warns him.

Because it goes quiet.

The hum beneath his ribs—constant for days now—thins to a filament so fine it almost disappears. Not slack. Not severed.

Muted.

He raises a hand.

They stop.

Silas is already watching the slope ahead, eyes narrowed. "That's not absence," he says quietly. "That's compression."

Dax scans left, then right. "Like the land folded something into itself and pretended it didn't."

Ryan swallows. "I don't like places that lie."

Rowan steps forward alone.

The terrain ahead looks unremarkable: a shallow rock shelf, fractured stone, a cleft where shadows collect too dark for the angle of the sun. Nothing dramatic. Nothing visibly wrong.

But the bridge does not extend into it.

It refuses.

Rowan kneels and presses his palm to the ground.

The answer is immediate.

Not welcome. Not resistance.

Redirection.

The contact slides sideways inside his awareness, like pressure diverted around a blockage instead of meeting it head-on. His breath tightens as the bridge attempts to orient—and fails.

He pulls his hand back sharply.

His pulse spikes.

Dax notices. "That hurt."

Rowan nods once. "It's a dead fold."

Silas crouches beside him, placing his own hand near—but not inside—the cleft's influence. He doesn't touch the ground. He listens.

"This isn't a doorway," Silas says. "It's a pocket that forgot where it belongs."

Ryan frowns. "So… trap?"

"No," Rowan says. "Worse."

He stands slowly, keeping his weight centered. The bridge hums again—but unevenly now, like tension redistributed through a structure not meant to carry it.

"This is where he stops running," Rowan continues. "And starts making us come to him wrong."

Dax's jaw tightens. "Meaning?"

Rowan looks at the cleft again. The shadow inside it does not behave like shadow. It doesn't deepen as clouds pass. It doesn't thin when light shifts.

It waits.

"He wants me to reach," Rowan says. "He wants me to pull on the bond directly."

Ryan's breath catches. "And if you do?"

Rowan doesn't answer immediately.

Because the answer is not abstract.

Because the land is already demonstrating it.

He steps one pace closer.

The world tilts.

Not visually—somatically. His inner ear stutters. His weight misreports itself. For half a second, Rowan feels like he's standing in two positions at once.

Dax grabs his arm without hesitation.

Rowan doesn't fight it.

"Enough," Silas snaps. "That's not a test. That's a snare."

Rowan steadies his breathing, forcing the bridge to retract a fraction—not release, just narrow enough to stop bleeding signal into the pocket.

The pressure eases. Barely.

Ryan exhales shakily. "That thing felt like it was trying to decide where you end."

Rowan nods.

Graham didn't build a door.

He built a place where context dissolves.

"He can't hold her in there forever," Dax says. "Whatever that is—it's expensive."

"Yes," Rowan agrees. "And he knows I know that."

Silas straightens, gaze hard. "Then why show it to us?"

Rowan's voice goes low. "Because he wants me angry enough to touch it wrong."

Silence settles.

The pocket does not react to their stillness.

It doesn't advance.

It doesn't retreat.

It simply remains—present, unresolved, requiring a mistake to function fully.

Ryan's hands curl into fists. "She's in there."

"No," Rowan says. "She's near it."

He closes his eyes—not to reach her, not to call—but to feel the bond's orientation now that he knows where not to pull.

The bridge responds cautiously.

She's close.

Close enough that the wrongness presses against her awareness.

Close enough that any misstep here would not miss.

Rowan opens his eyes.

"We don't engage," he says. "Not yet."

Dax stiffens. "We're right here."

"And that's why we don't," Rowan replies. "This thing doesn't reward speed. It rewards error."

Silas nods once. "Then we observe."

They pull back—not far, not retreating—but enough to let the land settle around the pocket without pressure. The dead fold remains visible, but its influence weakens at distance.

Rowan feels the bridge stabilize slightly.

Not relief.

Control.

He presses the comm stone once.

"Erin," he says.

Her voice answers quickly. "I felt that."

"Confirm," Rowan says. "That pocket—can you read it?"

A pause. Static shifts.

"I can't map it," Erin replies carefully. "But I can confirm this: it's not designed to contain her."

Rowan's jaw tightens. "It's designed to bait me."

"Yes," Erin says softly. "And if you force it—if you anchor too hard—it collapses through you, not away from you."

Dax exhales slowly. "So how do we crack it?"

Rowan watches the dead fold as the light shifts around it without touching it properly.

"We don't," he says. "Not directly."

He turns back to the others, expression set—not grim, not frantic.

Decided.

"He increased her load," Rowan continues. "Which means he's burning margin to keep control."

Ryan's voice is tight. "So we wait him out?"

"No," Rowan says. "We make him spend."

Silas's eyes sharpen. "How?"

Rowan watches the dead fold as light moves around it without ever touching it.

"We don't feed it," Rowan says. "We don't push. We don't try to open what he wants to collapse through us."

He looks at Dax, then Ryan.

"We step out of its reach," Rowan continues, "and we anchor somewhere it can't steal context from."

Dax nods slowly, understanding clicking into place. "Make him either follow… or keep burning margin holding it alone."

"Yes," Rowan says.

They move downslope—not retreating, not abandoning—just far enough that the dead fold's influence stops trying to decide where Rowan ends.

The bridge steadies by degrees. Not relief. Control returning.

Behind them, the dead fold tightens.

Not in pursuit.

In irritation.

Graham wanted a mistake.

Instead, Rowan has denied him one—and taken away the only kind of leverage a trap has: inevitability.

32
INTERFERENCE PATTERN

The land refuses to lie. That's how Rowan knows they're close again—not arriving, returning with a different question.

Not because it points — it no longer does that — but because it stops pretending coherence is free. Stone holds weight a fraction too long. Sound hesitates before deciding which direction to travel. Shadows stack where they shouldn't, darkening in places that don't deserve it.

This isn't pursuit anymore.

It's proximity.

Rowan lifts a hand, palm open.

They stop.

No one asks why.

The bridge beneath his ribs hums differently now — no longer stretched thin, no longer diffuse. It has narrowed into something dense and uncomfortable, like a wire pulled tight enough to cut skin if mishandled.

Ryan swallows. "That's him."

"Yes," Rowan says.

Not sight.

Not scent.

Interference.

They stand at the edge of a shallow rock shelf where the terrain ahead looks normal until you try to focus on it. The stone slopes down into a cleft that refuses depth — not shallow, not deep — just unresolved. The air there vibrates faintly, like heat without warmth.

Silas crouches, presses two fingers to the rock, and stills.

"It's load-bearing," Silas says. "Not an entrance—a lever." Dax exhales sharply. "So if we push it—"

"—it pushes back," Rowan finishes.

He steps forward alone.

The hum spikes immediately.

Not pain.

Recognition.

The bridge tightens so abruptly Rowan has to brace his stance to keep from pitching forward — not pulled, not dragged — but answered. Like pressure meeting pressure.

His jaw locks.

"She's under load," Rowan says quietly.

Ryan's voice tightens. "You can tell?"

"Yes."

Because the pull doesn't seek him.

It resists him.

That's new.

Rowan closes his eyes for half a breath — not to reach, not to call — but to feel how much of the bridge he's holding open without tearing himself apart.

Too much.

Too fast.

Graham knows this.

Rowan opens his eyes again.

"Back up ten paces," he says.

Dax blinks. "Rowan—"

"Now."

They obey.

As soon as distance increases, the pressure eases — not gone, not weaker — redistributed.

Rowan exhales slowly.

"He's using her as counterweight," Rowan says. "The closer I get, the harder it loads her side to stabilize the fold."

Ryan's face goes pale. "So every step you take—"

"—costs her," Rowan agrees.

Silence falls heavy and deliberate.

The land does not intervene.

It watches.

Dax's voice is rough. "So what do we do?"

Rowan doesn't answer immediately.

Because the answer isn't tactical.

It's relational.

Graham isn't blocking him.

He's listening.

Waiting for the bridge to behave like a weapon instead of a system.

Rowan turns away from the fold.

Just enough.

The hum shifts instantly — sharp, displeased.

Graham notices.

"Good," Rowan murmurs.

He takes another step back.

Then another.

The pressure resists — not violently — but insistently, like the system is trying to keep him engaged.

Rowan refuses.

He lowers himself to one knee and presses his palm flat against the stone beneath him — not to force, not to open — but to anchor.

The bridge tightens, then steadies.

Ryan stares. "You're… not advancing."

"No," Rowan says. "I'm equalizing."

Silas's eyes narrow. "You're taking load back onto yourself."

"Yes."

That costs him immediately.

Not pain.

Strain.

The hum under his ribs thickens into something heavy and bruising, like pressure held too long without release. His breath shortens. His shoulders tense.

But the resistance ahead falters.

Just a fraction.

Dax's jaw tightens. "He felt that."

"Yes," Rowan agrees.

Because the interference pattern wobbles.

Recalculating.

Rowan pushes more weight into the anchor — not emotionally, not violently — but deliberately. He lets the bridge retract a controlled amount, refusing to extend into the fold while still refusing to let go.

Balanced tension.

The land shivers faintly.

Somewhere inside the wrongness ahead, something shifts.

Ryan's breath catches. "The pressure's… changing."

Rowan nods once. "He increased the load on her to punish the approach."

Silas watches the fold with predatory focus. "And now?"

"And now," Rowan says, voice low and precise, "he has to decide whether to keep paying that cost without getting the reaction he wants."

The fold trembles again — sharper this time.

Not response.

Annoyance.

Rowan feels it then.

Not Graham's presence.

Graham's attention.

Cold.

Focused.

Irritated.

Rowan lifts his head and speaks into the distortion without raising his voice.

"You don't get me reckless," Rowan says.

The land tightens around him — not hostile — attentive.

"I'm not coming apart for you," he continues. "And I'm not trading her pain for my speed."

The pressure spikes — brief, punitive.

Rowan absorbs it.

Does not retaliate.

Does not advance.

The spike fades.

Dax exhales shakily. "That… worked."

For now.

Rowan pushes himself back to his feet, careful not to let the bridge flare.

"This is no longer about distance," Rowan says. "It's about cost management."

Ryan nods slowly. "So we slow it down."

"No," Rowan corrects. "We make him inefficient."

They pull back from the fold — not retreating, not abandoning — just enough to deny Graham the leverage he's trying to provoke.

The land eases slightly, like a muscle unclenching.

Rowan turns away from the interference pattern with intent still intact.

"She's still holding," Rowan says quietly. "I can feel it."

Ryan's voice breaks. "How?"

Rowan's jaw tightens. "Because the bridge still hasn't collapsed."

Because somewhere inside that load — inside that pressure Graham thinks he controls — Isorae is still present enough to resist becoming ballast.

Rowan looks back at the fold one last time.

Not in challenge.

In warning.

"This doesn't end with speed," Rowan says. "It ends with precision."

Behind them, the land begins to remember how to support weight again.

Ahead of them, the fold tightens — not triumphant.

Wary.

Because for the first time since taking her, Graham has encountered a problem his system wasn't built to solve:

A bridge that will not break.

A counterweight that will not disappear.
And a hunter who has stopped behaving like prey.

33
LOAD INCREASE

The interval tightens unevenly.

Isorae feels it first in her knees — not pain, not weakness, but a subtle misalignment, like gravity has tilted a degree too far to be honest. She corrects automatically, breath shallow, glow tightening under her skin to compensate.

The space allows the correction.

Then it corrects her correction.

Somewhere far off, a pressure that was braced outward is being forced to hold steady instead.

Isorae exhales slowly through her nose.

So that's how today is going to be.

Graham does not arrive immediately.

That, too, is new.

The interval hums without him — strained, unsettled, as if it's holding a posture it doesn't like for too long. Pressure slides along the inside of her awareness, not directional, not precise.

Waiting pressure.

She stands because the space prefers it. Because sitting invites instruction. Because stillness is the only protest it doesn't punish outright.

When Graham finally resolves from the distortion, the interval reacts like a muscle unclenching and then immediately locking again.

"You changed something," he says.

Not accusation.

Observation.

Isorae keeps her eyes level. "So did you."

His gaze sharpens. "Did I?"

"Yes," she replies. "You're compensating."

Graham steps closer, irritation flickering through his expression before discipline smooths it away. "Careful," he says. "You're extrapolating without sufficient data."

She almost smiles.

Almost.

"The space is doing more work," she continues calmly. "Which means you are."

The interval tightens along her spine in warning.

Graham notices.

"Interesting," he murmurs. "You feel margin now."

"You gave it to me," she says. "When you split the path."

For a moment, the silence stretches too long.

Then Graham exhales slowly — not angry, but displeased.

"He didn't take the bait," he says.

She doesn't ask who.

She doesn't need to.

Graham circles her once — closer than before, boots silent against a floor that still hasn't decided what it is. His presence drags the interval slightly out of alignment, like his weight costs more here than it should.

"That pocket should have provoked him," Graham continues. "It was elegant."

"It was obvious," she replies.

His head snaps toward her.

That was a mistake.

The interval tightens hard — not punishing, not violent — but immediate. Her ribs lock. Breath fractures shallow and sharp in her chest as the space insists on compliance.

Graham does not touch her.

He lets the space do it.

"Don't confuse restraint for mercy," he says quietly. "I'm still being gentle."

She forces her breath to slow anyway. In for four. Hold. Out for six.

The pressure eases a fraction.

"That wasn't the plan," Graham continues, more to himself now. "He was supposed to come apart."

She lifts her chin despite the strain. "He doesn't do that on command."

Graham stops directly in front of her.

Too close.

The interval corrects her posture again, pulling her upright, angling her chest toward him like a display she didn't consent to.

His eyes track the movement.

"Then I'll adjust the incentives," he says.

Her pulse spikes.

"You already are," she replies. "This place is louder today."

He studies her glow — the way it tightens, the way it flickers under sustained pressure — and something like satisfaction settles into his posture.

"Yes," he agrees. "Because now I'm holding you and the field."

He reaches out.

Not fast.

Not slow either.

He places his hand flat against the side of her neck.

The effect is immediate.

The interval surges to support the touch, reinforcing it, anchoring her there as if his hand is a point the space agrees with. Her glow recoils violently, light scraping inward hard enough to make her vision spark.

She gasps.

Graham feels it.

"There," he says softly. "That's the cost."

Her hands twitch — not reaching, not striking — instinctive motion the space interrupts before it can become action.

"You're using me as ballast," she rasps.

"Yes," he says. Honest. "And you're still holding."

His thumb shifts slightly — just enough to feel the way her pulse hammers too fast beneath his skin.

She hates that he can feel it.

She hates more that he's listening.

"This is why I can't let you rest now," Graham continues. "If you recover fully, you adapt. If you adapt, you stop being useful."

"Useful to what," she snaps.

"To pressure," he replies.

He removes his hand abruptly.

The space releases a fraction too late.

She sways, catches herself, jaw clenched hard enough to hurt.

Graham steps back, watching the aftereffects ripple through her posture, her glow, her breathing.

"You'll notice," he adds calmly, "that I didn't hurt you."

She glares at him. "You didn't need to."

"No," he agrees. "Not yet."

The interval tightens again — not sharply, not violently — but steadily, like a dial turned one click higher.

Her legs tremble now.

Graham observes it with interest.

"That's the new baseline," he says. "Consider it… encouragement."

He turns away.

This time, the space seals faster, sharper — a clean cut instead of a lingering close.

Isorae stands alone again, breath ragged, glow struggling to remain synchronized under the increased load.

Her body aches.

Her nerves hum.

The wrongness presses closer to the surface of everything.

But beneath it — buried deep enough that the interval hasn't learned how to reach it yet — the bond tightens in response.

Not pulling or calling.

Bracing.

Somewhere beyond the fold, Rowan has refused a trap.

So the pressure has come here instead.
Isorae plants her feet.
Adjusts her breath.
Lets the tremor settle into something she can hold.
If Graham thinks increasing the load will make her smaller—
He hasn't understood the system he's stressing.
Pressure doesn't only break things.
Sometimes—
It teaches them how to push back without moving at all.

34
LOSING MARGIN

The interval fails quietly.

Not a rupture. Not a scream.

A miscalculation.

Isorae feels it as a hesitation in the correction — a fraction of a second where the space doesn't decide fast enough what she is allowed to be. Her weight shifts forward before the interval catches her, knee buckling just enough that wrongness spikes sharp and hot along her spine.

She catches herself. Barely.

Breath comes hard. Teeth clenched. Glow flares on instinct — defense as reflex, not choice — and the light slams outward—

—and for the first time since she was taken, it does not fully rebound.

A filament shears sideways instead. Not a flare. Not a reach.

A timing slip.

It snaps back late, misaligned, as if the space doesn't know where to put it.

Isorae goes still.

That wasn't supposed to happen.

The interval reacts like a system embarrassed by its own mistake — tightening too fast, correcting too aggressively. Pressure clamps along her ribs and shoulders, forcing her upright with unforgiving precision, locking her into alignment as if perfect posture could erase error.

But something has changed.

She can feel it: a thin place in her glow that no longer answers cleanly. Not gone.

Out of sync.

The space hums — strained, uneven — compensating around a flaw it didn't anticipate.

Graham arrives mid-adjustment.

He doesn't step out of distortion this time.

He stumbles out of it.

Not dramatically. Not far. Just enough that his boot lands half a beat late, heel scraping against a surface that wasn't there when he expected it to be.

He stills immediately.

Eyes lift to her.

Then to the space.

Then — sharply — to the uneven banding of her glow.

"What did you do?" he asks.

Not accusation.

Assessment.

Isorae doesn't answer. She's too busy holding herself together — breathing shallow, grounding through the wrong kind of pain: not injury, not damage in flesh, but misfire. Her glow flickers unevenly now, bright in some bands, thin in others — like a constellation missing a star.

Graham steps closer.

Too fast.

The interval lags again.

Not enough to free her.

Enough to prove it can.

His jaw tightens.

"That wasn't resistance," he says quietly. "That was load failure."

Isorae lifts her chin. A bloodless smile cuts sharp across her face. "You said I was expensive."

The words land.

Graham's gaze snaps to the invisible structures holding her upright.

"You pushed before correction finalized," he says. "You forced a timing error."

"You trained me to," she replies.

That stops him.

Not anger.

Calculation grinding against new data.

His hand lifts as if to touch her — reflexive — then stills a hair's breadth away.

The interval reacts anyway, surging tight along her shoulder where his fingers would have landed.

Too tight.

Isorae gasps as pain flashes bright through her collarbone, sharp enough to steal breath. Her glow spasms in response—

—and the damaged filament lags again, tearing sensation sideways instead of outward.

Graham swears under his breath.

He steps back immediately.

The space eases.

Too late.

Isorae sags forward a fraction before forcing herself upright again, vision tunneling, jaw clenched hard enough her teeth ache.

"That's new," Graham says.

Not impressed.

Not pleased.

Concerned.

"You didn't hurt me," he continues, voice sharpening. "You destabilized the structure."

She breathes through the aftershock. "You built it around me."

"Yes," he snaps — and then catches himself, as if hearing the edge in his own tone. "And now it's failing because of you."

Silence stretches — heavy, humming, wrong.

Corrections arrive out of order now, overcompensating in one place while neglecting another. The geometry around them creaks like stressed metal.

Graham turns slowly, scanning the space like a man inspecting a cracked dam.

"This wasn't supposed to happen yet," he mutters.

Isorae watches him closely.

"You didn't account for fatigue," she says.

He looks at her sharply.

"You assumed I'd collapse," she continues. "Or comply. You didn't plan for endurance to change the system."

His eyes darken.

Not rage.

Cold assessment.

"You've introduced instability," he says. "That makes you dangerous."

She lets out a weak, bitter laugh. "You abducted a threshold. What did you think would happen?"

Graham closes his eyes briefly.

When he opens them, the fascination is still there — but it's edged now with urgency.

"This means I accelerate," he says.

Her stomach drops.

"Accelerate what?"

He steps closer again — slower this time, deliberate, as if every inch costs him something now.

"The collection," he says. "Before the interval degrades further."

She shakes her head, breath tight. "You're losing control."

"No," he corrects. "I'm losing margin."

That is worse.

He studies her glow — the uneven bands, the delayed rebound — and for the first time, his gaze lingers not on how she reacts…

…but on what might happen if the pocket collapses while she's inside it.

"You can't keep doing this," she says. "It won't hold."

Graham straightens.

"I don't need it to hold forever," he replies. "I need it to hold long enough."

"For what?"

He meets her eyes.

"To finish the experiment."

The interval shudders again — deeper this time — a low groan rippling through the wrongness like thunder trapped underground.

Far away — impossibly far — the bridge reacts.

Not pulling.

Not tearing.

Correcting.

Graham feels it.

His head snaps up, breath hitching as something answers strain he didn't expect to be shared.

So close.

His jaw tightens.

"This," he says quietly, "is the cost."

He steps back.

The space seals faster than before, sloppier — like hands closing on something already cracking.

Isorae remains standing, trembling now, glow flickering unevenly beneath her skin — altered, scarred in function, but alive.

And Graham knows it.

That knowledge follows him as he withdraws — not triumphant, not satisfied —

aware, for the first time, that the system he's forcing may break in a way that does not spare him.

Far beyond the interval, the bridge tightens under new strain.

Not snapping.

Adapting.

And the cost of holding Isorae has just gone from theoretical…

to permanent.

35
LOSS OF TOLERANCE

Rowan does not feel pain.

That would be simpler.

What he feels instead is loss of tolerance — the bridge tightening past comfort, past elasticity, into something narrower and exacting. The familiar hum sharpens as if honed, and his breath catches on sudden recalibration.

He stops mid-step.

Silas turns immediately. "Rowan."

Dax is already scanning the terrain, hand flexing once at his belt. "That wasn't terrain."

Rowan doesn't answer at first. He closes his eyes — not to reach, not to track — but to identify what just changed.

The pull is still there.

Isorae is still there.

But the bridge no longer forgives drift.

Margin is gone.

He exhales slowly through his nose.

"She paid something," Rowan says.

Ryan's stomach drops. "What do you mean, paid?"

"I don't know yet," Rowan replies. "But the bond just… narrowed."

Silas crouches, palm to stone. The ground responds sluggishly, like it's tired of being interrogated. "Compression," he says. "The land's being asked to carry a sharper load through fewer points."

Dax mutters, "That's bad."

Rowan opens his eyes.

The terrain ahead hasn't changed visibly — but the choices inside it have. Where there were once several plausible continuations, now there are fewer, steeper ones. The interval no longer tolerates exploration.

No wandering.

No second chances.

"She's still conscious," Rowan says. Not a guess. A fact — pulled from the way the pull refuses to soften.

Ryan swallows. "Then what happened?"

Rowan shakes his head once. "She forced something."

Silas looks up sharply. "She what?"

"She didn't break," Rowan says. "She shifted the system."

Dax exhales through his teeth, a fierce kind of pride. "That's our girl."

"That's dangerous," Silas counters.

Rowan's jaw tightens. "Yes."

The bridge hums again — deeper, less forgiving. It doesn't ask Rowan to slow down.

It demands precision.

He takes a step forward.

The land reacts instantly, correcting the angle of his foot placement by a fraction that would've sent him stumbling yesterday. Today, it simply informs him where he must be.

Ryan winces. "I don't like that."

"Neither do I," Rowan replies. "But it means we're closer."

They move again — no longer scouting, no longer testing.

Following.

The air thickens as they descend into a band of terrain that feels overused, like a corridor dragged too many times across the same reality. Sound dulls. Shadows cling too tightly to their sources.

Silas slows. "Reinforced."

Rowan nods. "Recently."

Dax's voice goes low. "He's compensating."

"Yes," Rowan says. "Badly."

The bridge tightens again — sharp enough that Rowan has to brace, hand going to the stone wall beside him. The contact grounds him, but the cost lands anyway: cold pressure behind his sternum, like breath being rationed.

Ryan reaches for him instinctively. "Rowan—"

"I'm fine," Rowan snaps — then immediately softens. "I'm fine."

But they all hear the truth beneath it.

Not weakness.

Load.

"He shifted it," Silas says quietly. "Put more of the stress onto you."

Rowan straightens, forcing breath into rhythm. "Because I can take it."

Dax's eyes darken. "And because he wants you angry."

Rowan looks ahead — to the seam beginning to show itself more clearly now. A distortion in the landscape like a held breath made visible. The place where coherence starts to argue with itself.

"Yes," Rowan says. "He wants me reckless."

Ryan's voice shakes despite his control. "Then don't be."

Rowan's mouth curves — not a smile. A decision.

"I won't be," he says. "But I will be unavoidable."

The land tightens around that statement.

Not resisting.

Aligning.

They move again — faster now, not rushing, but no longer cautious. Every step costs more, but every step strips away uncertainty. The path ahead has stopped pretending to offer alternatives.

And far away, in a corridor that has begun to crack, Graham feels the change register like a knife turning.

Isorae didn't just endure.

She forced the system into a posture that favors direction over flexibility.

The bridge no longer stretches.

It aims.

36
LOSS OF MANEUVER

Graham feels it the moment the bridge changes function.

Not when it tightens.

Not when it narrows.

When it stops responding to provocation.

The interval around him hums differently now — less elastic, more directional. He pauses mid-step, fingers flexing once as the geometry compensates a fraction too late.

Interesting.

He closes his eyes — not in fatigue, not in prayer — to listen.

The pressure signature has shifted.

Rowan is no longer stretching.

He is tracking.

Graham exhales slowly.

"So," he murmurs to the space, "she held."

That complicates things.

He turns his attention inward — toward Isorae's containment — not to touch her, not yet, but to reassess the load. The interval responds sluggishly, like a structure carrying more than its tolerances were designed to bear.

Her endurance has done something Graham did not anticipate:

It introduced error into the timing layer.

And timing errors propagate.

He steps closer to her position — not appearing, not engaging — letting proximity register through the system. The space tightens around her automatically.

Too automatically.

Graham frowns.

That reflex is new.

"You're forcing the interval to choose," he says aloud, more curious than angry. "That's inefficient."

Isorae does not answer.

She doesn't need to.

Her glow is muted but coherent — disciplined compression refusing to flare on cue. She has learned how to deny him feedback without denying function.

That is a problem.

Graham adjusts — subtly, carefully — shifting load into the structure instead of the subject. Reinforcing corridor integrity. Narrowing degrees of freedom.

The interval groans.

Not audibly.

Structurally.

Graham stills.

He doesn't like systems that argue back.

"Fine," he says quietly. "If you won't collapse, I'll reduce your options."

He escalates — not violence, not pain —

constraint.

The space responds.

Too eagerly.

Correction snaps into place faster than intended, overshooting tolerance by a measurable margin. The interval stiffens — losing adaptivity, becoming brittle where it should remain responsive.

Graham's breath stills.

That was a mistake.

He feels it immediately: a drop in responsiveness at the pocket's outer edges. Rigidity. The kind that prevents graceful recalibration.

"Undo," he murmurs.

The interval does not comply.

Not fully.

The structure holds — but now it holds one way only.

Forward.

Graham opens his eyes slowly.

Ah.

He has traded flexibility for control.

And somewhere far beyond the distortion, Rowan feels the consequence land like a clean, unmistakable vector.

Graham straightens.

"Too late," he says softly, to himself.

He steps fully into Isorae's presence.

She stands exactly where he left her — upright, controlled, glow compressed into a steady internal lattice. She doesn't look relieved.

She looks ready.

"You felt that," he says.

"Yes," she replies evenly.

Graham studies her for a long moment.

"You shifted the system," he says. "I didn't think you had the patience."

She meets his gaze without blinking. "You underestimated endurance."

A muscle jumps in his jaw.

"Perhaps," he allows. "But don't mistake this for leverage."

She lifts her chin. "You reinforced the corridor."

"Yes."

"And now you can't let it flex."

Silence.

Graham does not deny it.

Instead, he steps closer — not touching, not crowding — close enough that the interval has to choose between stabilizing her and accommodating him.

It chooses her.

That is new.

Graham feels the resistance press subtly against his own presence — polite, minimal, unmistakable.

The system has begun to prioritize continuity over control.

He smiles then — not pleased.

Challenged.

"Very well," he says. "If the bridge wants to narrow, we'll narrow together."

He turns away — not leaving, but repositioning.

Preparing.

Because now there is only one viable outcome left to manage:

Timing.

And timing cuts both ways.

Far from the interval, the land ahead of Rowan loses its last ambiguity.

The seam sharpens.

The path stops pretending it might diverge.

The bridge no longer hums.

It locks.

And for the first time since Graham initiated the game, he understands the risk he has just accepted:

He has removed his own room to maneuver.

37
LOSS OF PRIVILEGE

Graham does not arrive like a man.

He arrives like a decision the world didn't want to make.

One moment the seam ahead is only wrongness — shadow too dense for the sun, air too still to be wind — and the next, the wrongness gains posture. The rock shelf tightens. Sound falls inward. Even gravity hesitates, waiting to see what it's supposed to obey.

Rowan stops.

Not because he's surprised.

Because the bridge under his ribs goes cold.

Not pain.

Recognition without permission.

Silas shifts instantly — half a step forward, not to shield Rowan, but to make himself visible as part of the cost.

Dax's hand rests near his belt. Not eager. Not afraid. Ready.

Ryan swallows hard, eyes locked on the seam like looking away might make it bite.

Then Graham resolves.

Not fully inside their world, not fully outside it — standing in the shallow cleft of distortion as if the land has reluctantly agreed to host the outline of him. His boots don't quite press the stone. His shadow doesn't quite belong to him.

He looks at them the way someone looks at a set of tools.

And then, without moving his head, he looks at Rowan like Rowan is the only one that matters.

"So," Graham says softly. "You learned to refuse."

Rowan's voice is level. "You learned to overcorrect."

A flicker — irritation, quick as a blink — passes across Graham's expression.

The seam hums behind him — tight, held too rigid. A structure braced so hard it can't breathe.

"You're close enough now," Graham says, as if correcting an experiment's variables, "that every breath you take costs her."

"Shut the fuck up," Ryan bites out.

Graham's eyes move to Ryan with mild curiosity — as if he's briefly noticed a bird making noise — and then back to Rowan as if Ryan never spoke.

Rowan doesn't rise to it. Doesn't let the bridge flare.

He watches Graham the way he watches a storm front: not for beauty, not for threat — for pattern.

"You wanted panic," Rowan says. "You wanted speed. You wanted me to pull wrong."

Graham's mouth curves faintly. "I wanted you honest."

Rowan's gaze doesn't shift. "I'm honest now."

The land tightens around that statement.

Listening.

Graham's eyes dart briefly to the stone beneath Rowan's boots — to the way the ground holds him like it prefers him.

Then he smiles again, thinner.

"Tell me," Graham says lightly, "how much of yourself have you already spent?"

Silas answers without heat. "Enough to kill you."

Graham flicks his eyes to him, weighs him for a fraction, dismisses him.

Rowan steps forward one pace.

Not into the seam. Not into the bait.

Just enough for the bridge to hum once — dense, disciplined, held tight.

The seam answers.

A small, involuntary shudder runs through it, like a muscle trying not to twitch.

Rowan stops there.

And then he speaks — not to threaten, not to negotiate.

To force the universe into a single point.

"Where is she?"

The words are not loud.

They don't need to be.

They land like a hook in the fabric between worlds.

For the first time, Graham doesn't answer immediately.

Not intimidation.

Accounting.

The question forces the system to decide which reality it belongs to.

Behind Rowan, Ryan's breath catches like he can feel cost spike without knowing why.

Dax's eyes go narrow. "Rowan—"

Rowan doesn't look back.

Graham's expression changes by degrees. Curiosity remains. Reverence remains.

But beneath it: a dawning understanding that Rowan's discipline is no longer a variable.

"She is exactly where you think," Graham says finally, careful. "And still out of reach."

Rowan doesn't blink. "That's not an answer."

Graham's smile thins. "It's the only honest one."

Rowan shifts — not closer, but sideways, changing his stance so the bridge reorients without reaching.

The ground corrects with him. Helps him.

Graham's eyes sharpen at the accommodation.

"You're changing the load geometry," Graham says.

Rowan's voice is quiet. "I'm taking her out of your hands."

The seam trembles — an involuntary overreaction from something braced too hard.

Graham steps forward in the distortion without fully crossing, testing how much room he still has.

The pocket protests around his outline.

Not violently.

Reluctantly.

Everyone feels it — the world holding its breath to see whether it should allow him to exist here.

Graham stills.

"You're making it choose," he says, not quite accusing. "That's unstable."

Rowan's mouth doesn't move into anything like a smile.

"Good."

Silence spreads.

Held properly.

Graham's gaze slides, almost unwillingly, toward the coherent terrain behind Rowan — a place that can hold a campfire, hold men, hold ordinary physics without rewriting them.

Then his eyes return.

"You don't understand what you're asking," Graham says softly.

Rowan's voice doesn't change. "Try me."

Graham's breath is slow, controlled. "What I'm holding is not a room."

"It's a continuation," he continues. "A pocket that stays viable only while it's being paid for."

"And you're paying for it with her," Dax says.

Graham's eyes flick to him, annoyance flashing — then discipline.

"Yes."

The honesty lands like a blade.

Rowan's eyes narrow — not anger.

Calculation.

"You're spending margin," Rowan says.

Graham doesn't answer.

Rowan continues, steady and precise.

"You overcorrected. You narrowed it. You made it rigid."

The seam gives a faint, stressed groan, as if it hears itself named.

"And now you can't let it flex," Rowan finishes.

Graham's smile is gone now.

Not replaced by panic.

Replaced by something thin and managed.

"You should be careful," Graham says quietly. "You're close enough that your restraint is the only thing keeping her intact."

Rowan's voice drops.

"Then you should be careful too."

Graham's eyes darken. "Is that a threat?"

"No," Rowan says.

And that's the terrifying part.

"It's a fact."

The land tightens. The seam shudders.

Graham's outline flickers for half a beat — misregistered, like the pocket can't afford him and the bridge at the same time.

Silas leans forward a fraction — not toward Graham, toward the moment Graham loses the privilege of stability.

Graham exhales once, controlled, and steps back into the distortion.

Not retreat.

Repositioning.

Timing.

"I'll tell you something you can use," Graham says, smoothing his voice like a mask returning.

Rowan doesn't speak.

"You're going to have to choose," Graham says softly. "Between reaching her quickly… and reaching her safely."

Rowan's reply is immediate. "That's not my choice."

A flicker — annoyance again.

Then Graham smiles like a man who believes in the last move.

"Everything becomes your choice," he says, "when the system starts collapsing."

His outline trembles again — another micro-failure.

For the first time, he looks less like a man enjoying control—

and more like a man negotiating with something that no longer likes him.

"She's still awake," Graham says quietly. "Because she refuses to disappear."

Rowan doesn't waver. "So do I."

Then Graham folds sideways into the seam like slipping into a crack in the world.

The distortion snaps shut behind him like a clenched fist.

For a breath, nothing moves.

Then the land exhales.

Sound returns in the wrong order — wind first, then distance, then birds remembering they exist.

Ryan's knees unlock like he didn't realize he'd been braced.

Dax finally breathes out. "That was fucking stupid."

Silas's eyes stay on the seam. "That was necessary."

Rowan doesn't answer either of them.

He steps to the edge of the weight-bearing fold and lays his palm flat against the rock.

The bridge hums once.

Not reaching.

Orienting.

The seam answers with strain — and for the first time, the strain arrives late, a half-beat behind the contact, like the pocket had to think before it could react.

Rowan stills.

Feels it.

Maps it.

Then lifts his hand.

"There," he says quietly. "He's losing room."

Ryan swallows. "And Isorae?"

Rowan's jaw tightens.

"She's paying for it," he says.

Silas's voice is low, cold. "Then we stop letting her."

Rowan turns back to the seam, eyes steady.

"We don't chase him," Rowan says.

Dax's gaze snaps to him. "Then what?"

Rowan looks at the fold like it's a throat he intends to open with precision, not rage.

"We force the system," Rowan says. "Not him."

The land tightens around the words.

And far away — held upright inside a corridor now too rigid to forgive mistakes — the interval stutters.

Not collapsing.

Not yet.

But hesitating in a way that feels like uncertainty.

As if the world is beginning to decide who it wants to obey.

38
OVERCORRECTION

The interval snaps back wrong.

Not violently. Not all at once.

Like a muscle correcting after being held too long in a position it never agreed to.

Isorae feels it in the small places first — tendons behind her knees tightening too fast, the angle of her hips nudged a fraction off-center before the space catches it and overcorrects. Her spine is pulled straighter than necessary. Her shoulders are squared too precisely.

Alignment without mercy.

She inhales sharply and stills.

Do not flare.

Do not fight.

The damaged filament in her glow quivers — thin, unreliable — as the interval compensates for yesterday's failure by tightening everything else.

So this is the response.

The space has learned fear.

Graham arrives mid-correction.

Not resolving smoothly — never smoothly anymore — but stepping through distortion with a sharpness that scrapes the geometry around him raw. The interval firms at his presence, bracing the way a structure braces for load.

He doesn't look at her at first.

He listens.

"You shifted it," he says finally.

Not curiosity.

Controlled irritation compressed into discipline.

Isorae keeps her gaze forward. "You did."

He steps closer.

The interval reacts too fast — snapping pressure along her ribs, locking posture before she can adjust. Pain flashes white-hot under her breastbone, sharp enough to steal half a breath.

She hisses despite herself.

Graham's eyes narrow. "That reflex. Late. That means the structure is prioritizing containment over responsiveness."

He reaches out and anchors her upper arm — fingers spread, firm, not cruel.

The interval reinforces the contact instantly.

Her glow recoils hard, folding inward around the damaged filament until her vision sparks.

Graham doesn't squeeze.

He doesn't need to.

"Stand still," he says.

The command isn't loud.

The space agrees anyway.

Pressure locks her feet. Knees tremble. Thighs burn from the sustained correction.

Graham watches her breathing, the micro-failures in her posture.

Then, too softly: "Your bridge changed."

Her chest tightens.

"It stopped stretching," he continues. "It started aiming."

Isorae holds her face neutral, breath measured.

He searches her for reaction and finds discipline instead.

"You feel him closer now," he says. "Don't you?"

The pressure increases — exact, not violent — and her glow flickers unevenly under the combined demand of the space and his grip.

She breathes.

Holds.

Lets the tremor settle where it won't feed him.

"Yes," she says finally. "I feel him."

Graham studies her for a beat — then releases her.

The interval lets go a fraction too late.

She sways.

He catches her by the same arm immediately, preventing the fall the space would have punished harder.

Not kindness.

Damage control.

"Careful," he says. "You're operating closer to tolerance than you realize."

She looks at him, breath ragged. "You came back wrong."

His jaw tightens.

"You overcorrected," she adds.

The words land.

His grip stills.

"You made me spend margin," he says. "That has consequences."

"For you," she replies.

The pressure spikes — brief, punitive — snapping along her spine like a reprimand.

She gasps, then steadies.

Graham steps back.

The interval holds her upright without him now — tighter than before, less forgiving.

"That's the baseline," he says. "Courtesy."

Then, colder: "No rest."

She swallows. "You're afraid."

Graham pauses.

"Afraid," he says carefully, "is not the word."

He studies her glow again — the uneven bands, the delayed resonance — and this time his gaze isn't hungry.

It's managerial.

"It's management," he finishes. "And you just became more expensive."

He folds away into distortion.

The interval seals fast — sharp as a cut.

Isorae is alone again, legs shaking, glow flickering unevenly beneath her skin.

She does not fall.

She shifts her weight a fraction and feels the space hesitate before correcting.

That hesitation is everything.

She breathes into it.

Counts.

Lets her glow settle into a narrower pattern — not flaring, not calling.

Just present.

And underneath it, for the first time since being taken, she feels something ripple faintly through the bond.

Not a voice.

Not a pull.

A pressure change.

Rowan — testing the structure without touching it.

She closes her eyes for one controlled breath.

Not to reach.

To align.

And far beyond the interval — where land is remembering how to bear weight without breaking — something answers.

The space tightens again, irritated.

Too late.

She has the frequency now.

And she knows how to hold it without giving Graham anything at all.

39

LOSS OF CONTROL

The interval misfires again.

This time, it doesn't pretend otherwise.

The correction comes late — a half-beat delay that lets Isorae's weight shift before the space reacts. Her foot slides a fraction. Balance wavers.

She recovers. Barely.

The space snaps tight a moment later, furious at being caught slow, pressure slamming along her calves and spine with no nuance at all.

Isorae hisses and stills.

That delay shouldn't exist.

Graham feels it instantly.

Not through her.

Through the system.

He resolves from distortion hard — no grace left in the entry — boots striking a surface that solidifies under him only after impact. The interval stiffens at his presence, bracing instead of flowing.

He freezes.

Listens.

Jaw tightening.

"No," he says softly.

Isorae lifts her head.

Not defiant.

Ready.

"You lost it," she says.

The words land before he can stop them.

Graham turns sharply.

The space reacts late again — a flicker of indecision that costs him half a second of alignment.

That's all it takes.

He closes the distance in two strides and strikes her across the face.

Not measured.

Not calculated.

A backhand — sharp, frustrated, imprecise.

The sound cracks through the interval like something tearing that wasn't meant to.

Isorae's head snaps sideways.

Her vision blows white.

The space overcorrects violently in response — pressure slamming into her ribs and hips to keep her upright — but too late to spare her from impact.

She tastes blood.

The damaged filament spasms wildly, light shearing sideways instead of rebounding, feedback screaming through her nervous system.

Graham stills.

Instantly.

Breath fast — once, twice — then forced down, eyes tracking not her face but the geometry around them.

The interval is shaking.

Not collapsing.

But rattled.

"That," he says quietly, "was a mistake."

Isorae laughs — wet, breathless, unsteady. "You finally did something honest."

His hand twitches at his side.

He doesn't hit her again.

That restraint costs him visibly.

He steps back half a pace, palms flexing, forcing control back into his posture like a man assembling himself from fragments.

"I told you not to provoke instability," he says — to her, to himself, to the space.

She turns her head back slowly, cheek burning, pulse roaring.

"You lost control," she repeats. "That's what this looks like."

The interval tightens at her words — warning — but it's reactive now.

Not authoritative.

Graham sees it.

His expression shifts: irritation thinning into urgency.

"You're pushing past tolerance," he says. "That's not bravery. That's damage."

"And you hit me," she says. "That's not management."

Silence.

Corrections arrive out of sequence, struggling to decide whose priority to serve.

Graham exhales slowly.

"I don't need you broken," he says. "But I also don't need you believing you're untouchable."

He steps closer again, careful now, deliberate.

Not apologetic.

Not gentle.

"You learned something important," he continues. "The system won't always catch you."

"So did you," she replies.

He pauses — just long enough.

"What?"

"You can't afford to hesitate anymore," she says. "You don't have margin left."

That one lands deep.

Graham's mouth thins.

"Yes," he says quietly. "Which is why things change now."

He steps back.

The interval seals harder — brittle, over-tightened — like a door slammed on a warped frame.

Isorae remains standing. Barely.

Her cheek throbs. Her glow shudders unevenly, the damaged filament burning like a fault line that won't cool.

She does not fall.

But the line has been crossed.

Not symbolically.

Mechanically.

The space hums with aftermath — unstable, resentful, strained past elegance.

And far beyond the interval, the bridge reacts.

Not with panic.

Not with pulling.

With anger sharpened into restraint.

Rowan doesn't surge.

Doesn't reach.

He feels the failure anyway — not the blow, but the moment the system didn't correct in time.

And for the first time since Graham took her, the pocket doesn't feel like a cage.

It feels like a countdown.

Because now Graham has done the one thing he cannot take back:

He has proven that when pressure climbs high enough—

he stops calculating.

And starts striking.

40
OUT OF MARGIN

Rowan almost misses it.

That's what frightens him most.

There is no spike.

No surge.

No tearing pull that would justify panic.

The bridge doesn't flare.

It stutters.

A fractional hitch beneath his ribs — like breath catching mid-inhale — then a low, unfamiliar drag through the structure that has carried him this far without complaint.

Rowan stops.

Silas feels it instantly and raises a hand without looking back. Dax halts a step later. Ryan nearly runs into them before catching himself, breath sharp.

"What," Dax says.

Rowan doesn't answer.

He presses his palm to the stone beside him — not anchoring, not asking — listening through contact the way you listen for a familiar rhythm turning wrong.

The land answers late.

Too late.

Rowan's jaw locks.

That's new.

Ryan swallows. "Rowan?"

Rowan exhales through his nose, forcing breath into discipline before it can fracture into urgency.

"She's still present," he says.

Not reassurance.

Diagnosis.

Silas frowns. "Then what changed?"

Rowan keeps his hand on the stone, eyes unfocused. The bond hasn't weakened. It hasn't gone slack.

It has lost forgiveness.

"Something got through," Rowan says finally.

The words land like dropped glass.

Dax stiffens. "You mean—"

"I mean the system failed," Rowan cuts in, flat. "Not her. Not the bridge."

Ryan's face drains.

The air around them thickens, as if the corridor itself hears the statement and resents it. Sound dulls. Posture becomes expensive. Indecision becomes punished.

Silas's voice is quiet. "He crossed a line."

Rowan nods once.

The bridge answers that nod — not by pulling forward, not by urging speed — but by hardening. The hum condenses into something angular, directional, stripped of give.

Anger arrives then.

Not hot. Not wild.

Cold enough to shape.

Rowan lets it settle.

"That wasn't calculated," Rowan says. "If it were, the bridge would've absorbed it clean."

Dax bares his teeth. "So he lost control."

"Yes," Rowan replies. "And now he's out of margin."

Ryan's hands curl, then unclench. "And she paid for it."

Rowan closes his eyes briefly — not to reach, not to check.

To hold the bridge steady long enough to hear what it is asking now.

It does not want speed.

It does not want force.

It wants finality.

"He'll escalate," Rowan says. "Not cleanly. Not efficiently."

Silas straightens. "So we stop waiting."

Rowan opens his eyes.

Ahead, the seam they've been skirting no longer pretends ambiguity. Its edges sharpen. The wrongness loses subtlety — bracing for impact instead of hiding.

Rowan turns his head slightly, just enough to address them all.

"No more patience," he says. "No more letting him set the tempo."

Dax nods immediately. Ryan swallows hard and nods too. Silas doesn't nod — he simply shifts forward, ready.

Rowan steps away from the stone.

The bridge does not stretch.

It locks.

Not to a location.

To a decision.

The hunt is over.

What remains is extraction.

And Graham has just shortened the time he has left alive.

41

CASCADE FAILURE

The corridor stops pretending it is stable.

It doesn't collapse. It doesn't tear.

It reasserts itself — tightening with a jerky impatience that rattles Isorae's teeth. Planes fold too fast. Angles sharpen into shapes that hurt to look at. Corrections arrive out of order, like a system forced to work beyond tolerance.

She is already shaking when Graham appears.

Not drifting in.

Stepping out of the space itself, boots striking a surface that shouldn't exist with enough force to make the corridor flinch.

That's new.

His control is slipping.

"You're doing that on purpose," he snaps, voice clipped now — no trace of earlier fascination. "Every time you resist, you destabilize alignment."

Isorae lifts her head anyway.

Blood has dried along her lip. Her throat burns. Her glow flickers erratically — bright in some bands, absent in others — like a constellation that's lost its map.

"Good," she rasps. "I hope it fucking hurts."

Graham's jaw tightens.

He crosses the distance too fast.

No circling. No testing.

He grabs her arm — hard.

The corridor overcorrects instantly, snapping pressure through her shoulder, locking joints into place as if the space has decided she is no longer allowed to move independently.

She cries out despite herself.

Graham doesn't let go.

"This," he snarls, shoving her back into a plane that wasn't there a second ago, "is why ARIS failed. You make everything personal."

Her spine slams into hard geometry. Pain blooms sharp and nauseating. Her glow surges instinctively—

—and the corridor crushes it inward.

Not extinguished.

Compressed.

She gasps, ribs screaming as if something is squeezing her from the inside. Breath comes shallow and panicked, scraped thin against the space's refusal.

Graham leans in, forearm braced near her throat — not choking, but close enough that every inhale becomes expensive.

"Stop reaching," he growls. "Every time you do, you distort the system."

Isorae laughs weakly, tears hot. "You mean Rowan?"

The name lands like a blade.

Graham's composure fractures.

His hand lifts—

—and for half a heartbeat he hesitates, as if he feels the corridor watching him.

Then he strikes anyway.

Not a scientist's controlled correction.

A man's blunt override.

Isorae's head snaps sideways. Light bursts behind her eyes. The corridor shudders violently—

—and Graham freezes, breath catching, not at what he did to her—

but at what it did to the structure.

For the first time, fear flickers across his face.

Not of Isorae.

Of the cascade he's just triggered.

Isorae sags where the geometry holds her, blood sliding warm down her jaw. Her glow lashes against containment, wild and wounded.

"You're losing it," she whispers. "You're hitting because you're scared."

His eyes burn.

"I warned you," he says, breathing hard, anger bleeding into lecture. "When systems are stressed beyond tolerance, errors cascade. Control degrades."

She spits blood at his boots.

The silence afterward is terrifying.

Graham releases her abruptly and steps back.

The corridor wobbles.

His hands shake — barely, but enough.

He stares at the geometry around them, recalculating too fast now, skipping steps.

"No," he mutters. "No, no—this isn't supposed to—"

The corridor groans like metal under strain.

And Isorae feels it through the bond like a pressure wave.

Not rescue.

Not yet.

But impact.

A distant, answering force pressing into the system's outer skin.

Graham snaps his head toward her, eyes wild. "You did this."

Isorae lifts her head through blood and shaking, broken smile sharp.

"No," she whispers. "You did."

The corridor spasms again — hard enough that both of them stagger.

Graham snarls and folds sideways, vanishing in a violent slip.

The space snaps shut behind him like a slammed door.

Isorae collapses where the geometry finally allows it, body convulsing with shock, breath tearing in and out.

Her glow flickers weakly.

Still alive.

Still resisting.

And far away — closer now — Rowan feels the aftershock slam through the land hard enough to stagger him.

42
OVERFOLD

The land does not open for Rowan.

It negotiates.

Every step forward costs him something — time, precision, restraint. Stonewake does not surge the way it did when Isorae was first taken. It moves with colder intelligence now, weighing consequence against necessity.

Rowan lets it.

That is the difference.

Silas feels it too — a pressure behind his eyes that isn't threat so much as direction. He signals Dax without looking, two fingers cutting left. Dax adjusts instantly, rifle coming up, posture loose but lethal.

"This place hates him," Dax mutters.

"No," Silas replies. "It remembers him."

That's worse.

Erin's voice crackles through the comm stone, strained. "I'm losing clean vectors. He's overwriting his own corridors. That's not strategy — it's defense."

Silas's mouth tightens. "He's panicking."

Rowan nods once.

Good.

And dangerous.

Because overwriting has a cost:

It turns flexibility into brittleness.

It turns hiding into compression.

The corridor buckles again.

Isorae feels it like a punch behind the eyes.

She's barely aware of her position anymore — knees on a surface that isn't flat, shoulder pressed into a plane that keeps changing angle, wrists still bound by spatial refusal rather than anything visible.

Her body hurts in places she can't name.

Her cheek throbs. Her ribs ache with every breath. Her glow flickers weakly, flaring only when panic spikes too high to contain.

Graham stumbles in hard enough to make the space recoil.

He's breathing too fast now. Movements lack careful economy. The system responds late, like a tired muscle.

"You did this," he snaps, rounding on her. "Every time you resist, you destabilize the bridge."

She lifts her head with effort.

"Stop pretending it's my fault," she rasps. "You lost control."

Graham laughs — sharp and ugly.

"No," he says. "I adapted. The system is just—" he gestures as the geometry warps again, "—lagging."

The corridor groans.

Actually.

Isorae gasps as pressure snaps around her sternum, forcing air from her lungs in a choking rush. She folds instinctively — and the space refuses to give her anywhere to go.

Graham watches her struggle, something frantic behind his eyes now.

"Don't break," he mutters. "I didn't bring you this far to—"

The corridor lurches.

Graham stumbles sideways and slams a hand into the space to steady himself.

His fingers sink in farther than they should.

He freezes.

That wasn't supposed to happen.

Isorae feels it too — the moment containment slips.

Not enough to free her.

Enough to matter.

She drags in a ragged breath and laughs, broken and wet. "You feel that, don't you?"

Graham turns on her, eyes wild.

"They're too close," she continues hoarsely. "You can't hold it anymore."

His hand lashes out again—

—and the corridor resists him.

Just slightly.

Just enough.

Graham jerks back, shock flashing across his face.

"No," he breathes. "No—this isn't—"

The bond flares.

Hard.

Rowan staggers mid-step, pain tearing through his chest like a blade dragged along bone. He drops to one knee, palm slamming into earth as Stonewake tightens beneath him — not wild.

Furious.

Directional.

And for the first time since Isorae was taken, he doesn't feel distance.

He feels strain.

"Silas," Rowan says, voice dangerously calm. "He's overfolded the corridor."

Silas's eyes sharpen. "Meaning?"

"Meaning he's stacked corridor inside corridor until there's no slack left," Rowan replies, rising slowly. "He's running out of places to hide."

The land shifts.

Not opening a path.

Pressuring one.

Roots tighten. Stone firms. The forest ahead leans — not toward Rowan—

but against the distortion.

Graham feels it and goes still.

For the first time, true fear flashes across his face.

He looks at Isorae — not as specimen.

As liability.

"You did this," he snarls, voice cracking. "You're going to get us both killed."

She meets his gaze through blood and shaking, eyes burning.

"Good."

The corridor screams.

And somewhere between worlds, something finally tears.

43
SYSTEM REFUSAL

The corridor does not fail. It refuses.

Not dramatically — no rupture, no tearing seam — just a subtle reordering of priority that makes everything inside it feel suddenly unfamiliar.

Isorae feels it in the small places first.

The correction arrives a fraction late.

Not late enough to free her.

Late enough to prove the system is no longer answering the same authority.

Her glow flickers — not flaring, not collapsing — shifting into a tighter pattern she didn't choose but recognizes: conservation. A lattice held quiet on purpose.

Then the space tightens.

Not around her.

Around the idea of entry.

The distortion thickens, braces, and Graham steps through anyway.

He doesn't arrive like he used to.

No clean resolution. No practiced ease.

His boot lands half a beat wrong, heel scraping against a surface that decides to exist only after impact.

He stills instantly.

So does the corridor.

For a breath, neither of them moves — as if the system itself is waiting to decide whether it can afford him.

Graham's eyes lift, not to her face, but to the geometry around her.

He listens the way a man listens for a machine turning off-pattern.

"What did you do," he says.

Isorae doesn't answer.

She doesn't give him the dignity of reaction.

That silence is deliberate.

And the corridor — strained, jittery — seems to prefer it.

Graham steps closer.

The interval does not help him.

It doesn't clear space. It doesn't smooth his approach.

It resists him with a faint, polite pressure that isn't forceful enough to call hostility.

Just enough to make him adjust.

His jaw tightens.

That shouldn't be necessary.

"You're degrading the response curve," he says, voice clipped now, stripped of fascination. "Every time you hold through correction, you force desynchronization."

Isorae's throat burns. Dried blood pulls at her lip.

She lifts her head anyway.

"Good," she rasps. "Then it's working."

Something sharp flashes behind Graham's eyes — not anger.

Alarm.

He reaches toward her.

Not to hurt.

To test.

The corridor tightens immediately — but not in the direction he expects. The reinforcement that usually snaps into place around his contact hesitates, misroutes, and lands as a hard brace along Isorae's spine instead.

Protection.

Not for her comfort.

For continuity.

Graham freezes, hand hovering.

He can feel the system choosing without him.

He lowers his hand slowly.

The corridor eases a fraction.

A calculation passes across his face, fast and cold.

"You're teaching it to prioritize you," he murmurs.

Isorae forces a thin breath through her nose.

"No," she says, voice wrecked but steady. "I'm teaching it you're not worth the cost."

The corridor shudders — not collapsing.

Acknowledging load.

Graham's mouth thins.

For the first time, his composure has edges that look like desperation.

"This pocket is paid for," he says quietly. "It remains viable because I pay it."

Isorae's glow tightens.

Not as flare.

As pressure.

"And you're running out," she whispers.

The corridor convulses then — a jagged correction that snaps through the geometry like a fault line slipping. A plane folds wrong. A corner holds too long. The entire structure shudders as if it has briefly forgotten which way "stable" is supposed to point.

Graham staggers half a step.

Just half a step.

Enough.

His eyes go wide for a single heartbeat.

Fear.

Real and unmasked.

Then discipline slams back down over it, too late to erase what she saw.

He backs away into the distortion without fully turning his body, like he doesn't trust the space behind him to behave.

"This isn't supposed to happen yet," he says — to her, to himself, to the corridor.

Isorae doesn't smile.

She doesn't have energy for triumph.

But she lifts her chin anyway, and the system — irritated, brittle, alive — holds her upright without asking her permission.

Graham folds sideways.

The corridor seals behind him too fast, too hard, like a door slammed on a warped frame.

Isorae sways.

The space corrects her.

Late.

And far away — closer now — the bond answers with a pressure change so clean it makes her eyes sting.

Rowan.

Testing.

Not pulling.

Not begging the system to open.

Learning where it has begun to refuse.

Isorae closes her eyes for one controlled breath.

Not to reach him.

To hold steady enough that the corridor can't hide the truth:

It is starting to reject Graham.

And rejection, once begun, is a system behavior — not a mood.

It doesn't reverse for pleading.

It ends with collapse.

Or expulsion.

44
TOLERANCE EXCEEDED

The corridor no longer corrects cleanly. It reacts.

That is the difference.

The geometry around Isorae jerks instead of guiding, planes snapping into place too late, angles overshooting before pulling back. The space feels irritated — not sentient, not angry — but stressed beyond tolerance, like a structure that has stopped trusting its own calculations.

She tastes blood. Her head still rings from the strikes, a dull roar that makes the world arrive a half-second late. Her jaw aches where Graham's hand snapped it sideways. The interval has locked her upright again, spine too straight, shoulders pinned to an alignment she didn't choose.

Graham stands a step away from her. Breathing harder than he wants her to notice.

"You did that again," he says, voice tight, clipped. "You destabilized the response curve."

Isorae swallows. Her throat burns. Her glow flickers beneath her skin, ragged now, no longer smooth — light folding unevenly around the damaged filament that never quite realigns.

She lifts her eyes anyway.

"You hit me," she says hoarsely. "And it still didn't work."

The words land.

Not as accusation, but as data.

Graham's jaw flexes. He turns slightly, pacing a short arc, fingers curling and uncurling as if recalibrating his own margins. The corridor tightens with him, correcting his movement too eagerly, then shuddering when it overshoots.

That hesitation wasn't there before.

He feels it.

So does she.

"This system was not designed for defiance under sustained load," Graham says, more to the space than to her. "It's producing noise."

Isorae lets out a broken laugh. Blood slicks her lip. "You mean me."

Graham stops.

Slowly, deliberately, he turns back to her.

The interval firms at the shift, bracing like it expects impact.

"Don't provoke me," he says.

She meets his gaze, eyes bright with pain and something sharper underneath. "You already lost your temper. That was you."

For a fraction of a second, something ugly flashes across his face.

Then discipline slams down over it.

He steps forward.

Not fast.

Not careful either.

Decisive.

His hand comes up again — not striking this time — gripping her jaw where he already hit her, fingers digging into the tender ache left behind. The interval reinforces the contact instantly, locking her head in place, forcing her to face him.

Pain flares hot and nauseating.

She gasps.

"Look at you," Graham says quietly. "Still orienting. Still compensating."

She bares her teeth. "You're shaking."

He freezes.

The silence stretches, taut as wire.

Slowly, he becomes aware of his own hand — not the grip, but the tremor beneath it. The way the corridor tightens unevenly around his arm, as if uncertain whether to support the contact.

That should not happen.

Graham releases her jaw abruptly.

The interval lets go a fraction too late.

She sways. Before she can catch herself, he yanks her sideways and back, the motion violent enough that the corridor jerks to keep them upright. Geometry snaps into place too late, too hard.

She is slammed against him.

His body cages hers immediately — spine to chest, no space — his forearm sliding up across her throat, not choking, just locking her head in place. His hand clamps onto her jaw again, fingers digging in, forcing her face to cant upward.

The interval agrees.

Her breath fractures.

"There," Graham says quietly, mouth close to her ear.

Measured. Controlled.

Almost calm.

"Hold still."

Her hands jerk instinctively — the space kills the movement before it becomes resistance. Her arms lock uselessly at her sides, shoulders screaming as alignment tightens.

His other hand comes around her front.

Not hesitant.

Not exploratory.

Claiming.

The contact is wrong immediately — invasive — the way it disregards her entirely, treating her body as a surface to be tested, not a person to be acknowledged.

Her glow reacts violently — collapsing inward too fast, light scraping her ribs until pain sparks white across her vision.

She cries out.

Graham tightens his grip on her jaw.

"Don't waste energy," he murmurs. "The system will punish you for it."

His voice is close now — intimate in the most violating way — every word delivered precisely into the hollow beneath her ear.

"This isn't anger," he continues. "This is correction."

His hand presses harder between her thighs, deliberately slow, applying pressure in increments — measuring response, mapping thresholds.

The corridor groans — deep, structural — as the interval hesitates, caught between reinforcing the contact and preserving continuity.

"You keep forcing misalignment," Graham says. "So I'm removing variance."

Isorae gasps, breath coming shallow and broken as the space tightens around her ribs, compressing her posture into compliance.

"Stop," she manages.

His fingers flex once at her jaw.

"No," he says softly. "You don't get veto power."

The words land colder than the violence.

Her body shakes now — not collapse, not hysteria — systemic overload, nerves firing too fast, glow flickering wildly beneath her skin.

Graham stills.

Not because of her.

Because the space doesn't immediately obey.

The interval convulses — a jagged correction that snaps pressure down her spine and forces him to shift his stance to keep balance.

For a fraction of a second his grip falters. Fear flashes across his face. Unfiltered. Unmasked.

He shoves her forward abruptly, releasing her as the geometry slams back into place.

She stumbles, barely catching herself before the corridor wrenches her upright again, breath tearing in and out of her chest, body shaking violently now.

Graham backs away. Fast.

Hands flexing like he's recalibrating damaged equipment.

"No," he mutters. "No—this isn't how it's supposed to behave."

The corridor spasms again — harder — planes snapping out of sequence, pressure surging and collapsing in ugly waves.

Graham turns on her, fury bleeding through discipline now.

"You forced this," he snarls. "You destabilized the structure."

Isorae sags against the alignment barely holding her, blood warm at her mouth, glow flickering but stubbornly alive beneath her skin.

She lifts her head anyway.

"No," she says hoarsely. "You crossed it."

The corridor convulses violently.

Graham vanishes in a jagged sideways fold, the space snapping shut behind him like a door slammed hard enough to crack the frame.

Isorae collapses where the interval allows her to fall, knees hitting first, then her hands, breath tearing in and out of her chest.

Her glow flickers.

Far away — no longer far enough — Rowan staggers as the backlash rips through the land like a shockwave.

Silas swears.

Ryan goes white.

Rowan's eyes are dark with something colder than rage.

"He's out of time," Rowan says.

And the bridge — narrowed, locked, no longer negotiable — agrees.

45

AGENCY OVERRIDDEN

The land jerks. Not a quake. Not collapse.

A recoil.

Rowan staggers mid-step as the bridge beneath his ribs misfires violently, pressure snapping inward instead of extending. Breath slams out of him like he's been struck in the sternum. He catches himself on stone that isn't where it was a heartbeat ago.

Silas swears under his breath.

Dax is already braced, boots skidding. "That wasn't terrain."

Rowan doesn't answer.

He can't.

Because the bridge has gone wrong.

Not severed.

Not weakened.

Scrambled.

Information floods backward through it — not images, not memory — but force without context, sensation stripped of meaning.

Compression.

A sudden rearward pull.

Jaw restraint.

Alignment locking where it shouldn't.

Rowan's vision whites out.

He drops to one knee hard enough that pain spikes up his leg, but he barely feels it. His hands dig into the ground reflexively, fingers clawing stone as the bridge spasms again — not reaching outward, but collapsing inward on itself.

"She just took a hit," Rowan says hoarsely.

Ryan freezes. "What kind?"

Rowan shakes his head sharply.

"I don't—" He swallows. Forces breath. "I don't have clean signal."

Because that's the worst part.

The bridge is not showing him what happened.

Only that something crossed a line the system wasn't built to tolerate.

The land reacts late.

Too late.

A violent correction ripples outward through the slope, trees shuddering as if struck by wind that never arrives. Sound warps. Shadows tear loose from their sources and snap back wrong.

Silas crouches, palm down. "The fold just convulsed."

Rowan grips stone harder.

The sensation hits again — sharper this time.

Not pain.

Violation translated into physics.

Pressure where there should be choice.

Constraint where there should be agency.

A sudden, brutal certainty of proximity she did not consent to endure.

Rowan retches.

Dax is beside him instantly, one hand on his shoulder, grounding without asking. "Rowan."

Rowan shakes his head once.

"No," he says. "Don't—"

Another backlash surges through the bridge.

This one carries emotion without narrative — not fear, not panic — containment under force.

The kind that leaves marks even when it stops.

Rowan snarls — low, feral — and the land answers.

Stone fractures uphill with a sharp report. Not collapse. Warning.

Ryan's voice breaks. "She's still alive. I can feel that much."

"Yes," Rowan says.

Because that, at least, is clear.

The bridge didn't go dark.

It screamed and came back wrong.

Which means she's still holding.

But something irreversible just happened.

Rowan pushes to his feet too fast. The bridge protests, pain flaring hot behind his sternum as if punishing haste.

Silas catches his arm. "Easy."

Rowan shrugs him off — not violently, but with intent that doesn't allow argument.

"He put hands on her again," Rowan says.

Dax goes very still. "You sure?"

Rowan's eyes lift, black with focus. "The bridge doesn't echo impact like that unless agency was overridden."

Silence drops hard.

Even the land seems to pause.

Ryan whispers, "Is she—"

"No," Rowan cuts in. "Not broken."

Because if she were—

The bridge would have collapsed.

Instead it has reoriented.

Rowan closes his eyes for half a breath and does something dangerous.

He doesn't reach for her.

He listens to the absence where consent should be.

The signal is ragged. Misaligned. But alive.

And threaded through it — unmistakable now — is Graham's interference, frantic and uneven.

Rowan opens his eyes.

His voice is quiet.

Deadly.

"He lost control."

Dax's jaw tightens. "And hit back."

"Yes," Rowan says. "And the system punished him for it."

Another tremor ripples through the slope — deeper this time — a fold snapping shut somewhere ahead with violent finality.

Silas exhales slowly. "He ran."

"Good," Rowan says.

Because running means fear.

And fear means mistakes.

Rowan straightens fully now, the bridge no longer thrumming — no longer humming —

Locked on vector.

"She's still holding," Rowan says. "But the cost just changed."

Ryan swallows. "How?"

Rowan's mouth curves into something sharp and merciless.

"He crossed from control into impulse."

The land tightens around them — not resisting.

Aligning.

"And systems don't forgive that," Rowan finishes.

Somewhere ahead, the fold continues to tear itself apart trying to contain what it was never meant to.

And Rowan starts moving.

Not faster.

Final.

46
THE BRIDGE ARRIVES

Rowan starts moving.

Not because he chooses to.

Because stopping is no longer a neutral act.

The moment his weight commits forward, the land answers with something it has not offered since the beginning of this search:

agreement.

Not guidance.

Not generosity.

A hard, structural alignment—like a joint snapping into place after days of strain.

The bridge beneath his ribs doesn't hum anymore. It doesn't stretch. It doesn't seek.

It locks.

Rowan feels the difference in his teeth.

Silas keeps pace without speaking, eyes scanning the slope the way you scan a room after you've heard the first gunshot and realized no one is leaving. Dax stays on Rowan's left, close enough to catch him if the land lies. Ryan holds the right flank, silent, gaze too sharp like he's trying to see through the air itself.

No one asks where they're going.

They can all feel it.

The world has stopped offering questions.

Ahead, the terrain tightens—not narrowing into a corridor, but shedding its unused options. A line of rock that should be climbable becomes too sheer. A slope that should be passable turns slick with an invisible refusal. A hollow that should hold shadow simply… doesn't.

Paths don't close behind them.

They fail to exist in front of them.

Dax glances sideways at him once, quick. "You're not… tracking anymore."

Rowan doesn't look at him. He keeps his eyes forward, jaw set.

"I'm not," he says.

Silas's voice is low. "Then what is this?"

Rowan swallows carefully, feeling the bridge settle tighter under his sternum.

"Consequence," he answers.

Ryan makes a small sound—half breath, half disbelief. "You mean—"

"I mean the system chose a direction," Rowan says. "And it's not letting go."

Silas crouches, palm to stone.

The ground replies sluggishly, reluctant, like it's tired of being interrogated.

"It's not stable up there," Silas says.

Rowan's eyes flick forward. The rock shelf ahead looks ordinary—granite, pines, scrub—but the space around it carries the wrong kind of quiet.

Not absence.

Containment.

Dax's hand flexes once at his belt. "We going straight into it?"

Rowan listens.

Not outward.

Inward.

The bridge doesn't offer more information. It offers only insistence.

A line.

A destination.

A refusal to detour.

Rowan exhales once, slow.

"Straight," he says.

Ryan swallows. "Rowan… if the bridge is locked—if it's doing this without you—"

Rowan cuts his eyes to him, hard but not unkind.

"It's not without me," Rowan says. "It's through me."

That's the difference.

That's the danger.

He reaches for the comm stone.

His fingers are steady.

Static answers first—distance translated into noise, interference stripped of sentiment.

Then Erin's voice cuts through, clipped and sharp.

"Rowan."

"You felt it," Rowan says.

"I felt the backlash," Erin replies immediately. "And then the field reoriented."

Dax's mouth tightens. "So you saw him run."

"I saw a closure event," Erin says. "Not clean. Not planned. Like someone slammed a door that wasn't meant to close yet."

Rowan's jaw works once.

"He lost margin," Rowan says.

"Yes," Erin confirms. "And the system is compensating."

Silas's eyes narrow. "Meaning?"

Erin hesitates—rare, brief, but there. Like she hates what she's about to say.

"Meaning the interval has stopped trying to stay flexible," she says. "It's choosing stability over responsiveness."

Rowan's grip tightens on the comm stone. "It's making itself brittle."

"Yes," Erin says, voice low. "And brittle systems break fast when they break."

Ryan whispers, "Is that good?"

Erin's answer is immediate and merciless.

"It depends who it breaks on."

Rowan closes his eyes for half a beat.

Not to reach Isorae.

Not to call her.

To measure his own body against the locked vector inside it.

The bridge isn't only aimed.

It's loaded.

He opens his eyes.

"Can you tag the current trend," Rowan says. "I don't need coordinates. I need… confirmation."

A faint clicking sound. Erin working.

Then: "You're within the highest interference band I've seen," she says. "You're at the edge of the pocket's support structure."

Silas straightens. "So we're at the frame?"

Erin's voice tightens. "Yes."

Rowan's gaze goes to the rock shelf again—the place where shadow refuses to behave, where sound hesitates before it chooses a direction.

He can feel it now without touching it.

Not Graham.

Not Isorae.

The architecture.

A stressed hinge.

A corridor forced to carry more than it can.

Dax watches him. "How bad is it?"

Rowan doesn't answer right away.

He takes one step forward.

The land corrects the angle of his boot placement before his heel even meets stone.

It doesn't shove him.

It places him.

Ryan's voice breaks in a whisper. "That's… not normal."

"No," Rowan says.

His breath comes out through his nose, controlled, cold.

"It's done pretending."

Silas's hand hovers near his shoulder as if to steady him. Rowan doesn't allow it—not because he's proud, but because contact is information now, and he can't afford noise.

Dax shifts his stance. "We go in together."

Rowan's eyes flick to him. "You stay coherent."

Dax's brow furrows. "What does that mean?"

"It means don't let the field pull you into my vector," Rowan says. "If I go down, someone needs to be able to pull me back out."

A silence falls.

Not because they don't understand.

Because they do.

Ryan swallows. "And if she's—"

Rowan's gaze snaps to him, sharp enough to cut.

"Alive," Rowan says. "Still alive."

He doesn't say more.

Because the bridge refuses to give him more than that.

Because the absence where consent should be has not returned to presence—but the signal hasn't collapsed either.

Alive is enough.

Alive is everything.

The land shifts again, a subtle tightening—like the world drawing its shoulders back before impact.

Rowan steps forward.

This time, the system doesn't simply allow it.

It demands it.

The rock shelf accepts his weight like it has been waiting for it.

The air thickens.

Shadows pool too dark.

And somewhere ahead, beyond the last place the terrain can convincingly pretend it is terrain, the interference pattern holds—wary, strained, misaligned.

Not inviting.

Not retreating.

Just waiting to be tested by the one thing it no longer knows how to handle:

A bridge that has stopped reaching…

…and started arriving.

Rowan's voice is quiet when it finally comes, not said to the others, not said to the land—said to the structure itself.

"Enough," he tells it.

And the interval—brittle, stressed, out of room—tightens like it heard him.

Not in defiance.

In preparation.

47
COUNTERWEIGHT

The interval tightens like a jaw.

Not closing.

Holding.

Rowan feels it in the air first—pressure that refuses to give, the way a cracked structure refuses to flex once it's braced. The rock shelf accepts his boots with a precision that makes his ankles itch. The land places him before he finishes the step.

It isn't guidance.

It's constraint shaped like cooperation.

Behind him, Silas moves like a man entering a room that might rearrange itself around his bones. Dax holds Rowan's left, close enough to catch him if the field decides to lie. Ryan keeps right, breathing like he's afraid to spend oxygen on words.

The seam ahead isn't fog.

It's behavior.

Shadow pooling too dark. Sound arriving wrong, then snapping into place as if embarrassed. The edge of it is a hinge under stress.

Rowan takes one more step.

The vector tightens.

And somewhere far beyond the shelf, through layers of wrong geometry, the far end of the bridge answers with a small, involuntary recoil—load transfer.

Rowan stops so abruptly Silas almost collides with him.

Dax's voice is rough. "That was her."

Rowan doesn't deny it.

Ryan's throat works. "You didn't even—"

"I didn't need to," Rowan says.

He shifts his weight forward a fraction without stepping.

The bridge answers—immediate, ugly.

Consequence without distance.

Silas crouches, palm hovering above stone. He doesn't touch. He listens like he's standing near a live wire.

"It's load-bearing," Silas says.

Rowan keeps his eyes forward. "Say it."

Silas's jaw tightens. "The frame stabilizes by transferring stress to the far anchor."

"Costs her," Dax mutters.

Rowan says it flat because anything else would become weather.

"Yes."

Ryan's voice goes thin. "Then we don't go in."

Rowan turns his head slowly.

"We go in," he says.

Ryan flinches.

Rowan doesn't raise his voice. He makes it denser.

"But not on his timing."

He reaches for the comm stone.

Static.

Erin's voice cuts through, clipped and immediate. "Rowan."

"Confirm transfer," Rowan says.

A beat. Then—quiet, precise:

"It's dumping on the far end when you advance," Erin says. "Preferred failure mode looks like catastrophic load on her."

Rowan's fingers go numb around the stone.

Silas's eyes harden. Dax goes very still. Ryan's breath breaks.

Rowan closes his eyes for half a heartbeat.

Not to reach Isorae.

To measure his own body against the locked vector inside it.

Then he opens them.

"Can you read her layer?" he asks Erin.

A pause—like she hates the answer.

"It's flattening," Erin says softly. "Not gone. Preserving continuity."

Rowan's stomach turns cold.

If the system spikes her again while she's doing that—

He doesn't let himself finish the thought.

He lowers the comm stone.

The seam waits—brittle, eager, preparing for the mistake it was designed to exploit.

Rowan doesn't give it the pleasure.

He widens his stance.

Not forward.

Down.

Anchoring himself to the shelf, letting the bridge settle into bone instead of pulling through ribs.

Dax watches him. "Rowan."

Rowan doesn't look back. "No contact."

Dax stills.

Silas's expression sharpens. "What are you doing?"

Rowan's voice is quiet.

"Taking weight."

He steps forward—slow, placed before correction can steal the angle.

The system tries to dump load—

Rowan catches it.

Not stopping it.

Redirecting it into himself, bracing through sternum and spine until his breath constricts and his vision narrows at the edges.

The cost lands like a fist under his heart.

He doesn't stagger.

He refuses.

Ryan whispers, voice breaking. "Rowan…"

Rowan shakes his head once.

No noise.

No mercy for the system's impatience.

He takes another step.

The transfer begins—

Rowan absorbs it again, letting it compress him instead of her.

Heat blooms behind his sternum, then cold, then heat again—his body translating structural stress into survival language.

He keeps moving anyway.

The seam is close now. Not a door.

A decision the world hasn't made yet.

Rowan looks at it and speaks like architecture can hear—because it can, in the only way structures ever listen:

through load.

"You don't get to use her against me," Rowan says.

The air tightens.

Not in defiance.

In preparation.

Rowan's mouth curves into something sharp and merciless.

"Wrong lever," he murmurs.

He steps forward again.

And the corridor—stressed, out of margin, tired of pretending—begins to decide whether it will break open…

or break down.

On him.

48
IRREVOCABLE

Graham stops pretending.

The careful cadence is gone. The measured distance. The tone that tried to pass curiosity off as restraint.

Graham enters the corridor already angry.

Not the measured irritation from before.

Not the disciplined recalibration.

This is impatience that has lost its vocabulary.

The space resists him immediately — angles tightening too late, pressure lagging behind his movements like a system that no longer trusts his inputs. He stumbles once, catches himself, snarls at nothing.

Enough.

Isorae is where he left her.

On her knees now.

Not because she chose it. Because the corridor finally allowed her to stop pretending her legs could hold her.

Her head hangs forward. Her hair hides her face. Her glow is barely visible — not extinguished, not dimmed — compressed, folded inward so tightly it barely interacts with the field at all.

That should alarm him.

Instead, it infuriates him.

"You don't get to shut down," he snaps.

No response.

That silence is the last thing that breaks him.

When he steps into alignment this time, it is fast—too fast—his movement snapping the corridor's geometry into compliance like it flinches for him now.

Isorae feels it before she sees him.

"Get up," Graham snaps.

She doesn't move fast enough.

His hand closes in her hair and yanks.

Pain explodes across her scalp as her head is forced back, neck screaming in protest. She cries out—raw, broken—and the sound seems to anger him further.

"I said get up."

He hauls her to her feet with brutal force, fingers tangled in her hair, other hand slamming hard into her ribs to keep her vertical. Something cracks. She feels it immediately — sharp, blooming pain that steals her breath.

Her glow flares reflexively—

—and Graham hits her.

Open hand. Hard. Across the face.

The sound echoes through the corridor like a gunshot.

Her head snaps sideways. She stumbles, vision blurring, ears ringing. She tastes blood.

"Stop that," he snarls. "Every time you flare, you fight me."

She laughs—hoarse, broken. "That's the point."

Graham's composure shatters completely.

He slams her backward into the corridor wall—if it can be called that—hard enough to drive the air from her lungs. The space hardens at his command, holding her there, arms spread, chest exposed, spine arched painfully, ribs screaming.

"You don't get to antagonize me," he spits. "You don't get to decide how far this goes."

Her breath comes in ragged pulls. Her glow flickers weakly now, uneven, like it's struggling to stay coherent.

"You think this is about dominance?" Graham continues, voice shaking with rage. "You think I'm proving something to you?"

Her mouth fills with blood. She spits it at his feet.

"Fuck you."

That is the wrong answer.

He crowds her space, presses in close enough that she can feel the heat of him, the tension vibrating through his frame. His hand closes around her throat. A clamp that turns breath into a variable.

"Every time you fight me," he says, voice shaking with rage he's trying to dress up as method, "you make this take longer."

He doesn't wait for her to answer. He pins her harder—shoulders, ribs, pelvis—forcing the corridor to harden around her like a mold. Planes snap into existence at her back and sides, holding her in a spread of angles that hurts to inhabit.

His other hand slides—deliberate, invasive, crossing from violence into violation with full awareness of what he's doing, forcing himself between her legs.

"No," she gasps, panic tearing through her voice now. "No—don't—"

"This is what you're for," he spits. "This interface. This bond. This reaction."

The corridor pulses.

Not randomly—precisely.

Pressure rises in measured increments, then drops a fraction, then rises again, hammering her sensory pathways until her body can no longer tell signal from threat. Her glow flares on reflex and is immediately forced inward, each correction arriving faster than her nervous system can recover.

Reminder. Punishment. Calibration.

Graham feels it.

That's what he wants.

"Yes," he breathes. "There—feel that? That's him. That's Rowan feeling you."

She can feel Rowan then—not clearly, not consciously—but as a tearing pressure inside her chest, like something sacred being ripped open from the inside.

"Stop," she sobs. "Please—"

Graham's face twists.

"Too late."

He pushes harder.

Isorae sobs—one harsh sound torn loose when the next pulse hits and her lungs misreport themselves. Her vision tunnels. The corridor roars like rushing water.

She reaches for breath and finds only mathematics.

Something sacred inside her chest—something that has stayed hers through every correction—shudders under the demand and withdraws.

Not surrender.

Emergency evacuation.

The world tilts sideways. Pain moves away from the center of meaning. Her limbs become heavy, unreal, as if they belong to someone else wearing her skin.

Graham feels the change and panics.

"No," he snaps, shaking her once—hard. "Stay with me."

Her eyes don't track properly.

Her body is still there.

But she isn't fully inside it.

Time fractures. Seconds disappear. Sound loses language. The corridor keeps trying to correct a person who has moved to a place correction cannot reach.

Graham lets go like he's been burned.

She drops to the floor in a boneless heap, hitting the surface hard. Blood threads from her mouth onto geometry that doesn't know how to be a floor.

The corridor recoils.

Violently.

Planes shudder. Alignments shear. The structure screams—not in sound, but in refusal.

Graham stumbles back, suddenly unsteady, breath breaking.

"No," he mutters, panic bleeding through his anger. "No, no—this wasn't—"

She wasn't supposed to leave.

She was supposed to transmit.

Graham stares at Isorae's dissociated body, fear crawling cold along his spine now.

The space no longer answers him cleanly.

The bond he tried to weaponize has changed state.

And Isorae—lost somewhere deep behind her own eyes—does not feel the corridor begin to fail.

She does not feel Graham retreat.

She is gone.

And Graham has just discovered the cost of forcing a bond to scream.

49
THE SHAPE OF ABSENCE

The bridge goes silent.

Not quiet.

Silent in the way a body goes silent when shock sets in—systems still firing, but nothing translating correctly anymore.

Rowan is mid-step when it happens.

There is no warning hum. No tightening. No narrowing.

The locked vector simply… empties.

The force that had been pressing forward through his sternum vanishes so completely that he pitches forward, catching himself on stone with a sharp, uncontrolled grunt. His palms scrape rock that feels suddenly unreal—too solid, too late.

His breath leaves him in a sound that is not language.

Not pain.

Absence.

Dax swears sharply. Silas is already moving, hand out, bracing Rowan's shoulder before he can collapse fully.

Rowan doesn't register any of it at first.

Because the bridge didn't recoil.

It didn't misfire.

It went blank.

The land around them reacts a beat later—trees shuddering, stone groaning low in the ground, the air compressing as if reality itself just inhaled too sharply. A ripple tears through the slope, snapping loose dust and sending birds screaming up from branches they were never supposed to occupy.

Silas's voice cuts through it. "Rowan."

Rowan doesn't answer.

He can't.

Because where Isorae should be—

There is nothing.

Not gone.

Not dead.

Worse.

Unreachable.

Rowan's hands curl into the rock until his knuckles burn.

The bridge is still there. He can feel its structure.

But the signal—the presence—the answer—has withdrawn behind something dense and absolute.

The backlash comes in fragments now—no narrative, no images—just raw translation of violation into physics.

A violent compression that doesn't belong to him.

A forced proximity that scrapes wrong against his nervous system.

A sudden, catastrophic absence of consent.

Rowan's vision tunnels.

His jaw locks so hard his teeth ache.

The land reacts again—this time not correcting, not aligning, but bracing. Stone tightens under his palms. The slope leans subtly inward, as if the world itself has decided it needs to hold him upright.

Dax's voice is tight. "Rowan. Talk to me."

Rowan drags in a breath that feels like broken glass.

"She's still alive," he says.

His voice is hoarse, scraped raw by the effort of forcing sound through a body that wants to fold in on itself.

Silas swears softly. "You're sure?"

"Yes."

Because the bridge didn't collapse. It didn't sever.

It went mute.

Which means she didn't disappear.

She retreated.

Rowan closes his eyes for half a heartbeat… and makes a choice.

He does not reach for her. He does not push the bridge. He does not try to force contact through the silence.

Because whatever just happened—

If he pulls now, he will tear something that cannot be repaired.

Instead, he listens to the shape of the absence.

It's dense.

Localized.

Contained behind a structure that is no longer pretending to be stable.

The corridor is no longer managing her.

It is holding damage.

Rowan opens his eyes.

Something in him has gone very still.

Not rage or panic.

Decision.

"He crossed a hard threshold," Rowan says quietly.

Ryan looks up at him, eyes red, shaking. "Rowan—what just happened?"

Rowan says immediately, "She's inside."

That distinction matters.

Dax's jaw tightens. "Inside what?"

Rowan pushes himself upright, every movement precise now, economical, stripped of anything that might waste energy or signal.

"The corridor," he says. "And herself."

The land answers that statement with a low, resonant groan—like a structure acknowledging its own stress fractures.

Silas looks ahead, eyes narrowing. "It's not hiding it anymore."

"No," Rowan agrees. "It can't."

He takes one step forward.

The bridge does not guide him. It does not resist either.

It simply permits.

That is worse.

Ryan swallows. "Rowan… if she's not reachable—"

Rowan cuts his eyes to him, sharp but controlled. "She is reachable."

"How can you tell?"

Because the silence is not empty.

It's intentional.

A retreat that preserved something vital by pulling it out of range.

Rowan exhales slowly.

"She's not responding," he says. "But she's still holding enough to be found."

Silas nods once. "And Graham?"

Rowan's mouth tightens—not into a snarl, not into a smile.

Into something colder.

"He lost her," Rowan says.

The land tightens around them—not collapsing, not surging—

aligning.

Because whatever Graham did in that corridor—

It broke the system's tolerance for him.

Rowan steps forward again. This time, the ground does not correct him. It makes room.

The silence remains. The absence stays dense.

But the vector reasserts—not as pressure, not as pull—as inevitability.

Rowan's voice is quiet when he speaks again.

Not to the others.

Not to the land.

To the broken architecture ahead of them.

"Hold," he says.

And the corridor—cracked, overstrained, no longer pretending—does.

Not for Graham.

For what is coming next.

Rowan moves. Not faster. Not reckless.

Unstoppable.

Because now there is nothing left to negotiate.

Only retrieval. Only aftermath. Only the cost of getting her back— from a place she survived by leaving herself behind.

50
EJECTION

Graham does not leave cleanly.

He is already running before he admits that he is.

The corridor rejects him in increments—small refusals that arrive too late to be useful, corrections that overshoot and snap back wrong. Angles stiffen where they should flex. Pressure lags behind his movements like a system buffering inputs it no longer trusts.

This is not resistance.

Resistance implies intent.

This is failure.

He stumbles once—just once—and the space answers with a sharp, humiliating misalignment that forces him to plant his hand against a plane that shouldn't exist yet. His palm slides. The surface resolves too late. His fingers scrape against something that feels like unfinished geometry.

Graham swears.

Not at her.

At the interval.

At himself.

At the cascade he can no longer slow.

"No," he mutters. "No—this is a timing issue."

He forces his breath into discipline. In through the nose. Hold. Out slow. He reaches for the familiar lattice of metrics in his head—load, margin, feedback latency—tries to reorder the system by naming it.

The system does not care what he calls it anymore.

Behind him, Isorae lies still.

Too still.

That is the problem.

Her silence is not compliance.

It is absence.

And absence is catastrophic for a system that requires response.

Graham turns back despite himself.

She has not moved.

Her body remains where it fell, folded at the joints in a way that suggests gravity finally won an argument the corridor was too tired to keep fighting. Her glow is nearly gone—not extinguished, not dimmed—withdrawn. Collapsed inward to a point that refuses to transmit.

No signal. No modulation. No usable data.

His stomach drops.

"No," he says again, louder now, as if volume could restore authority. "That's not an acceptable state."

He steps closer.

The corridor resists him this time—not by force, but by indecision. The plane he expects to step on arrives half a beat late, and his weight shifts wrong. His balance wavers.

The system is no longer prioritizing him.

That thought lands cold.

He reaches—not to touch her, not yet—but to ping the field around her, a diagnostic sweep meant to reestablish baseline.

The response is jagged.

Feedback spikes. Noise floods the channel. The corridor tightens around him instead of her, a brief, ugly inversion that snaps pressure up his spine and makes his vision blur.

Graham staggers back.

Hands up.

"Stop," he snaps reflexively—to the space, not to her. "That's not what I told you to do."

The corridor does not correct.

It holds.

Not in obedience.

In tension. Like a structure deciding whether to fail now or fail later.

Graham's breathing goes shallow.

This is bad.

This is worse than resistance.

This is a system that has lost its hierarchy.

He backs away from Isorae slowly, eyes never leaving her, as if she might suddenly reassert herself—flare, scream, reach, give him something to grab onto.

She does not.

Her dissociation is total enough that the bond no longer behaves like a conduit.

It behaves like a wound.

And wounds do not negotiate.

The realization hits him in a sequence of clean, terrible steps:

She is no longer routing through him.

The interval is compensating around her, not through her.

The bridge—whatever Rowan is doing on the other end—is no longer stretching. It is bearing down.

Graham feels it then.

Not the man.

The vector.

A pressure moving with intent instead of curiosity.

Rowan is not trying to reach the corridor.

He is approaching the frame.

Graham swallows.

This was not how the model ended.

He pivots sharply and the corridor punishes him for haste—geometry snapping tight, a violent correction wrenching his shoulder sideways. Pain flares, bright and immediate.

He snarls, shoves through it, forces motion.

"I need space," he says aloud, voice shaking now. "I need time."

The corridor gives him neither.

A fold ahead collapses prematurely—sealing with a brittle crack that sends a shock through the structure. Graham stumbles again, catches himself on nothing, then something, then nothing.

The interval is shedding options.

Just like the land did for Rowan.

That should not be happening here.

That should not be happening to him.

Graham's control fractures into panic.

He stops trying to manage the corridor.

He starts trying to escape it.

He reaches for a higher-level fold—an exit that bypasses the local architecture entirely. It's sloppy. It's risky. It requires margin he no longer has.

He doesn't care.

He initiates the tear anyway.

The corridor screams.

Not audibly.

Structurally.

Planes shear. Alignments misfire. The space convulses in protest, trying to preserve continuity while he rips a hole through it like a man clawing at drywall during a fire.

Behind him, Isorae does not react.

Her stillness is an accusation.

Graham throws himself into the fold.

The transition is violent.

Not a smooth dissolution—an ejection.

He is flung sideways through unfinished space, slammed into a holding pocket that barely stabilizes in time to keep him from fragmenting. He hits the floor hard, breath knocked from his lungs, vision tunneling.

The fold snaps shut behind him with a soundless violence that leaves a ringing pressure in his skull.

For a long moment, Graham lies there.

Panting.

Shaking.

Alive.

The space around him settles—slowly, grudgingly—into a configuration that does not belong to him but is no longer actively hostile.

He laughs once.

A short, broken sound.

"Okay," he whispers. "Okay. That was… premature."

He pushes himself up on unsteady arms, every nerve screaming with the aftermath of correction backlash. His hands are trembling now. He cannot stop them.

That terrifies him more than the pain.

He takes stock.

He is intact.

The system did not collapse here.

Which means it collapsed there.

Which means—

Graham stills.

Rowan will reach the corridor before it fully stabilizes.

The frame will be compromised.

And Isorae—

Isorae is no longer transmitting.

Not pain. Not resistance. Not anything.

Graham presses his palm to the ground beneath him and feels the faint echo of the interval's distress ripple outward like a bruise spreading under skin.

The bond has changed state.

From tool.. to liability.

He bares his teeth, a snarl without sound.

"Fine," he mutters. "Then we revise."

He pulls himself to his feet, already recalculating—not with elegance now, not with patience—but with desperation sharp enough to cut.

He made one mistake.

He will not make the second here.

Graham turns away from the damaged pocket, from the corridor that is already failing without him, and retreats deeper into unfinished space—toward contingency, toward distance, toward anything that buys him time.

Behind him, the interval continues to unravel.

Ahead of him, something far worse is aligning.

And for the first time since he began managing systems instead of understanding them, Graham runs not from consequence—but from a hunter whose approach the structure itself has decided to assist.

51
WHITE ROOM

The corridor holds her the way a hand holds a thing it has already dropped.

Not with care.

With refusal to admit gravity exists.

Isorae is on the floor where she fell.

Her cheek is pressed to a surface that cannot decide whether it is stone, metal, or the idea of a plane. It is cold in the way systems are cold—clinical, indifferent, consistent. The cold does not comfort. It does not punish.

It simply is.

Her body breathes.

Shallow. Uneven. Automatic.

Like a machine running on emergency power.

She watches it happen from somewhere behind her eyes.

Not above her.

Not outside her.

Just… back.

A single step removed from the place where sensation becomes meaning.

There is blood in her mouth.

She tastes it without tasting it.

The flavor registers like a line of data: iron, salt, heat.

No narrative attached.

Her ribs hurt. Her jaw hurts. There is a bloom of pain in places that try to sharpen and fail, like nerves sending messages into a room that has already been emptied of listeners.

The corridor corrects around her every few breaths.

Small, impatient recalibrations.

A plane stiffens.

An angle adjusts.

As if the space keeps checking whether she is still compliant enough to be worth holding.

She does not move.

Not because she cannot.

Because the part of her that decides movement is not currently staffed.

There are holes in her time.

They do not feel like blanks.

They feel like pages removed.

She tries to reach for the last moment she remembers clearly—tries to find the edge where her mind let go—and her thoughts slide off it, unable to get purchase.

Like the memory has been lacquered over.

That's what it feels like.

Lacquer.

A glossy seal placed over something volatile.

You can see the shape beneath it if you tilt your head.

You cannot touch it.

If she tries, her chest tightens and her breath catches wrong, and the corridor responds by tightening too—mistaking awareness for resistance.

So she stops trying.

It is easier to float.

To let the body be the body.

To let the corridor have its measurements, its alignments, its rules.

Her glow is barely there.

Not extinguished.

Folded so far inward it has stopped interacting with the space at all. She can feel it like a small star sunk under thick water.

Distant.

Still burning.

But refusing to flare.

Because flaring is invitation.

Because flare is feedback.

Because everything that happened happened because feedback got weaponized.

Her body shivers once.

A tremor that starts in her thighs and travels upward like a delayed aftershock.

The corridor answers with a correction so sharp it almost looks like violence—planes snapping tighter, pressure cinching her shoulders as if to say: *Do not do that.*

Isorae blinks.

Slow.

Uninvested.

The corridor settles.

Satisfied.

It wants her still.

She can do still.

Still is easy.

Still is the safest shape she has had in days.

Somewhere far away—far enough that far is a concept, not a distance—something tests the bridge.

Not like a call.

Not like a pull.

Like a hand checking whether a door is locked without turning the knob.

Rowan.

The name arrives without sound.

Without voice.

Only the recognition of a frequency her body has known too long to need translation.

For one thin, fragile second, her glow twitches.

Not outward.

Toward him.

Instinct attempting reoccupation.

The corridor reacts immediately.

Pressure clamps her ribs. A brutal tightening at the base of her skull pins her head at an angle she did not choose. The space learns fast, punishes fast—like a frightened animal with teeth.

Her breath stutters.

Her awareness steps back again.

Fine.

If contact costs this much, then contact becomes unaffordable.

She will not pay that price with his hands on the other end of the bridge.

She will not let connection become a leash.

So she withdraws.

Not in despair.

In strategy older than language.

When pain becomes inevitable, the mind becomes small.

When the body becomes unsafe, the self relocates.

Her thoughts simplify.

Count breaths.

Don't signal.

Don't flare.

Don't fight.

Somewhere in the corridor's geometry, something trembles—a brittle system trying to convince itself it can still hold what it no longer understands. A faint groan runs through the planes now and then, like metal cooling after fire.

The corridor is damaged.

She knows this without caring.

Damage is information.

It means failure is possible.

Not through strength.

Through endurance.

She tries to smile.

Her lip splits.

The sensation registers.

Warm.

Wet.

External.

She releases it.

Time stretches. Collapses. Resets.

Sequence loses authority.

She closes her eyes and discovers it changes nothing.

The darkness looks the same as the corridor.

Flat.

Bright.

Unconcerned.

A white room.

Not literal.

A mental architecture.

A place the world cannot enter because she has removed the parts of herself it would need to reach.

In the distance—closer now, but still unreachable—the bridge shifts again.

This time it is not a test.

It is weight.

Rowan is coming.

She knows it by the way the corridor flinches.

By the defensive impatience in its corrections.

The space has begun to anticipate.

Good.

Let it anticipate. Let it waste its strength preparing.

Isorae lies still, eyes half-open, breath shallow.

Her body remains.

Her glow remains.

But her self—the part that hurts, remembers, screams—stays sealed behind the lacquer.

Protected.

Preserved.

Waiting.

Because if Rowan finds her like this—alive, injured, not present—then the survival problem changes.

Then endurance becomes extraction.

Then the question is no longer whether she can hold.

It is whether she can return.

The thought does not arrive as words.

It arrives as release.

A loosening behind the eyes. A forbidden easing in her chest. The sudden absence of effort that comes when a body realizes it might not have to brace anymore.

If it ended now, she would not resist.

The understanding settles without drama.

That is what breaks her.

No fear spike.

No refusal.

No reaching.

Only the quiet, shameful relief of imagining stillness that asks nothing.

No corrections.

No vigilance.

No requirement to remain present inside something that keeps editing her existence.

Her glow would stop being measured.

The bridge would go slack.

And she would not have to choose.

For one suspended moment, the idea feels like rest.

Then something recoils.

Not outward.

Inward.

A collapse of warmth into nausea. A tightening beneath her sternum that has nothing to do with pain and everything to do with recognition.

She hates herself for how easy it felt.

For how quickly her mind accepted the idea of not continuing.

For the way relief arrived before grief, before anger, before loyalty.

The shame is not loud.

It is precise.

It cuts cleanly and leaves understanding behind:

She is tired enough that ending feels merciful.

Her breath fractures—not into sobs, not into sound—but into shallow pulls that fail to complete.

Her glow spasms beneath her skin, flickering in tight, incoherent bands.

Not resisting.

Not flaring.

Ashamed.

The corridor tightens, misreading the internal collapse as instability. Pressure clamps her ribs and spine, firm and corrective, reminding her that even now, even like this, she is still required to hold shape.

Her awareness retreats again.

Fine.

If awareness costs this much, she will ration it.

She does not argue with the thought she despises.

She does not justify it.

She does not forgive it.

She carries it the way a body carries shock—quietly, deeply, without ceremony.

Somewhere far beyond the corridor, the bridge tightens again.

Not sharply.

Not urgently.

A steady pressure.

Careful weight.

Rowan.

The recognition does not pull her back.

It hurts too much for that.

But it interrupts the thought.

The relief does not complete itself.

It remains unfinished.

Her body stays.

Her glow stays.

Her self remains folded behind the white, behind the lacquer—protected from hope and despair alike.

She does not choose to stay.

She simply does not leave.

And in the arithmetic of survival,

that is enough.

For now.

52
ALMOST

The corridor stops pretending.

It doesn't disguise itself as terrain anymore. It doesn't bother smoothing its edges or hiding its seams. Reality gives up the performance and shows its scaffolding—planes intersecting at wrong angles, shadows detaching and reattaching without apology, sound arriving in pieces instead of waves.

Rowan steps into it anyway.

Not because the path is clear.

Because the bridge will not allow hesitation.

The moment his boot crosses the threshold where the land should decide whether it is still land, the interval reacts openly. Pressure ripples outward in visible distortions—air folding, light stuttering like a skipped frame. The ground under his feet corrects too late, then too hard, snapping him into alignment that feels less like placement and more like enforcement.

Silas curses softly behind him.

Dax inhales sharply, steadying.

Ryan makes a sound that might be Rowan's name.

Rowan doesn't answer.

Because the first thing he feels is not the corridor.

It's her.

Not the bond.

Not signal.

Body.

Weight.

The sudden, devastating certainty of mass without movement.

Rowan's breath stutters.

He doesn't see her.

He knows her—somatically, catastrophically—the way you know a body when you carry it too long or lose it too fast. The bridge doesn't transmit thought or pain or emotion now.

It transmits orientation.

She is close.

She is down.

She is still.

Rowan's knees almost buckle.

The corridor punishes the micro-failure immediately—pressure snapping up his spine, forcing him upright, insisting on continuation. His teeth clench hard enough to ache.

Not yet.

Not yet.

The space around them convulses.

Not subtly.

A visible shear rips through a nearby plane, splitting shadow from stone. The shadow drags for a half-second before snapping back wrong. Sound shatters—Ryan's breathing arriving twice, Silas's footstep echoing before it lands.

The corridor is no longer stable enough to maintain sequence.

Rowan moves anyway.

Each step forward costs more than the last—not physically, not exactly—but internally. The bridge has narrowed to a blade-edge channel through his chest, every deviation punished with brutal efficiency. He cannot rush. He cannot slow.

He can only proceed.

And then—

Something gives.

Not distance.

Not structure.

Her.

The change is subtle enough that it almost passes as fatigue in the bond. Almost.

But Rowan has lived inside this connection long enough to know the difference between strain and release.

The resistance that has been holding the bridge taut eases.

Just a fraction.

Not collapse.

Letting go.

Rowan's stomach drops.

This is wrong.

This is worse.

His breath catches hard in his throat.

Because the bridge is no longer pushing back against her weight.

Because her presence is no longer insisting on being here.

Because somewhere inside the interval, something essential in her stopped bracing.

Not unconsciousness.

Not injury.

Choice.

No—

Not choice.

Acceptance.

The knowledge hits him sideways, brutal and intimate, like suddenly realizing the person you love has gone quiet not because they can't scream—but because screaming stopped feeling useful.

Rowan swallows hard.

His vision blurs at the edges.

"She's here," Ryan whispers behind him, voice breaking.

"Yes," Rowan says.

The word feels inadequate.

The space ahead tightens—not into a doorway, not into a chamber—but into something like an aperture that can no longer decide what it is containing. Geometry flickers, half-resolving and collapsing again, like a structure trying to remember how to be a place.

Rowan reaches the edge of it.

The corridor reacts violently.

Pressure slams into him from the side, forcing him to brace with one hand against nothing that becomes something just in time to keep him upright. The contact sends a shock through his arm, numbness blooming from fingers to shoulder.

Silas grabs his other arm, anchoring him.

"Rowan," Silas says, tight. "The frame's tearing."

"I know," Rowan replies.

Because he can feel it.

The corridor is failing openly now—no longer attempting to preserve itself for later use. Planes peel away like skin from a wound. The interval prioritizes containment over coherence, locking down sections too late, too aggressively, trapping pressure where it shouldn't be trapped.

And somewhere inside that—

Her.

Rowan takes another step.

This one nearly drops him.

The sensation hits without warning: a hollow under his ribs, a deadened slackness where resistance should be. The bond doesn't strain.

It yields.

"She's not… she's not answering," Ryan says, panic bleeding through discipline.

Rowan shakes his head once, sharp.

"She's alive," he says.

Then, quieter—because the truth is a blade—

"But she stopped pushing."

The words feel like treason in his mouth.

He can feel her now with terrifying specificity—not thought, not awareness, but physical truth. The way her body occupies space without asserting it. The way her presence no longer demands anything from the world holding it.

Not absence.

Withdrawal.

Presence without participation.

Rowan's chest caves inward.

He understands it all at once.

The exhaustion.

The relief.

The moment where fighting stopped feeling like survival and started feeling like prolongation.

The moment she realized she wouldn't resist if it ended.

And hated herself for how peaceful that felt.

Rowan's hands shake.

Not from fear.

From fury so controlled it threatens to break bone.

He takes another step.

The corridor screams.

Not sound.

Stress.

The architecture spasms, a massive overcorrection ripping through the space like a convulsion. Dax is thrown sideways, barely catching himself before a plane snaps shut where his leg was a heartbeat ago.

"Rowan!" Dax shouts.

Rowan doesn't turn.

Because now—

Now he can feel the outline of her.

Not visually.

Somatically.

The shape her body makes against the floor. The angle of her spine. The way her weight settles wrong, like gravity has finally claimed something it's been arguing with for too long.

Rowan's chest caves inward.

He wants to run.

The bridge forbids it.

He wants to stop.

The corridor will not allow that either.

Almost.

He is almost there.

Close enough that the bridge begins to misfire again—not collapsing, not screaming—but hesitating. Like it doesn't know whether it should continue functioning once the distance it was built to span is gone.

Rowan reaches the final interference band.

He can see her now.

Not clearly.

Not cleanly.

A body-shaped interruption in the corridor's failing geometry—hair spilled across a surface that refuses to decide whether it is floor or wall, limbs folded wrong, glow barely perceptible, withdrawn to a point that hurts to look at.

Not extinguished.

Hidden.

He takes one more step.

The corridor slams shut between them.

Not fully.

Not cleanly.

A partial seal—a violent compression that forces him to stop inches from her, pressure roaring through the space like a held scream finally released.

Rowan cries out despite himself, the sound ripped from his chest as the bridge locks hard, preventing contact.

His hand hovers in the air where her shoulder should be.

But the space will not let him touch.

Not yet.

Silas swears.

Ryan sobs once, sharp and broken, then clamps down on the sound.

Rowan's vision blurs.

He is close enough to feel the heat leaving her skin.

Close enough to feel how little she is asking of the world now.

Close enough to understand that if this lasted any longer, she might let go completely—not because she wants to die—but because she is so tired of being required to stay.

Rowan presses his forehead against the invisible barrier, breath shaking now despite every effort to control it.

"I'm here," he says—not to her, not to the others, but to the corridor itself. "I'm not leaving."

The interval shudders.

Not in refusal.

In strain.

Because the structure is failing.

Because Graham ran.

Because the system no longer knows how to reconcile containment with arrival.

Rowan stays where he is.

Hand hovering.

Body braced.

Heart breaking in slow, measured increments.

Almost is worse than absence.

Almost is the cost.

And somewhere inside the failing corridor, the space begins to understand that it can no longer keep them apart without tearing itself completely in half.

53
THE COST OF PASSAGE

The corridor breaks.

Not all at once. Not cleanly.

It fails the way exhausted things fail—by letting go of one rule at a time.

The barrier between Rowan and Isorae doesn't shatter. It thins. Pressure bleeds sideways instead of holding. Geometry loses confidence. The invisible plane between his outstretched hand and her shoulder begins to slip—not opening, not yielding, but forgetting why it was ever there.

Rowan feels it in his teeth.

In his wrists.

In the bridge, which screams once—high, sharp—and then falters, like it regrets making noise.

His throat tightens.

For one violent, stupid half-second, fear claws up his spine—not of what's ahead, but of what might still be taken away.

Afraid the corridor will remember itself.

Afraid it will correct again.

Afraid he will be forced to stand there, close enough to see her, unable to touch.

"Now," he says.

The word comes out low. Stripped.

Not to the others.

Not to the system.

To the part of himself that might freeze.

He steps through.

The space punishes him immediately.

A brutal correction snaps into his sternum like recoil. Pain lances hot and blinding through his chest, and something inside him tears—not muscle, not bone—orientation itself ripping loose as the bridge overextends past what it was ever meant to carry.

Rowan makes a sound he doesn't recognize.

Short. Animal. Broken off halfway through breath.

His knees hit the ground beside her.

The first thing he does is not touch her.

Because he has learned what sudden contact costs systems already in shock.

Because he knows the corridor is watching for excuses.

He forces breath into himself.

Once.

Twice.

Then—slowly, reverently, like approaching a wild thing that has already been wounded—he places his hand flat against her shoulder.

She is warm.

Alive.

The warmth nearly guts him.

It's not comfort-warm. It's body-warm. Human. Fragile. The kind that fades if you wait too long.

His mouth fills with iron.

"Isorae," he says.

The name slips—rougher than he intends. Smaller.

No response.

Up close, the wrongness multiplies.

Her weight is wrong. Settled unevenly, like gravity finally won an argument it had been losing. Her ribs don't lift together. Breath stutters shallow and uncertain, like her body is keeping the smallest promise it can still afford to keep.

Blood crusts at her mouth. Along her jaw. In her hair.

Her scent hits him then—copper, ozone, skin overheated by fear and containment—and something feral snarls behind his eyes.

Her glow is barely perceptible now. Folded so far inward it doesn't feel dim.

It feels hiding.

Her eyes are open.

But they are not here.

Rowan's vision blurs.

He swallows hard enough his throat aches.

The bridge inside him surges reflexively and he clamps down, jaw tightening until his molars scream.

Not yet.

Not like this.

He leans closer, lowering his voice—not urgent, not pleading. Controlled. Exact. The way you speak to someone standing on the wrong side of themselves.

"Stay in your bones," he says.

The words are not metaphor.

They are instruction.

They land.

Not as meaning.

As orientation.

Her breath catches.

Just once.

Rowan's chest shudders violently before he stills it.

He hates how desperate the relief is.

"Good," he whispers—too soft, almost not sound. "That's it. I've got you."

He slides one arm behind her back with surgical slowness, supporting without lifting yet, testing what her body will tolerate. The corridor twitches in irritation—planes tightening like it resents gentleness.

Pain spikes behind Rowan's eyes as the bridge flares again—angry now, overloaded.

He bares his teeth.

Does not look away from her.

Her head lolls toward his shoulder, heavy, unresisting. When he shifts her even slightly, she makes a small sound—not pain.

Disorientation.

Rowan stills instantly.

His grip firms—gentle, absolute—like he can physically hold her in place inside herself.

"I know," he says, voice cracking once before he crushes it flat. "I know. Don't go. Just—"

He swallows.

"Stay."

He presses his forehead briefly to the side of her head.

Not comfort.

Orientation.

A fixed point.

His breath shakes against her hair.

"I'm here," he says again. "You don't have to come back yet. Just don't leave."

Behind him, the corridor convulses.

A violent shear rips overhead. Planes collapse inward like ribs. Silas shouts Rowan's name—sharp, afraid in a way Rowan has never heard. Dax braces hard enough his boots scrape stone. Ryan breaks, a raw, helpless sound tearing out of him before he clamps a hand over his mouth.

Rowan doesn't turn.

Because he can feel the system preparing to correct.

Can feel it searching for the fastest way to regain control.

And he knows—cold, absolute—what it will choose.

It will dump the load.

On her.

Rowan's grip tightens around her back.

His decision happens before language can interfere.

He pulls the bridge through himself.

Not reaching outward.

Not extending.

He collapses it inward—forcing the alignment to route through his body instead of the space around them.

The pain is immediate and catastrophic.

His vision whites out. Something ruptures inside his chest with a wet, wrong sensation—nerve, vessel, something vital that will never regenerate. Blood floods his mouth and he chokes on it, a sound tearing out of him that he cannot stop.

He does not let go.

Cannot.

Because if he releases—

the corridor will take the easiest anchor.

Her.

The corridor screams.

Not in sound.

In structure.

Then it gives.

Not because it wants to.

Because it has no other option.

Rowan gathers Isorae fully into his arms.

Her body folds into him like it has forgotten how to hold itself. Her head drops against his shoulder. Her breath—thin, stubborn—touches his throat.

He moves.

The world fractures behind them—geometry folding in on itself, containment failing completely now. The corridor collapses into raw interference.

Rowan stumbles.

Silas and Dax are there instantly, hands brutal and sure, anchoring his weight because they understand exactly what it means if he falls with her in his arms.

Ryan is openly sobbing now, unashamed, one hand clamped over his mouth. His eyes never leave her face.

"She's breathing," he gasps. "Rowan—she's breathing."

"Yes," Rowan manages.

His left arm is numb.

He does not acknowledge it.

They clear the threshold as the corridor implodes—not exploding—

ceasing to be a place at all.

Interference collapses inward with the soundless release of a held breath.

Silence.

Real silence.

The land accepts them like it has been holding itself rigid for days.

Rowan drops to his knees and lowers Isorae carefully onto solid ground.

Outside the corridor's cruelty, the damage looks human.

That hurts worse.

He cups her face with reverent precision, thumbs brushing dried blood from her cheek.

His hands are shaking.

He lets them.

"Stay in your bones," he says again.

Not command.

Prayer.

Her gaze flickers.

Barely.

Enough to shatter him.

Rowan folds forward until his forehead rests against hers.

Not orientation now.

Need.

Because he cannot hold himself upright without this contact keeping him from coming apart.

The bridge inside him is wrong.

Irreversibly misaligned.

He knows it.

Accepts it.

Love did not fix this.

Love did not undo what was done to her.

Love did one thing.

It made him take the cost instead of letting the system spend her.

Rowan closes his eyes, pain blooming everywhere he has not yet allowed himself to feel.

"I've got you," he whispers.

Not a promise of healing.

A statement of fact.

Whatever comes next—

she will not face it alone.

54
THE LONG WAY BACK

They turn toward Stonewake without ceremony.

No declaration. No relief. No sense of victory to mark the change in direction. Rowan adjusts his grip on Isorae and steps forward, and the land—tired, scraped thin, but still functional—allows it.

That is all.

She is light in his arms in a way that has nothing to do with weight. Her body is present, warm enough, breathing shallow but steady. Her head rests against his chest where his heartbeat should be reassurance. He doesn't know if she can feel it.

He doesn't test.

Testing would be hope, and hope has teeth right now.

Silas takes point without being asked. Dax drifts to Rowan's left, close enough to intercept a stumble, far enough not to crowd. Ryan stays to the right, eyes tracking the terrain with a medic's attention—watching for the kind of wrong that announces itself too late.

No one speaks for a long while.

The corridor behind them does not follow.

That, more than anything, tells Rowan they are truly leaving.

The interference thins with each step—not gone, not healed—but no longer gripping. Reality resumes behaving like something that expects to be walked on. Sound arrives when it should. Shadows keep their shape. Gravity remembers its manners.

The land exhales.

Rowan does not.

He walks carefully, adjusting his pace to Isorae's breathing without looking down at her. If he looks, he might search her face for recognition, and he knows better now than to demand that from her. Her body has already given enough.

By midday, they stop for water.

Silas scouts the perimeter while Dax sets down packs. Ryan approaches Rowan quietly, hands visible, movements slow the way you approach a skittish animal or a bomb you're not certain has finished deciding what it is.

"She needs fluids," Ryan says.

Rowan nods once.

He kneels with deliberate care, lowering Isorae onto his coat. Her limbs move when he places them, compliant but distant, like she's letting him arrange something that no longer belongs to her. He hates that thought and sets it aside because it will not help her drink.

Ryan crouches and offers the canteen, speaking softly—not to Isorae, but to the space around her, like he's negotiating with the air.

"Just a little," he says. "You don't have to wake up. Just swallow if you can."

Rowan slides a hand behind her neck, supporting her head. His thumb presses lightly at the pulse point beneath her jaw. It's there. Fast, but there.

She swallows.

Once.

Then again.

Rowan exhales through his nose and doesn't let himself close his eyes.

After, he lifts her again, settling her against him. Her head finds the same place at his chest without instruction. Muscle memory, maybe. Or gravity. He doesn't care which.

They walk.

Hours pass in increments Rowan can measure only by the ache in his shoulders and the way the light shifts through the trees. The land does not hurry them. It also does not offer shortcuts.

Fair.

They camp before dark. Not because they can't go on, but because pushing now would be about fear instead of necessity.

Silas builds the fire. Dax takes first watch without discussion. Ryan hovers near Isorae, checking her breathing again, then looking at Rowan with the careful expression of someone who knows better than to say what he's thinking.

"She's stable," Ryan says quietly. "For now."

Rowan nods. He sits with his back against a tree, Isorae cradled against him, wrapped in blankets that smell like Stonewake even out here. Erin packed them that way on purpose. Rowan notices. He files it away as something to be grateful for later.

The fire crackles.

The forest does not intrude.

At some point, Silas returns and sits across from Rowan, gaze steady and unflinching.

"He's not following," Silas says.

"I know," Rowan replies.

Dax glances up from his watch. "We looking for him?"

Rowan doesn't answer immediately. He adjusts Isorae's blanket where it has slipped, careful not to touch her skin without necessity. She does not react. He doesn't know whether that's mercy or absence.

"No," Rowan says finally. "Not now."

Dax nods. No argument. Just acceptance.

"He'll turn up," Dax says. "Or he won't."

"He will," Rowan says. Not conviction. Assessment. "He has nowhere else to go."

Silence settles again.

Rowan does not sleep much that night. When he does, it is shallow and easily broken, his body waking at every shift of Isorae's weight, every change in her breathing. Once, she jerks suddenly, a sharp inhale tearing out of her chest like she's falling.

Rowan tightens his hold.

"Stay in your bones," he murmurs, so quietly it's barely sound. "You're safe now."

He doesn't know if she hears him.

He knows the words matter anyway.

Morning comes pale and cool. They eat. Rowan eats because he has to, not because hunger exists. Ryan hands him a ration without comment. Silas refills water. Dax stretches and rolls his shoulders like a man preparing for another long day.

They walk.

By the second day, the land begins to recognize them.

Not opening—not welcoming—but easing. Slopes that would have resisted yesterday hold steady. Stones stay where they're placed. The path does not lie.

Stonewake is still far.

Rowan feels the distance like a held breath that has not yet decided to release. But the bridge beneath his ribs, locked and scarred, remains intact. It does not reach anymore. It does not search.

It holds.

And that is enough to keep him moving.

They stop again before nightfall. This time, Rowan notices that Isorae's fingers curl faintly into his shirt when he lowers her. Reflex, maybe. Or anchoring. He does not comment. He does not smile.

He simply adjusts so she can keep hold.

The long way back is quiet.

Not peaceful.

But survivable.

And for now—for this narrow stretch of time—that is everything.

55
STILLNESS

Isorae is still where Rowan lowered her.

That's what Ryan registers after a minute or two — not immediately, not as a shock, just as something that fails to change. She hasn't shifted. Hasn't leaned. Hasn't reacted to the ground cooling beneath her.

Rowan kneels in front of her, quiet, methodical, hands steady as he offers her water. She doesn't take it until he presses it gently into her palm. Even then, she holds it without drinking, eyes fixed somewhere past his shoulder.

"Isorae," Rowan says once.

Not loud. Not urgent.

Her gaze shifts a fraction.

Not to him.

To the sound.

That delay lodges itself under Ryan's ribs.

She drinks when Rowan tips the container slightly. Swallows too carefully. Stops the instant the pressure eases. Hands the water back without looking at it.

She never asks for more. She never refuses.

She simply… waits.

Ryan watches her eyes.

They don't wander. They don't track. They don't search for threat or safety or meaning.

They rest, unfocused, like she's listening to something happening very far away.

When Dax shifts his weight behind her, boots scraping stone, she flinches.

Not dramatically.

Just a sharp, involuntary contraction — shoulders tightening, chin tucking, breath stopping for exactly three seconds before restarting.

Rowan doesn't move.

He counts silently.

Ryan can see it in the way Rowan's jaw flexes once.

When the count finishes, Rowan reaches out — slow, visible — and places his hand over hers.

She doesn't react.

Not withdrawal. Not acceptance.

Just contact without registration.

Ryan's stomach twists.

"She's alive," he thinks.

"And she is not here."

Minutes pass.

Or hours.

It's hard to tell.

Isorae doesn't speak.

Not a word. Not a sound.

Her mouth opens once — Ryan's pulse spikes — but nothing comes out. She closes it again, expression unchanged, as if the impulse never fully formed.

Rowan murmurs something too quiet for Ryan to hear.

Isorae does not answer.

Rowan stays anyway.

Eventually, her breathing slows.

Not sleep. Not rest.

Something shallower.

Rowan leans forward until his forehead nearly touches hers.

"Stay in your bones," he whispers.

Her breath hitches.

Just once.

Then smooths.

That is the only response Ryan sees.

He memorizes it.

Because later — Evan will ask questions.

And Ryan will need to explain that whatever happened to Isorae did not take her voice.

It took her location.

She is alive.

That is not the same thing as being present.

And for now, no one tries to bring her back.

They sit.

They wait.

They let her stay where she went — because something in her chose it as the only place left that was safe.

56
JURISDICTION

Stonewake does not announce itself. It does not flare, or rise, or sing them home.

It simply stops resisting.

Rowan feels it first—not as relief, but as a redistribution of weight. The pressure that has ridden his spine for days doesn't vanish; it slides sideways, easing out of his joints and into the land beneath his feet, like Stonewake is quietly saying *I've got it from here.*

The bridge doesn't unlock.

It unloads.

His breath stutters at the change. Not because he's tired—he passed tired days ago—but because his body has learned to brace against resistance that suddenly… isn't there.

The path widens.

Not dramatically. Just enough to allow four people carrying one broken center to pass without argument.

Ryan notices the air first. "Sound's back," he murmurs, like he's afraid to scare it away.

He's right.

Wind stops arriving late. Footsteps land when they're supposed to. The shadows under the pines stop smearing at the edges, return to behaving like shadows instead of afterimages.

The land is no longer correcting them.

It's receiving them.

Rowan doesn't look back.

He can't.

Isorae's weight in his arms is different now—less contested. The interval that kept trying to claim her posture, her breath, her alignment has loosened its grip, passing responsibility to muscle and bone and skin.

Human things.

She is warm.

She is breathing.

She is not present.

Stonewake's outer boundary registers them before the structures do. Rowan feels the shift like a deep joint popping back into place, something long-dislocated finally allowed to settle.

Then Evan is running.

He doesn't shout. Doesn't call Rowan's name. He moves like a man who has already accepted what he's about to see and is sprinting to minimize consequences, coat flaring behind him, hands already bare.

Erin is with him—faster than her build suggests, eyes flicking not to Isorae first, but to the field around them. The residue. The interference that hasn't fully let go yet.

"Rowan," Evan says—then stops short.

Because now he's close enough to see her.

The way her head rests against Rowan's chest, face turned inward. The bruising along her jaw, her throat. The way her body does not react when Evan's shadow falls over her.

Alive.

But not tracking.

Evan's fingers are on her wrist before Rowan fully stops walking.

Pulse. Breath. Pupils.

His jaw tightens.

"Inside," Evan says. Not sharp. Not panicked. Absolute. "Now."

Rowan nods once.

Does not ask where.

Does not ask how long.

He crosses the threshold with her still in his arms, and the moment he does, Stonewake closes behind them—not sealing, not trapping—but claiming jurisdiction.

The wild releases them.

Inside, the air changes again.

Not magic.

Function.

Walls that know how to hold sound. Floors that don't flinch under weight. Light that doesn't interrogate.

Evan directs without slowing. "Bed."

Rowan lowers Isorae only when Evan tells him to. Every movement is measured, precise, like if he misjudges an inch, the world might punish her for it.

She doesn't stir.

Her body accepts placement with terrible compliance.

Rowan stays close enough that his knee touches the bed frame, his shadow overlapping hers.

Evan works quickly now—checking ribs, spine, airway. His voice is calm, clipped, professional, but his eyes keep flicking to Rowan, assessing him too.

"Consciousness is… displaced," Evan says carefully, more to Erin than to Rowan. "She's dissociated deeply. Protective response."

"How deep," Erin asks.

Evan exhales. "Enough that we don't rush it."

Rowan presses two fingers to Isorae's wrist again.

Counts.

She doesn't react.

"Stay," Rowan says, quiet but unyielding.

Evan doesn't look up. "I wasn't planning to move you."

Good.

Outside the room, Ryan lingers at the doorway. He hasn't come closer. He's learned better than to crowd the injured.

Evan glances up once. Meets Ryan's eyes.

"Later," Evan says gently.

Ryan nods. Steps back. Lets the door close.

Down the hall, Erin catches Dax's arm as he passes. Their relief is brief, sharp, swallowed immediately by the gravity of what followed them home.

No one celebrates.

No one collapses.

This is not an ending.

Evan finishes the initial exam and finally straightens.

"She's alive," he says.

Rowan nods.

"And," Evan continues, choosing every word with care, "she's not all the way inside herself yet."

Rowan already knows.

Still, he lowers his head, presses his forehead briefly to the back of her hand, grounding himself in the warmth of her skin.

"Stay in your bones," he murmurs.

She does not answer.

But her breath stays steady.

Outside, the wind shifts direction.

Stonewake settles deeper into itself.

And far beyond its boundary—where the land no longer opens paths and the interval has nowhere left to negotiate—something begins to understand that it has crossed into a territory that remembers.

And does not forget.

57
HOLDING PATTERN

Evan does not call it recovery.

Not yet.

Recovery implies direction.

What Isorae is doing is stabilizing.

He works in careful layers, the way you do when you don't know which system will panic if you move too fast. He dims the lights first—not dark, just softer—then checks her pupils again. Still reactive. Still slow.

Good.

He listens to her lungs longer than necessary, not because he expects collapse, but because listening is how you show a body it's allowed to stay.

Rowan sits on the edge of the bed, unmoving.

He hasn't let go of her hand since they came inside.

Not gripping.

Anchoring.

Isorae's fingers don't curl back. They don't withdraw either. Her hand remains where it was placed, like it hasn't received updated instructions yet.

Evan straightens quietly. "No internal bleeding that I can hear," he says. "At least not catastrophic. Ribs are likely cracked—maybe fractured—but she's breathing through it."

Rowan nods once.

"What about—" He stops. Swallows. "What about the rest?"

Evan doesn't pretend not to understand. He washes his hands slowly at the basin, buying himself time to choose accuracy over comfort.

"She dissociated hard," Evan says. "That kind of retreat doesn't happen unless the nervous system decided presence was more dangerous than absence."

Rowan's jaw tightens.

"It's not permanent," Evan adds immediately. "But it won't be linear."

Nothing is.

Evan moves back to the bed and adjusts the blanket—careful not to surprise her. Even unconscious bodies can startle.

"She'll need prompting," he continues. "Food. Water. Sleep. Sometimes breathing."

Rowan's eyes flick to Isorae's face.

"I'll handle that."

"I know," Evan says gently. "But you can't be the only one."

Rowan doesn't answer.

Because he doesn't know how to promise that.

Evan places two fingers lightly at Isorae's pulse again. Steady. Present.

"She may not remember large stretches," he says. "Or she might remember everything, just not from inside herself."

Rowan exhales slowly.

"What do I say," he asks, finally.

Evan considers him carefully.

"You don't ask questions she can't answer," Evan says. "You narrate the safe things. Time. Place. What her body is doing."

Rowan nods. He already knows how to do that.

"You tell her what's real," Evan continues. "Without demanding she participate."

He steps back, giving Rowan the space without leaving.

Isorae shifts then. Barely.

A small movement of her shoulder, a tightening of her brow, like her body has brushed up against sensation and isn't sure whether to retreat again.

Rowan leans in immediately—not crowding, not loud.

"You're at Stonewake," he says softly. "You're inside. Evan's here. I'm here."

Her breathing hitches.

Then steadies.

Evan watches the response with careful interest.

"Good," he murmurs. "She heard that."

Rowan keeps his voice low, steady. "You don't have to do anything. Just stay where your bones are."

Her fingers twitch.

Not a grasp.

Not withdrawal.

Just… signal.

Evan releases a breath he didn't realize he was holding.

Outside the room, footsteps pass quietly. Erin pauses at the doorframe, takes in the scene without intruding.

"How is she," Erin asks.

"Alive," Evan replies. "And that's doing a lot of work right now."

Erin nods. She looks at Rowan—not with pity, not with questions—but with something like shared vigilance.

"I'll stay close," she says. "If you need to sleep."

Rowan shakes his head once. *Not yet.*

Later, when Evan finally leaves the room to prepare fluids and pain management that won't overwhelm Isorae's system, Rowan remains.

Time stretches.

Minutes pass.

Then another small movement.

Isorae's lips part.

No sound comes out.

Rowan still answers it.

"I know," he says quietly. "You're not ready yet."

Her breath trembles.

He tightens his hold on her hand just enough that she can feel it if she's still anywhere nearby.

Outside, thunder rolls—distant, low.

Stonewake doesn't storm yet.

It waits.

And somewhere far beyond its borders, something that thought it could disappear into the folds of the world begins to realize the land is no longer offering exits.

Inside the room, Rowan stays exactly where he is.

Because keeping her alive is not about fixing.

It's about not letting go until she can find her way back on her own.

And that, he can do.

58
CLINICAL HOURS

(POV: Evan)

Evan keeps his hands visible.

It's instinct more than strategy, but it matters.

He announces everything he does before he does it—even the things that shouldn't need announcing.

"I'm going to check your pulse."

"I'm sitting here."

"I'm not going to touch you yet."

Sometimes Isorae nods.

Sometimes she doesn't respond at all.

Both count as information.

Her vitals are steady in the way that worries medics the most—nothing alarming enough to justify intervention, nothing strong enough to reassure. Her pulse runs fast at rest. Her blood pressure dips when she stands too quickly. Her pupils lag a fraction longer than they should when light changes.

Trauma does that.

So does prolonged dissociation.

He doesn't write any of this down.

There's no chart that will help more than attention.

When he checks her ribs, he does it through the fabric first, slow pressure, one finger at a time. She winces at the third rib on the left, breath catching—not a sharp pain response, more like a memory of pain that hasn't decided whether it's done.

"Healing," Evan murmurs. "Still tender. That's expected."

She stares at the wall.

He waits.

After a moment, she says, "Okay."

The word is barely audible. Flat. But it's an answer.

He leaves it there.

Hygiene becomes a medical decision on the second day.

Not because she smells.

Because she doesn't notice.

She sits where she's placed. She eats when food is given. She drinks when prompted. She sleeps in shallow, uneven stretches that leave her body stiff and cold.

The body needs to be reminded it belongs to itself.

Evan explains what he's going to do before he suggests it.

"I'm going to help you wash," he says. "Just to keep your skin from breaking down. You don't have to do anything."

No reaction.

Rowan is in the room already, seated against the wall, close enough to be seen but not close enough to intrude. Evan notes the way Isorae's gaze drifts—not toward Rowan, but toward the place where he is. Orientation without engagement.

Good enough.

Evan keeps everything clinical.

Warm water. Neutral soap. Towels pre-warmed and laid out where she can see them. No sudden temperature changes. No surprises.

"I'm going to wash your hands first," he says.

He waits.

Her fingers don't move.

He proceeds anyway—slow, predictable, narrating pressure and placement like he would with a patient under light sedation.

She flinches once when the cloth touches her wrist.

Evan pauses immediately.

"Stopping," he says.

The flinch doesn't deepen.

After a moment, her breathing evens.

"Continuing," Evan says.

This time, she doesn't react.

Rowan doesn't move the entire time.

Evan clocks that too.

When the washing is done, when she's dry and dressed in clean clothes that don't cling or scrape, Isorae sits exactly where she's placed again. No resistance.

Compliance without presence.

Evan files it under expected and moves on.

Hydration remains the constant battle.

She doesn't feel thirst. Or hunger. Or fatigue the way people usually do. Her body sends signals; her awareness doesn't always receive them.

Evan notices patterns before Rowan does.

She drinks more when the cup is warm.

She eats better if the food is pale and simple.

She tolerates touch better in the morning than the evening.

She startles less if the room smells like stone and smoke instead of herbs.

He tells Erin all of this quietly.

Erin adjusts the space without comment.

That's how it works here.

Rowan is a variable Evan watches carefully.

Not because Rowan is unsafe.

Because Rowan is exhausted.

He sleeps in fragments—twenty minutes here, forty there—always waking to check Isorae's breathing like his body has learned that vigilance is oxygen. Evan sees the tremor in Rowan's hands when he thinks no one is watching. Sees the way his posture never fully relaxes.

Evan says nothing.

Not yet.

Because Rowan is holding something together that does not survive being named.

Once, while Evan is checking Isorae's pupils, Rowan shifts his weight too quickly behind her.

Isorae flinches hard.

Not away from Rowan.

Into herself.

Her shoulders snap tight. Her gaze drops. Her breathing goes shallow and fast, like she's bracing for something that hasn't arrived.

Rowan freezes instantly.

"I'm stopping," he says. Calm. Immediate. "I'm not moving."

Evan watches the way Isorae's body responds to that information—not relief, exactly, but recalibration. Her breath slows by degrees. Her hands unclench.

It takes a full minute.

But she comes back.

That night, Evan sits alone on the steps outside and stares at his hands.

He's treated broken bones. He's treated blood loss. He's treated shock.

This is different.

This is a system that learned the world was not safe and then learned it very precisely.

There is no antidote for that.

Only time. Repetition. Safety that does not demand proof.

When he goes back inside, Isorae is asleep.

Rowan is awake, watching her.

"She eat today?" Rowan asks quietly.

"Yes," Evan says. "More than yesterday."

Rowan nods once, like that information slots somewhere critical.

Evan hesitates.

Then, gently: "You don't have to be perfect at this."

Rowan doesn't look at him. "I know."

But his voice says he doesn't.

Evan lets it go.

Healing, he knows, is not about doing things right.

It's about doing them again.

And again.

And again—

until the body believes the danger has passed, even if the mind isn't ready to agree yet.

59
HELD WITHOUT ASKING

(POV: Rowan)

The nights are the hardest.

Not because she screams.

Because sometimes she doesn't.

Rowan learns quickly which is worse.

When Isorae cries out, there is direction to it—sound, movement, a place to put his hands where they won't do harm. He can speak then. He can say her name. He can say *Stonewake, inside, safe,* like coordinates pulled tight enough to hold.

When she goes silent, her eyes open but not to the room.

Those nights, he doesn't touch her at all.

He sits on the floor beside the bed, back against the frame, close enough that his presence registers without becoming a demand. He counts her breaths. He counts his own. He lets time pass without trying to drag her back into it.

Evan told him once, quietly: "Don't chase her out of dissociation. That just teaches the body it isn't allowed to leave."

So Rowan waits.

The flinching is unpredictable.

Some days she lets him hand her a cup of water without reaction, fingers brushing his like it means nothing at all. Other days, the same motion makes her shoulders snap tight, eyes widening in a way that has nothing to do with him.

Those days, he freezes mid-reach.

"I'm stopping," he says immediately. Not apology. Information. "I'm here. I'm not moving."

Sometimes she nods.

Sometimes she doesn't.

Either way, he steps back.

Food happens only because it's brought to her.

Evan leaves small plates—nothing overwhelming, nothing with strong smells. Erin sits with her sometimes—sometimes Ryan sits with her—talking softly about ordinary things: the way the light changes in the east rooms, how the creek shifted after the last storm, which stones are warmer in the afternoon.

Isorae listens.

That's all.

When she eats, it's slow and mechanical, like she's following instructions written somewhere just out of reach. Rowan doesn't comment. He learned early that praise makes her stop.

Water is harder.

She forgets it entirely.

Rowan keeps track instead. Sets the cup within her line of sight. Moves it closer when it goes untouched too long. When she drinks, it's only a few sips at a time, like her body hasn't remembered thirst yet.

Evan checks her ribs every few days. He explains what he's doing even when she doesn't respond.

"Still healing," he says once, gently, after she winces. "You're doing fine."

She doesn't answer.

Later that night, she speaks for the first time in days.

Rowan is half-asleep in the chair when he hears it.

"Too loud," she says.

Her voice is thin. Careful. Like it's been rationed.

He stills instantly. "What is?"

She swallows. "The fire."

He nods, even though she isn't looking at him. "I'll fix it."

He does it slowly. No sudden changes. He dampens the flames until the room settles into shadow instead of glow.

When he looks back at her, her eyes are closed again.

But her shoulders have eased.

That counts.

The nightmares come in waves.

Some nights she wakes clawing at the blankets, breath tearing out of her chest like she's still being crushed by space that won't let her move. Those nights, Rowan stays seated, voice low and steady, repeating the same things Evan taught him to say.

"You're on a bed."

"You're breathing."

"No one is touching you."

He never says *I won't hurt you.*

Evan told him not to.

Promises invite comparison.

Days pass.

Then weeks.

Healing doesn't look like progress. It looks like accumulation.

One morning she accepts a bowl of broth without flinching.

Another day she startles anyway when Rowan shifts his weight too fast.

Once—only once—she reaches for his sleeve when he stands up.

Doesn't grip.

Doesn't pull.

Just enough pressure to say *don't leave yet.*

He sits back down immediately.

Doesn't comment.

Doesn't smile.

He knows better than to turn survival into a moment.

At night, when she finally sleeps without tension locking every muscle, Rowan allows himself to rest too. Never deeply. Never fully.

Always half-aware of her breathing.

Always listening for the smallest change.

He does not think about Graham.

Not yet.

The land is handling that.

Rowan's job is smaller now.

Harder.

He is not here to fix.

He is here to stay.

And for now, that is enough to keep her tethered—not to him, but to the idea that presence does not always lead to pain.

That some spaces hold.

And do not demand anything in return.

60

SMALL RETURNS

(POV: Isorae)

There is a place she goes that has no edges.

It is not darkness.

It is not sleep.

It is a room without walls where nothing asks anything of her.

She does not always choose it.

Sometimes she arrives there because the world comes too close—because sound sharpens, because hands move too fast, because memory presses up from underneath like water finding cracks.

When she is there, time behaves politely.

It does not rush. It does not insist.

Coming back is harder.

She knows she has come back when weight returns first. The pull of gravity. The pressure of fabric against skin. The ache in her ribs that never quite leaves.

Pain is an anchor.

She is learning that.

Someone has placed a cup near her hand.

She stares at it for a long time before touching it.

The surface is warm.

That helps.

Her fingers curl around it without instruction. Muscle memory does the work her mind doesn't want to.

She drinks because her throat hurts, not because she's thirsty.

The water tastes like stone.

Stonewake, she thinks distantly.

That word still means something. She doesn't examine what.

When she sets the cup down, her hand shakes.

She notices without judgment.

That, too, is new.

There are gaps in her days.

Not lost time exactly—more like sections of film spliced out and replaced with still images. Rowan sitting on the floor, back against the bed. Erin's shadow crossing the doorway. Evan's voice explaining something she doesn't remember hearing.

No one asks her to fill in the blanks.

She is grateful for that.

Once, Rowan says her name too softly.

She startles anyway.

Her body reacts before meaning arrives—muscles locking, breath stuttering, awareness collapsing inward like a fist.

Rowan stops instantly.

"I'm here," he says. Not closer. Not louder. "You don't have to answer."

She nods because nodding feels safer than speaking.

Later—much later—she says, "I heard you."

It takes everything she has.

Rowan doesn't respond right away.

When he does, his voice is steady in a way that tells her he had to work for it.

"That's enough," he says.

At night, she dreams in fragments.

Not scenes.

Sensations.

Pressure without location. Sound without source. The certainty that something is about to happen and the knowledge that she cannot stop it.

She wakes with her heart racing and no memory of why.

Sometimes Rowan is already awake.

Sometimes Erin is there instead, quiet and solid like the floor.

No one touches her unless she asks.

Most nights, she doesn't.

Her body flinches at kindness as often as it flinches at threat. She doesn't trust the difference yet.

In the morning, Evan checks her eyes again.

"Any headaches?" he asks.

She thinks about it.

"No," she says. Then, after a pause, "Not sharp."

Evan smiles—not big, not hopeful. Just acknowledging.

"That's useful information," he says.

She almost smiles back.

Almost.

The effort exhausts her.

When she is alone, she practices being present in small ways.

Naming things.

The grain of the wood on the floor.

The weight of the blanket.

The sound of wind moving through leaves instead of through corridors.

Sometimes she whispers, "Here."

Just to see if it stays true.

It does.

Not always.

But more often than before.

She is not healing.

Not yet.

She is returning in pieces.

And for now, that is enough to keep her from disappearing entirely.

61

What Lets Her Stay

He learns the difference between watching and hovering.

Hovering makes her smaller.

Watching lets her decide when to exist.

Rowan sits where he can see her without being in her way—back against the wall, boots off, hands loose on his knees. The room is quiet in the way Stonewake gets when it's listening instead of guarding. The fire is low. No one moves fast.

Isorae is awake.

That, by itself, is not a victory. It is a condition.

She's wrapped in a blanket Ryan brought—heavy, woven, textured enough to give her something to feel that isn't skin on skin. Her eyes track the room in short, careful arcs. When she settles on something, she stays there longer than she needs to.

Anchoring.

Rowan recognizes it now.

He does not interrupt.

Evan's instructions echo in his head, clinical and gentle in equal measure.

Offer options. Don't stack demands. If she forgets, remind—not correct.

So Rowan waits until her hand drifts, uncertain, near the cup.

"Water's still warm," he says. Neutral. Informational.

She hesitates.

Then reaches.

Her fingers shake. The cup rattles faintly against the saucer.

Rowan does nothing.

She drinks. A few swallows. Enough.

When she sets it down, her breath lets out in a way that tells him the effort cost more than it should have.

"Good—" he starts, then stops himself.

Praise sounds like pressure.

"Thank you," he says instead.

That lands better.

At night, he still sleeps in fragments.

Not because he's afraid to rest—because his body doesn't trust time anymore. He wakes every hour or two, listening for changes in her breathing, the shift that means she's pulled too far inward or jolted too far awake.

Sometimes she's staring at the ceiling.

Sometimes she's gone somewhere he can't follow.

When she flinches—because a log pops in the fire, because someone laughs outside—Rowan stills like a held breath.

He waits.

If she looks at him, he says her name.

If she doesn't, he stays quiet.

There are moments when he wants to touch her so badly it aches—just to prove to both of them that he can. That the world can contain contact without harm.

He does not.

Consent is not a single word.

It is an environment.

Evan stops by in the afternoon, checks her vitals without fuss, speaks to her as if she is fully present even when she isn't.

"How's the light today?" Evan asks.

Isorae considers. "Soft," she says, after a pause.

Evan nods. "We'll keep it that way."

After he leaves, Rowan notices she's watching the window.

"The trees moved," she says quietly.

Rowan follows her gaze. The branches sway, slow and ordinary.

"They do that," he says.

She nods once.

The smallest acknowledgment.

Later, when the room empties and the fire sinks lower, Rowan feels the weight he's been carrying finally press through him—anger, grief, the memory of the bridge screaming back wrong.

He does not put it on her.

He lets the land take it instead.

Stonewake answers—not with reassurance, not with absolution—but with steadiness. The floor holds. The walls don't lean in. The night stays outside where it belongs.

Isorae shifts, just slightly, and her shoulder brushes his arm.

Accidental.

Rowan freezes.

She doesn't pull away.

After a long moment, she says, barely audible, "Don't go."

Rowan's chest tightens.

"I'm here," he says. No promise beyond what he can keep.

She nods, eyes closing again—not asleep, not gone. Resting at the edge of herself.

Rowan stays where he is.

Holding nothing.

Offering everything that doesn't ask.

More days pass.

The cabin still doesn't feel like shelter.

It feels like a place the world has been asked not to touch.

Rowan closes the door behind him one evening and does not turn the latch. He leaves it exactly as it is—not sealed, not open—because sealing feels like panic and leaving it open feels like exposure.

The lamp throws low amber light across the room. It does not reach the corners. He lets it stay that way.

Finally, he says her name.

Soft. Once.

"Isorae."

Her gaze flickers. Not toward him—through him—like a radio catching half a signal.

"I don't know how long I've been here," she says.

Rowan swallows. "Long enough."

That seems to satisfy something. Her breathing shifts—not deeper, not calmer—just… present.

"I keep expecting it to happen again," she continues. "Like if I move wrong, I'll be back there."

"You won't," Rowan says.

Not because he believes it blindly.

Because she needs the words to exist in the room.

Her fingers twitch against the blanket, then curl, then go still again like the instruction chain stops halfway through.

"My body feels borrowed," she says quietly. "Like I'm renting it."

Rowan reaches for her then—slowly, visibly—and lays his hand over hers on the blanket. He does not lace fingers. He does not grip.

Weight. Heat. Proof.

"You're not required to live in it yet," he says. "Just don't leave it completely."

Her glow responds faintly—a dull, uneven pulse beneath her skin, like light seen through fogged glass.

That scares him more than the flares ever did.

She turns her head a fraction, eyes finally finding his face.

"He's still loud," she whispers. "Not here. But… echoing."

Rowan nods. "I know."

"How?"

"Because echoes don't mean presence," Rowan says. "They mean impact."

She considers that.

Silence stretches—not empty, not strained—simply unfilled.

Then her breath catches.

Wrongly.

Her hand tightens under his, fingers digging into the blanket like she's bracing against a slope.

"Something's moving," she says.

Rowan stills completely.

Not toward the door.

Not outward.

Here.

"What does it feel like," he asks.

"Like the world is remembering me," she says. "And not agreeing on what that means."

"You don't have to answer that," Rowan says. "You don't have to interpret it."

Her eyes glass slightly, focus slipping again.

"I don't want to disappear," she says. Not pleading.

Statement. Fear.

"You're not," Rowan says.

He shifts closer, sitting fully now, knee against the bed, shoulder within reach without touching her again.

"Stay in your bones," he says gently.

The words land.

Her glow shudders—not collapsing, not flaring—catching. Like something slipping that finds friction at the last second.

She blinks. Once. Twice.

Her gaze steadies just enough to lock onto his.

"I'm trying," she whispers.

"I know," Rowan replies. "That's enough for tonight."

Outside, Stonewake adjusts—a soft redistribution of pressure, like the land testing whether it's allowed to breathe again.

Inside the cabin, Isorae's fingers curl around his hand—weak, uncertain—but intentional.

Rowan doesn't move.

Weeks edge forward in uneven increments.

She begins to walk again. Slowly. At first with his full support, later insisting on doing it herself even when her knees shake.

"I don't want my body to think I'm still trapped," she says.

Rowan doesn't argue.

Sometimes she talks.

Sometimes she doesn't.

Once, late one evening, she says calmly, "He doesn't feel loud anymore."

Rowan stills. "Does that scare you?"

She considers. "No. It scares me that it doesn't."

Stonewake hums beneath all of it—steadier now, but alert. The valley holds its breath not because it expects disaster, but because it remembers what disaster sounds like when it approaches quietly.

Nothing explodes.

Nothing resolves.

Life resumes in careful, deliberate motions.

And everyone knows—without saying it—that this calm is not peace. It is consequence.

Not because something is happening.

But because something already has—

and it has not finished deciding what it cost.

62
ORIENTATION

By the fourth week, the nightmares change.

They don't stop.

They lose their teeth.

Isorae still wakes in the dark, breath catching, heart racing like it's forgotten the difference between past and present. But the terror no longer arrives fully formed. It doesn't seize her whole body and drag her under before she knows what's happening.

Now, there's a moment.

A thin sliver of awareness where she knows she's waking.

Rowan recognizes the difference before she does.

Her body tenses, but it doesn't thrash. Her breath stutters, but it doesn't lock. Her glow flickers — uneven, muted — and then holds.

She blinks at the ceiling.

For several seconds, she just breathes.

Rowan stays still.

He's learned that stillness matters more than reassurance.

"You stayed," she says quietly.

It isn't fear.

It isn't relief.

It's orientation.

"Yes," Rowan answers.

She exhales, slow and shaky, as if checking that the word means the same thing in her body as it does in her mind. Then she turns her face slightly toward him, eyes unfocused but present.

"I dreamed about the orchard again," she murmurs.

Rowan's chest tightens. "The one near the river?"

She nods. "The trees were wrong. Younger than they should be." A pause. "But I knew where I was."

"That counts," Rowan says.

She considers that, lips pressing together faintly. "I didn't feel hunted."

Rowan lets himself breathe.

"I'm glad," he says.

Evan insists on food the next morning.

Not forcefully. Not gently either.

Relentlessly.

"Protein first," he says, placing the bowl in her hands. "Then we negotiate."

Isorae squints at him. "You're very bossy for someone I technically outrank metaphysically."

Evan doesn't blink. "Three bites."

She eats four.

Erin is there too, seated on the floor with her back against the wall, boots kicked off, presence deliberately casual. She talks while Isorae eats — about Parker reorganizing tools without telling anyone, about Sera turning inventory into a color-coded system that no one asked for but everyone secretly appreciates, about Jalen volunteering for watch rotations he doesn't need to take.

"It's like everyone's trying to prove the place still works," Erin says. "Like if we keep moving, nothing else will break."

Isorae stares into her bowl.

"That's what he did," she says quietly.

No one asks who.

Erin just nods.

That afternoon, Isorae walks to the doorway on her own.

Not far.

Just far enough to feel the air change.

The outside hits her all at once — sound, movement, depth. Her hand twitches, reflexively reaching for Rowan's sleeve, but she doesn't grab it.

Rowan stays exactly where he is.

She stands there for a long moment, eyes tracking the clearing like it might rearrange itself if she looks too closely.

Then she steps out.

Stonewake does not react.

No surge. No recoil.

Just the low, steady hum of the land continuing to exist.

Isorae exhales, breath shaking but real.

From across the clearing, Evan watches, relief and concern tangled so tightly he doesn't bother trying to separate them.

That night, Isorae eats without being prompted.

Later, she asks for water.

Rowan doesn't comment on either.

When the cabin settles and the dark presses in again, she speaks without opening her eyes.

"I don't remember parts of it," she says.

Rowan waits.

"And I don't want to," she adds. "But I'm scared of what it means that I can't."

Rowan shifts closer, careful, deliberate. "It means your mind chose survival."

"That sounds like something people say to make it easier."

"It is," Rowan agrees. "And it's also true."

She nods slowly.

"Will it come back?"

Rowan doesn't lie. "Some of it might."

She swallows. "Okay."

It isn't peace.

But it's progress.

And for now, that is enough.

63
COLD WATER, LIVING SKIN

Night returns quietly.

Not all at once — not like it used to — but gradually, the way it does when a body has learned that sleep can be entered without being taken. The cabin cools. The air settles. The last warmth of day fades from the floorboards.

Isorae sleeps.

Longer than she has in days.

Deep enough that dawn becomes memory instead of threat.

And then — somewhere past midnight, somewhere between dreaming and waking — something shifts.

Not fear.

Not pain.

Attention.

Her eyes open in the dark.

She doesn't bolt upright. She doesn't gasp. There's no spike of panic, no violent return. Just a sudden, razor-clear awareness that she is awake — and that her body is not.

She feels… suspended.

Like her weight hasn't quite come back to her bones yet.

Her glow is tight to her skin, compressed, dim but alert — not flaring, not collapsing. Waiting.

She lies still, breathing slow, cataloging sensation the way Evan taught her to. The bed. The blanket. The warmth beside her.

Rowan.

He sleeps close, one arm loose but present, his breath steady enough that it anchors the room by existing. The sight of him should settle her.

It almost does.

But the sensation doesn't fade.

It sharpens.

Not him — not now — and not Graham exactly.

The imprint.

The memory of being handled with intent. Of being decided.

Her skin prickles, not where she was hurt, but where she was assessed. Every place her body was treated like information instead of self.

Her glow flickers — uneven, restrained.

Rowan feels it.

He stirs instantly, the way he always does when her body shifts before her mind does. His hand slides to her back without waking fully, grounding pressure instinctive.

"You're here," he murmurs, voice low with sleep but certain. "Stay."

She nods, though her throat tightens around the motion.

She swallows hard. "I feel… wrong."

He doesn't ask for explanation. He never does when the truth lives in the body instead of language.

"Breathe with me," he says.

She tries.

The air won't go deep enough.

Her chest tightens. Every place Graham touched feels loud, like it's still being observed from the inside.

"No," she whispers. "No, no—"

She's moving before Rowan can stop her — slipping out of bed, feet silent on the floor, glow flaring sharp and thin like a blade drawn too fast.

"Isorae—"

The door opens.

Cold night air crashes over her, and suddenly she needs it — needs the shock, the sting, something real enough to drown out the memory.

She runs.

Not blindly.

Purposefully.

The stream.

Rowan is after her immediately — not chasing, not calling her name — tracking the way he always does, reading the land the way some men read maps. She veers past the shallows, past the bend where the water runs gentle and deep, heading for the darker stretch where the stream widens and drops.

"Isorae," he calls once.

She doesn't stop.

She doesn't slow.

By the time Rowan reaches the bank, she is already wading into the deepest channel, skirt gathered in shaking fists, breath tearing out of her chest as the current pushes hard against her thighs. She doesn't ease herself in.

She hits the water — stumbling forward until the cold slams into her hips, her ribs, her lungs — and the shock pulls a broken cry from her throat.

The stream is brutal tonight. Fast. Icy. Unforgiving.

Good.

She scrubs at her arms like she's trying to peel something off, nails dragging red lines across skin, hands frantic at her throat, her collarbone, her chest.

Hard.

Desperate.

"Get him out," she gasps, words barely forming. "He's in my skin — he's still in me —"

Rowan is in the water before the sentence ends.

The cold doesn't slow him. It never does.

He moves carefully now, feet braced against the current, approaching from the side so he doesn't startle her, so she doesn't feel cornered. His hands come first — open, visible — before his body closes the distance.

He catches her wrists gently but firmly, not stopping her movement at first, just meeting it.

"Stay in your bones," he says, voice low, steady, unbreakable. "You're here. You're now. You're with me."

She shakes violently, teeth chattering, glow flaring wild beneath her skin like it can't decide whether to burn or hide. The water roars around them, loud enough to swallow everything except breath and touch.

"I can still feel where he decided things," she sobs. "Like my body forgot it was mine."

That hits him harder than any scream ever could.

Rowan slides one arm around her middle, anchoring her weight against him, the other hand still at her wrists — not restraining, holding. He presses his forehead briefly to her temple, grounding himself before he grounds her.

"Your body didn't forget," he says, rough and certain. "It survived."

Her knees give out.

He's ready for it.

He pulls her fully against his chest, water surging around them as he bears her weight without hesitation. She clutches at him like a drowning woman, fingers digging into his soaked shirt, face pressed into the place where his heart beats strong and real and now.

She sobs there, breath hitching, whole body trembling like it doesn't know where the edges are anymore.

"I don't want him in me," she whispers. "I want to feel me. I need to feel you."

Rowan freezes.

Not pulling away.

Not tightening his hold.

Just… still.

Because the words land heavy, and for a split second he doesn't trust himself to answer them cleanly.

His hand flexes once at her back.

"Isorae," he says quietly — not a warning, not a refusal — her name used as a pause. "Listen to me."

She nods against his chest, breath hitching.

He exhales slowly, choosing each word like it might bruise if mishandled.

"You don't have to decide anything right now," he says. "You don't have to do anything to prove you're still here. Not for me."

She pulls back just enough to look at him, eyes glassy but present. "I know. I'm not—" Her voice shakes. "I'm not trying to fix it. I just— I need to feel my body answer me again. I need your touch to make his disappear."

That breaks something open in him.

Not hunger.

Recognition.

Rowan's jaw tightens. He searches her face — not for consent alone, but for coherence, for agency, for the part of her that is choosing instead of fleeing.

"This isn't something you owe me," he says finally, slower now, rougher. "And it's not something you need to do to be whole."

She nods, swallowing hard. "I know."

He doesn't let it go yet.

"Say it because you mean it," Rowan says. Not demanding. Steady. "Say it so I know you're here with me — not running from him."

Her hands tighten in his shirt, anchoring herself before she speaks.

"I choose this," she whispers. "I choose you. I want to be here."

Only then does Rowan move.

Not urgently.

Not greedily.

With care that borders on reverence.

He shifts his grip, one arm firm around her waist, the other sliding down her spine as he eases her back toward the bank. The water resists, tugging at her skirt, at her legs, but he doesn't rush it. He lets her feel each step, each change in pressure, each place where cold gives way to warmth.

"Come with me," he murmurs, mouth brushing her temple. "I've got you."

She lets him lead her out of the stream, knees weak, breath uneven, skin hypersensitive from cold and fear and relief all tangled together. The night air kisses her wet skin as he lowers her carefully onto the moss and damp earth, one hand never leaving her body, never letting her feel abandoned between movements.

The ground is cool beneath her back.

Solid.

Real.

Rowan kneels over her, water-dark hair clinging to his forehead, chest rising and falling in slow, deliberate control even as his eyes burn. He cups her face, thumbs warm and sure as they brush away the last traces of tears. Then his hands slide down her sides, following the curve of her ribs, her waist — learning her again — before settling between her thighs.

Not hurried.

Not hesitant.

Intent.

"Stay in your bones," he murmurs, voice low now, intimate, his mouth close enough that she feels the words against her skin. "Stay right here with me."

She arches into his touch without thinking, a broken sound leaving her throat as his fingers press into her — firm, grounding — not asking, but listening. His mouth finds her jaw, her throat, her collarbone, kisses slow and lingering, each one anchoring her deeper into herself.

This is your body.

This is now.

This is yours.

Her glow answers — not flaring, not retreating — but warming, spreading, a low ache blooming through her that makes her gasp. She grips his shoulders, nails biting into skin she knows, heat she trusts.

"Don't be gentle," she breathes, need threading through the words. "Don't disappear on me."

Rowan exhales shakily against her skin.

"I'm not going anywhere."

He shifts closer, one hand steady at her hip while the other slides higher, pushing damp fabric aside, baring her inch by inch to the night. The sound of cloth slipping away feels loud in the quiet — deliberate, unavoidable. Cool air kisses her skin where he's just uncovered her, and she shivers, breath catching.

He pauses there.

Just long enough for her to feel the want sharpen.

"Tell me," he murmurs.

She doesn't hesitate. She hooks her leg around his waist, drawing him in, anchoring him exactly where she needs him. "Now."

That's all it takes.

When he moves into her, it's slow only for a moment — just enough for her body to register the stretch, the heat, the undeniable fact of him filling her completely. She gasps, a broken sound tearing free as her fingers bite into his shoulders, nails pressing hard enough to leave marks.

Rowan stills, jaw clenched, breath shaking against her mouth. "God," he exhales. "You feel—"

She cuts him off with a sharp roll of her hips, pulling him deeper, refusing hesitation. Her body answers before thought can interfere, muscles tightening around him with a certainty that steals the air from his lungs.

"That," she says, voice wrecked. "Right there."

The restraint snaps.

He starts to move — deeper now, firmer — every thrust deliberate, heavy with intention. Not taking. Meeting. The sound of skin against skin fills the night, wet and unmistakable, her breath breaking into sharp, helpless gasps with each motion.

Heat coils low and urgent inside her, spreading fast, erasing distance. She clutches at him, legs locking around his waist, dragging him closer, needing more — more pressure, more friction, more proof.

Rowan groans, forehead dropping to her shoulder as he drives into her again, harder this time, the force of it rocking her back against the earth. His grip tightens at her hips, fingers digging in as if to anchor himself, to stay present inside the intensity instead of being lost to it.

"You're here," he breathes, voice rough. "You're so fucking here."

Her body answers with a broken cry as the rhythm sharpens, urgency building fast and undeniable. Each movement sends sparks tearing through her, pleasure stacking, climbing, her glow flaring bright and hot beneath her skin — not out of control, but alive, demanding.

She meets him thrust for thrust now, hips rising, chasing the friction she needs, the pressure that makes her whole again. The pleasure burns — too much, perfect — coiling tight until her muscles tremble and her breath shatters completely.

"Rowan—" His name rips out of her, unguarded.

He feels it — the way her body tightens suddenly, pulse racing wild beneath his hands — and he follows, thrusts turning relentless, breath ragged, control fraying as the sound of her gasps and the heat of her pulling him in undo him completely.

When she breaks, it's with a cry she doesn't try to swallow, body arching hard into his as release tears through her, pleasure crashing outward in hot, blinding waves. Her glow spills bright and radiant, flooding the space between them as if the night itself has split open.

Rowan follows with a hoarse groan, burying himself deep as release hits him hard and fast, his body shuddering with it, weight collapsing over her as he holds her through every aftershock.

They stay like that — tangled, breathless, hearts hammering — the stream roaring behind them, the earth solid and unyielding beneath her back.

She is here.

She is present.

She is whole.

Rowan presses his forehead to hers again, breathing her in, grounding them both as the world slowly widens back out.

Not taken.

Not lost.

Chosen.

Alive.

The earth is solid beneath her. The night holds. The stream rushes behind them like something that has already passed.

They don't rush away from it.

For a long while they stay exactly where they are — her body heavy against the earth, Rowan's weight still anchoring her, his breath slowing until it matches hers. He doesn't move first. He doesn't assume the moment has ended just because the intensity has softened.

His hand remains at her hip. Warm. Certain. Real.

She notices small things returning: the cool air against her skin, the steady rush of the stream, the ache in her thighs that feels earned instead of imposed. When she shifts, the earth answers her weight without resistance. When she exhales, nothing tightens in response.

Rowan presses a slow kiss to her temple, then her hairline — not possession, not urgency. Check-ins disguised as tenderness. Each one asks the same question without words.

Are you still here?

She is.

Eventually she rolls onto her side, drawing her knees in slightly, and he follows without crowding, staying close enough that she can feel him without being held in place. He pulls her clothes back into reach, helps her into them only when she leans into his hands first. The fabric is cold, damp, grounding.

When they stand, he waits again — watching her balance, watching her breathe — ready but not reaching.

She takes his hand this time.

The walk back is quiet. Not heavy. Not fragile.

Just… integrated.

Their footsteps fall in rhythm with the stream as it fades behind them, the night opening instead of closing. Her body carries the memory of him without flinching. The place Graham touched without permission no longer feels exposed — it feels occupied.

By the time the cabin lights appear through the trees, her breathing has settled into something steady and her thoughts have weight again.

She hasn't disappeared.

She hasn't scattered.

She's still inside herself.

And when they finally return to the cabin — wet, cold, breathing slowly back into themselves — the interruption does not erase the progress she made earlier.

It belongs to it.

Because healing doesn't move in straight lines.

It circles.

It revisits.

And sometimes, in the middle of the night, it asks the body to remember who it belongs to now.

By morning, Isorae sleeps again.

Not unbroken.

But grounded.

And that, too, is progress.

64

Hard, But Not Bad

Morning comes slowly to Stonewake.

Not with birdsong or brightness, but with the careful way light tests whether it's allowed to enter. Dawn presses against the cabin windows like a question asked softly enough not to wake anyone who isn't ready.

Rowan wakes before Isorae does.

That has become habit.

She lies curled toward him, breath warm against his chest, one hand fisted in the fabric of his shirt like it anchored her sometime in the night and never quite let go. Her glow is faint but present—a low, steady warmth instead of the jagged flicker it used to be.

He doesn't move.

Not because he's afraid to wake her.

Because stillness, right now, is part of the care.

Outside, Stonewake hums—low, narrow, watchful. The land has not relaxed, but it has settled into a stance. Like a body bracing around an old injury instead of flinching from it.

A knock comes at the door.

Soft.

Measured.

Rowan waits a beat longer, then carefully eases Isorae's fingers loose from his shirt. She stirs but doesn't wake, breath hitching once before evening out again, her body settling back into the mattress like it trusts the landing.

He opens the door just enough.

Evan stands there with a mug in one hand and a folded cloth in the other, eyes already scanning Rowan's face before he speaks. Not just exhaustion—something deeper. A different kind of aftermath.

"How was the night?" Evan asks quietly.

Rowan considers the question honestly. "Hard. But not bad."

Evan's gaze flicks—briefly—to Rowan's collar, the damp curl of hair at his temple, the way his shoulders are braced like someone who carried weight and didn't put it down yet.

He nods.

"I figured," he says, not unkindly.

Rowan doesn't ask how he knows.

"Is she awake?"

"No."

"Good." Evan lowers his voice further, shifting the cloth in his hand. "When she is, she'll need water before anything else. Small sips. And she's going to be sore—physically and neurologically. Cold shock, adrenaline burn-off… and re-entry." A pause. "Sometimes the body remembers safety all at once. It can feel like impact."

Rowan's jaw tightens. "I know."

Evan studies him for a second longer, then adds gently, "You did right by her."

Rowan exhales—slow, controlled—not relief exactly, but something adjacent.

Evan pauses, then hands him the mug. Steam curls up between them.

"Drink," Evan says. "You didn't sleep either."

Rowan almost smiles.

Almost.

Behind Evan, Erin crosses the clearing with a tablet tucked under her arm, hair braided back in a way that says she expects to be interrupted repeatedly. She stops when she sees Rowan in the doorway.

"Morning," she says softly.

"Anything changed?" Rowan asks.

Erin exhales. "The field is quieter."

Rowan waits.

"Not stable," she adds. "Not resolved. Just… compressing. Like something is being denied room."

"Where?" he asks.

Erin doesn't gesture toward a location. She doesn't need to.

"Everywhere he isn't," she says. "And fewer places he can be."

Rowan nods once.

Inside the cabin, Isorae shifts.

A small sound leaves her throat—not fear, not pain—orientation. The sound of someone checking where they are.

Rowan turns back immediately.

She's awake when he kneels beside the bed, eyes open but calm, tracking him instead of the corners of the room. That alone feels like a victory.

"Hey," he says softly.

Her gaze sharpens slightly. "You didn't leave."

"No."

She swallows. "Good."

He offers her the mug, helping guide her hands around it when her fingers hesitate. She takes a careful sip, then another.

"Cold?" he asks.

She shakes her head. "Just… loud."

"Everything or just your body?"

She considers. "Both. But less than before."

Rowan nods. "That counts."

A shadow crosses her expression—not fear, not panic—memory. She glances toward the window, toward the direction of the stream.

Rowan waits.

"I don't regret last night," she says quietly.

He doesn't answer immediately.

He shifts closer instead, forearm resting against the bed so she can feel him there without being crowded.

"I know," he says finally. "And if that changes, you tell me."

She looks at him sharply. "It won't."

"That's not the point," Rowan replies gently. "The point is that you don't owe consistency to anyone but yourself."

That earns him a long look.

Then she nods. "Okay."

A pause.

"Stay," she adds, softer.

"I am."

Later, Evan returns to check her vitals, careful and unhurried, explaining each touch before he makes it. Erin sits on the chair near the window—not observing, not intruding—just present in a way that doesn't ask Isorae to perform recovery for anyone.

Outside, Dax and Silas rotate watch without discussion. Not hunting. Not waiting.

Listening.

Ryan passes the cabin once.

He pauses this time—not long, not intruding—just enough to look in through the window.

Rowan catches his eye.

Ryan lifts a hand in a small, wordless acknowledgment. Relief, restrained. No urgency. No fracture. Just confirmation that she's upright, drinking, breathing.

That's enough.

He moves on without comment, falling back into the quiet rhythm of the place.

Inside, the morning continues.

Isorae eats a little. Drinks more. Lets Erin help her braid her hair because lifting her arms that high still feels like asking too much.

Rowan stays.

Stonewake holds.

And somewhere beyond its borders—where paths have begun to refuse and space has started to narrow its patience—someone is learning what it means to be slowly deprived of options.

But for now, that is not their concern.

For now, the day passes without crisis—not because everything is fixed, but because enough of it is working.

Progress, slow and uneven.
But real.
And today, that is enough.

65
JURISDICTION ERROR

Graham retreats in increments.

That is how systems survive failure: not with panic, but with managed withdrawal. Controlled losses. Calculated pauses that preserve authority even when territory must be conceded.

He leaves the corridor behind him in stages, moving outward through bands that should still be permissive—zones that have historically tolerated his presence without objection. He expects resistance eventually. He does not expect dissent.

At first, the world complies.

Distortions open when requested. Folds hold long enough to pass through. Terrain reforms behind him with professional neutrality, the kind that implies continued cooperation rather than forgiveness.

He allows himself—briefly—to categorize the collapse as localized.

An anomaly.

A variable spike.

Distance, he assumes, will restore margin.

Days pass under that assumption.

He measures time by recalibration cycles, by the number of times he stops to assess the field and finds it still technically functional. He eats only when necessary. Rests only when the space permits it—which is less often than it used to. Sleep comes shallow and procedural, stripped of narrative, leaving behind irritation instead of fear.

The first deviation is subtle.

A fold hesitates.

Not refusal.

Delay.

Graham freezes mid-transfer, body suspended between states, breath held—not because he is afraid, but because hesitation introduces inefficiency. Geometry resolves after a beat too long, accepting the input with reduced tolerance.

The passage feels thin.

Like a system honoring a request it no longer respects.

He logs it as interference.

The second deviation is directional.

He notices it only after several days, when he realizes he has been walking without increasing distance. The horizon behaves incorrectly—never blurred, never broken, simply… uncooperative. Features recur at new angles. Ridges reappear with altered contours.

The terrain is not looping.

It is compressing.

Graham adjusts his course.

The ground accepts the first step.

Accepts the second.

Corrects the third.

Not violently.

Decisively.

His boot lands on stone that did not exist a moment ago—flat, exact, irritatingly precise. The correction carries no hostility.

Only certainty.

Graham exhales through his nose and continues.

Weeks pass.

The space does not trap him outright. That would be crude. Inelegant. Instead, it pares away options with careful restraint. Paths do not close behind him. They fail to exist ahead of him. Routes that once allowed variance now present a single viable angle of progress—and that angle bends, gradually but insistently, back toward the valley he has avoided naming since leaving it.

Stonewake.

He does not allow the word full articulation, even in his own mind.

Naming confers relevance.

The third deviation is scale.

Distance begins to misbehave. A full day's travel yields less separation than it should. The sky adjusts too quickly. Cloud formations gather and disperse with suspicious obedience, stacking into patterns that resemble weather without fully committing to it.

Storm logic.

No storm.

Yet.

Irritation sharpens.

Weeks in, he attempts a clean exit.

A lateral fold—one he has used before to disappear from hostile terrain. The distortion forms, thin but present, and he steps—

—and it collapses.

Not violently.

Not dangerously.

It simply fails.

The shape of escape dissolves like wet paper, leaving him exactly where he started.

Graham stumbles forward half a step before catching himself. His pulse spikes—then is reined in, controlled, disciplined.

Again.

Different input. Different angle.

Same result.

The space permits the outline of departure to appear just long enough to insult him with possibility—then withdraws it without explanation.

Graham does not swear.

Swearing implies loss of composure.

He stands very still and listens.

What he registers is not pursuit.

It is jurisdiction.

The land is not chasing him.

It is reorganizing itself around him.

Another week passes.

Sleep degrades—not from fear (fear is inefficient), but from the absence of rest the space now allows. He wakes with the sensation of having been… evaluated.

Not watched.

Counted.

The pressure is not on his body.

It is on his options.

Every outward vector thins into impracticality. Every detour corrects into something steeper, slicker, more punishing than the path being offered.

The offered path always bends the same way.

Inward.

Toward Stonewake.

The realization settles fully when he stops walking and the world does not widen in response.

He turns slowly.

The horizon does not move.

Not fixed.

Withheld.

That is when irritation tips into something colder.

This is not residual interference.

Not collapse.

This is the land identifying a variable it no longer consents to host.

A brief, unwelcome memory intrudes: the corridor screaming back instead of obeying. The moment control inverted. The instant the system refused to stay abstract.

Not guilt.

Not regret.

A more dangerous recognition:

He has forced the environment to acknowledge a boundary.

And boundaries, once enforced, propagate.

Thunder rolls in the distance.

Not close.

Not yet.

But closer than it was yesterday.

The clouds stack with unnatural patience, drifting against winds that have not earned authority over them.

Stonewake is no longer avoidable.

Not because someone is hunting him.

Because the problem is no longer permitted to remain external.

You do not do what he did and retain infinite outward movement.

Graham recalculates.

If arrival is inevitable, then timing becomes the only remaining leverage.

He starts moving again.

Not fast.

Speed wastes margin.

And margin—thinned, shrinking, but not yet exhausted—is all he has left.

Behind him, paths retract without drama.

Ahead of him, the world narrows in increments he can feel in his teeth.

And somewhere beyond the closing distance—where a valley has been holding, remembering, waiting—the land finishes aligning itself.

Stonewake is awake now.

And neutrality has been formally revoked.

66
PRESSURE SYSTEM

Erin feels it before the sky admits it.

Not rain. Not wind.

Load.

She's standing at the edge of the clearing with the tablet idle in her hands, not because there's nothing to read, but because the data stopped being the point sometime during the night. Stonewake doesn't need instruments when it's this awake. It announces itself through posture—through the way the ground tightens, through the way the air holds still like it's waiting for permission to move.

She closes her eyes.

The land answers immediately.

Not with images. Not with sound.

With constraint.

It's the same sensation she felt weeks ago when the interval stopped negotiating—when flexibility gave way to enforcement. Only now it's broader. Distributed. The pressure isn't localized to a fold or a corridor. It's systemic, spreading outward in bands that overlap and reinforce each other.

Containment logic.

Erin exhales slowly and opens her eyes.

The clouds have begun to stack.

Not storm clouds yet—too neat, too patient—but the architecture is there. Vertical development where the atmosphere should be diffusing. A slow, deliberate thickening that ignores the usual rules about temperature gradients and prevailing winds.

The sky is building something it hasn't decided to unleash.

Stonewake is preparing.

She turns back toward the structures—cabins low and quiet, paths held in careful neutrality—and feels the way the valley braces around them. Not defensively.

Selectively.

"Okay," Erin murmurs, mostly to herself. "So that's how it's going to be."

Footsteps approach on gravel that doesn't crunch as much as it should.

Silas stops beside her without comment, gaze already lifted to the sky. He doesn't ask what she sees. He's learned better than that. Instead, he asks the only useful question.

"How wide?"

Erin doesn't look away from the clouds. "Widening."

"Directional?"

"Yes."

"Inbound?"

She nods once.

Silas swears softly under his breath—not angry, not afraid. Just acknowledging a reality that doesn't care how anyone feels about it.

"It's early," he says.

"It's timely," Erin corrects. "Those aren't the same thing."

She finally glances down at the tablet, not to check readings but to confirm what her body already knows. The numbers align too cleanly. Pressure differentials forming without sufficient cause. Microfronts organizing where randomness should still dominate.

Storm logic without weather.

Stonewake is no longer reacting.

It's anticipating.

"I haven't felt it like this since—" Silas stops himself.

Erin finishes the thought anyway. "Since it decided something needed to end."

Silas's jaw tightens. "And we're sure it's him?"

Erin hesitates—not because she doubts it, but because certainty carries weight.

"Yes," she says finally. "Not because the land hates him. Because it recognizes him."

That gets Silas's attention.

"Recognizes him how?"

"As unresolved," Erin replies. "As a variable that broke a constraint and never paid the cost."

She scrolls absently, more out of habit than need. The readings bloom and stabilize, bloom and stabilize, like the system is rehearsing escalation without committing yet.

"He hasn't crossed the boundary," Silas says.

"No," Erin agrees. "But the boundary has crossed him."

They stand in silence for a moment, listening to the valley breathe.

Somewhere deeper in Stonewake, a low roll of thunder mutters—not close enough to be a threat, not distant enough to be coincidence. The sound doesn't travel like normal thunder. It doesn't fade.

It settles.

Silas glances toward the cabins. "Rowan's going to feel it."

"He already does," Erin says. "He just hasn't named it yet."

"And her?"

Erin's gaze flicks—briefly, carefully—toward the cabin where Isorae rests. "Not directly. The land isn't touching her. It's… adjusting around her."

"Protective?"

"Yes," Erin says. "But not gentle."

Silas exhales through his nose. "Of course not."

Another rumble rolls through the valley, deeper this time. The clouds thicken perceptibly, edges sharpening, vertical columns knitting together like a system finally agreeing on a solution.

Erin's tablet pings.

She doesn't look at it.

She doesn't need to.

"He's closer," Silas says.

"Yes."

"And he doesn't have a choice anymore."

"No."

Erin closes her eyes again—not to reach, not to intervene—but to witness.

The land is doing exactly what it always does when something violates its deepest agreements.

It is tightening the rules.

Storm systems continue to gather, no longer pretending they're incidental. The air grows heavy with static, with the kind of charge that makes skin prickle and animals go quiet. Stonewake hums—not loud, not dramatic—but present in a way that demands attention.

Everyone will feel it soon.

They won't need explanation.

When the first real thunder breaks overhead, Erin opens her eyes and finally allows herself to say it out loud.

"He's coming," she says.

Not as warning.

As fact.

And all around them, the valley settles into its stance—not bracing for a fight, but preparing to enforce an answer that has been deferred long enough.

67
THE STORM

The first thunder arrives without rain.

It rolls across Stonewake like a warning issued too late to be useful—deep, slow, and carrying a pressure that makes the trees lean as if they've remembered something they didn't want to.

Erin is the first to stop moving.

Not because she hears it.

Because the land changes temperature under her feet—an almost imperceptible drop, a tightening of permission. The valley's usual quiet doesn't break; it condenses. Like breath held inside a clenched jaw.

She steps out of the cabin and looks at the sky.

The clouds are wrong.

Not just dark.

Organized.

Layered the way muscle layers.

A storm system built with intent.

Rowan is already outside.

He didn't decide to be.

He's been living at the threshold for weeks — even when he's indoors, some part of him never leaves the land—always listening through his bones for shifts in the field, always tracking what the land won't say out loud. His body learned a new kind of vigilance after the corridor.

After what it did to her.

He stands near the edge of the clearing, shoulders loose the way a predator's shoulders look loose right before it springs. His hands are bare. His knuckles, still tender from weeks of contained force and nowhere to spend it, flex once, slow.

Silas comes out behind him, scanning the tree line without speaking.

Dax follows, jaw set hard enough to grind teeth.

A moment later, Erin hears Ryan inside the cabin—quiet footfalls, careful. He doesn't come out. He stays where Isorae is, because even now, even after weeks, the valley won't forgive anyone for leaving her alone when the air turns mean.

Evan appears at the threshold with a blanket half-folded over one arm, eyes flicking between Rowan and the sky.

"What is it," Evan asks.

Erin answers without looking at him. "Pressure."

Dax exhales. "That's a nice word for it."

A second thunderclap hits closer—sharp enough to vibrate in their teeth. The ground seems to listen to it and decide it agrees.

Silas shifts his stance, widening his base. "He's coming."

Rowan doesn't move.

But the land around him does.

Not visible.

Somatic.

The valley leans into him the way it leans into its own spine—readying itself for load.

Erin's throat tightens. "He doesn't get to choose that."

Silas glances at her. "He can't anymore."

No one says the word Graham.

They don't need to.

The land says it for them, in the way the wind stops behaving like wind and becomes directionless pressure. In the way distant leaves turn their faces away from nothing.

Rowan's voice comes quiet, almost conversational, because if he raises it he will start screaming and he doesn't trust what will happen after that.

"Take her further inside," he says, not looking back.

Evan hesitates. "Rowan—"

"Now," Rowan says. Not a command. A boundary.

Evan swallows and turns back in.

Erin watches Rowan's shoulders, the set of his neck. Watches the way his breath is too controlled—controlled like a man gripping a blade by its edge to keep it from falling.

"You don't have to do this alone," Erin says softly.

Rowan's mouth twitches once. Not a smile.

"I'm not alone," he answers.

And the land—fierce, furious, awake—seems to bristle at the statement like it agrees.

The first rain finally falls.

Not drops.

Needles.

Cold and hard, slanting sideways as if the sky has decided gravity is optional today.

Lightning flickers somewhere behind the ridge—silent, distant, like a diagnostic test run before the real discharge.

Silas steps closer to Rowan, voice low. "When he appears, don't let him talk you into—"

Rowan cuts his eyes to him.

The look is a knife.

Silas stops.

Because that's the point.

Rowan can feel it already—the pressure gradient, the tightening spiral, the land closing paths the way it closed paths around Graham for weeks. Only now it's happening here, in front of them, where the valley has chosen to finish what it started.

Erin feels it too: the architecture of Stonewake flexing, bracing. The valley isn't waiting for a visitor.

It's preparing for a collision.

Then—

a seam forms in the clearing.

Not a door.

Not a tear.

A wrongness. A hesitation in what the air is allowed to be.

The grass beneath it bends in opposite directions at the same time.

Rain strikes it and vanishes.

Sound thins there.

Time stutters.

Dax's hand goes to his belt—habit, muscle memory, useless against this kind of physics.

Silas murmurs, "There."

Rowan's breath slows even further.

A figure resolves from the seam like a mistake deciding to become real.

Graham.

He doesn't arrive cleanly.

He arrives the way someone arrives after being pushed down a flight of stairs and still insists they meant to.

He stumbles once, catches himself, and his expression flashes—irritation at the world for not obeying him fast enough.

He is thinner than before. Dirt-streaked. Clothes torn in places like the land has been grabbing at him for weeks.

And still—

still his eyes lift with that same cold, pleased intelligence, like he's amused by the fact that he's alive.

Lightning cracks overhead, close enough to make the clearing glare white.

In the flash, Graham turns his head slightly, as if listening.

Then he smiles.

Not relief.

Not fear.

Recognition.

"Stonewake," he says, tasting the word like it's an inside joke. "Of course."

Erin takes an involuntary step back, not from him, but from the wrongness of hearing his voice in this place.

Dax's jaw goes rigid. "You shouldn't be here."

Graham's gaze slides to Dax without interest. "And yet."

Then—inevitably—his eyes find Rowan.

And something in Graham brightens.

Like a match struck in a dark room.

"There you are," Graham says softly.

Rowan doesn't speak.

He can't.

The storm fills the space where language should go.

Graham's grin widens, rain washing blood—old or new—out of the corner of his mouth.

"You feel it," Graham says. "Don't you?"

Rowan's hands curl into fists.

Graham's voice becomes almost gentle, like he's explaining a concept to a student.

"The land brought me back," he continues. "It herded me. Like an animal. Like a problem it couldn't ignore anymore."

He laughs once—short, delighted.

"And you're standing here like you think that makes you righteous."

Rowan's breath shudders.

Silas shifts closer, ready to grab him if he has to.

Erin's pulse pounds, suddenly aware of how thin the line is between Rowan's restraint and Rowan's ruin.

Graham tilts his head, studying Rowan like he's trying to decide how to break him fastest.

Then he says, conversationally, casually—like it's a weather report:

"She screamed."

The word hits like a brick.

Rowan's posture changes.

Not visibly.

Structurally.

The land responds to it too—pressure rising, the valley tightening its jaw.

Graham watches the reaction with visible pleasure.

"Not at the end," Graham adds, smiling wider. "That would be… predictable."

Rowan makes a sound.

Not words.

A low, feral vibration that doesn't belong in a human throat.

Silas starts, "Rowan—"

Graham lifts his voice just slightly, like he wants an audience.

"In the middle," he says. "Like she still thought you might—"

Rowan moves.

Charging.

Arriving.

He crosses the clearing like the storm has borrowed his body, like gravity belongs to him now, like the land itself is throwing him forward.

His fist meets Graham's face with a crack that would have been thunder if the sky hadn't stolen the job.

Graham drops hard into the mud.

Rowan is on him before anyone can breathe.

"YOU DON'T GET TO SAY IT!" Rowan roars—finally—voice shredding, raw enough to tear the air. "YOU DON'T GET TO SPEAK HER!"

He hits him again.

And again.

The strikes are not controlled.

They are not elegant.

They are a man trying to beat a moment out of existence.

Graham coughs blood and laughs.

It is the worst sound in the valley.

It's not bravery.

It's not defiance.

It's pure psychosis: joy at being able to provoke this exact outcome.

"Yes," Graham wheezes through broken breath. "There it is. That's the animal."

Rowan's hands shake as he grabs Graham by the collar and hauls him up just to slam him down again.

"You touched her," Rowan growls, words barely shaped. "You touched her."

Graham's eyes glitter. Rain streams down his face like tears he doesn't deserve.

"She's still inside you," Graham whispers. "Every time you hold her now, you'll wonder where I—"

Rowan howls.

Not a shout.

A tearing sound that comes from someplace older than language.

He drives his knee into Graham's ribs.

Graham jerks, choking—

then laughs harder, almost giddy with the pain.

"Oh," Graham gasps. "Do it again. I want you to remember how easy it is to become—"

Rowan slams his fist into Graham's face again.

"SHUT UP!"

Another strike.

"SHUT UP!"

Another.

"SHUT UP!"

The land convulses around them—trees bending, thunder detonating so close it seems to split the sky right above Rowan's head.

Erin stands frozen, heart racing, watching Rowan unravel in real time.

This isn't justice.

This is a man watching the last thread of his restraint snap and realizing he can't put it back.

Silas finally moves.

He throws himself into Rowan from behind, hooking his arms under Rowan's, trying to pull him off.

"Rowan!" Silas shouts into his ear. "ROWAN—LOOK AT ME!"

Rowan thrashes like a trapped thing, breath ragged, voice breaking into snarls.

"He—" Rowan chokes, unable to finish the sentence without turning into something else. "He—"

Dax steps in too, grabbing Rowan's shoulder, grounding with his full weight.

"Rowan," Dax says hard. "If you kill him with your hands, you'll feel it forever."

Graham coughs, spits blood, then smiles up at them like he's watching a show.

"You hear that," Graham rasps, laughing weakly. "They're saving you."

Rowan surges again.

Silas locks tighter, jaw clenched, muscles straining.

Rowan's eyes are gone dark—no iris, no mercy, just vector.

"Let me go," Rowan growls.

Silas's voice breaks with effort. "No."

Graham's grin spreads like infection. "You want to be a monster so badly," he says. "You want to crawl into the same kind of control I used and pretend it's different because you—"

Rowan screams.

A full, shredding scream—grief turned into sound, rage turned into earthquake.

The valley answers.

Lightning strikes the far edge of the clearing, blowing a tree apart in a burst of steam and splinters.

Graham's smile falters for the first time.

Not because of Rowan.

Because the land has turned its face toward him.

And it isn't curious.

It isn't negotiating.

It is furious.

Erin's breath catches.

She can feel it like static in her teeth: the valley making a decision.

Silas tightens his hold on Rowan like he can physically keep him human.

Dax plants himself between Rowan and Graham, even though it's absurd, even though if the land decides to act, Dax is just a body in the way of a god.

Rowan's chest heaves.

His hands drip blood.

His voice comes out low and broken, almost not his.

"I will not become you," Rowan says—like a vow forced out through teeth.

Graham laughs again, but it's smaller now. Thinner. A crack in the performance.

"Sure," Graham whispers. "Tell yourself that."

Thunder cracks directly overhead.

A detonation.

The ground shudders beneath Graham's back like it's lifting its shoulders.

Rain comes down harder.

The clearing darkens.

The air thickens until breathing feels like pushing through water.

Erin takes one step forward, eyes on Rowan—on the fact that he's trembling now, not from fear, but from the aftermath of almost crossing a line he would never come back from.

And Graham—mud-caked, laughing, broken—tilts his head as if listening to the storm like it's speaking directly to him.

For the first time since he arrived, his eyes flicker—not pleading, not bargaining—calculating.

Because he understands what's happening.

He can't manipulate this.

The land isn't a subject.

It's a system.

And it has finally classified him correctly.

Rowan's voice breaks, quiet now, wrecked.

"Enough," he says.

He isn't speaking to Graham.

He's speaking to himself.

To the valley.

To the part of him that wants to keep swinging until nothing is left.

The storm answers anyway.

The air drops another degree.

The clearing tightens like a fist.

And Graham's laughter, finally, starts to sound like a man realizing he has run out of places to stand.

68
FINAL CORRECTION

The land does not wait for permission.

It has been waiting long enough.

Graham is still laughing when it starts.

Not loud laughter. Not hysterical. A wet, broken sound pulled from a chest that refuses to accept consequence. Blood streaks his teeth. One eye is already swelling shut. His ribs are a mess beneath his skin, breath hitching wrong, but the grin stays—feral, unrepentant.

Rowan's fists are shaking.

Not from exhaustion.

From the effort it is taking not to finish this himself.

The rain thickens suddenly, no longer falling but slamming into the clearing. Wind tears sideways through the trees. Thunder cracks overhead so close it rattles bone. The ground underfoot shifts—not violently, not yet—but with intent.

Graham's laughter stutters.

He feels it.

The land has stopped bracing.

It is advancing.

Graham scrambles backward, boots sliding in the mud, balance already failing. His hands fling out instinctively, palms skidding against earth that no longer behaves like earth.

"No—this isn't—"

The ground seizes him.

Roots burst from the mud in thick, pale coils, wrapping his ankle, his calf, his knee. They tighten brutally, yanking his leg flat and twisting his hips sideways as his weight collapses fully onto his back.

He hits hard, spine slamming into sodden earth.

Before he can roll, more roots snap up across his other leg and waist, pinning him spread and helpless, rain plastering his hair to his face as he thrashes uselessly.

Then the stone answers.

It erupts straight up through his trapped calf.

The force is vertical, surgical—bone splitting, flesh tearing as the spike punches through and locks him in place. His scream rips out of him, back arching off the ground as far as the roots will allow.

Blood pours down his leg, steaming faintly in the rain.

He claws at the mud, fingers digging uselessly as the soil hardens beneath his hands.

A second spike erupts through his thigh, higher, driving clean through muscle and pinning his leg completely. His hips slam back down as the roots cinch tighter, preventing any roll, any escape.

The clearing contracts.

Trees lean inward, roots tearing free with wet, grinding sounds. The air thickens, pressure crushing down on his chest until each breath comes shallow and panicked.

Stone begins to curl up around his ankles and knees, locking his lower body into a growing lattice of earth and rock.

"Stop—STOP—"

Thunder answers.

Not above him.

Behind him.

The ground beneath his shoulders buckles, then surges upward in a brutal, heaving motion, forcing his upper body to lift as stone punches through his lower back.

His scream shatters into something raw and unrecognizable as the spike tears through him, lifting his torso off the ground, ribs cracking audibly under the pressure.

Blood explodes outward, splattering rain-slick stone.

Rowan staggers back, breath tearing out of him, stomach turning.

Silas swears, the word breaking in his throat.

Dax goes rigid, jaw clenched hard enough to crack.

No one intervenes.

No one can.

Stone continues to bloom upward in merciless succession—through ribs, through shoulder, through neck—impaling him again and again, lifting his ruined body fully off the ground.

He hangs there, pinned open, blood pouring down jagged stone grown directly from the valley's judgment.

His mouth opens.

No sound comes out.

Lightning strikes.

Not random.

Deliberate.

The bolt slams into the stone skewering him, electricity ripping through his body in a blinding flash. Flesh chars instantly. The smell is immediate and nauseating. His body locks rigid as the current overwhelms every nerve at once.

Still, the land does not stop.

The stone tightens.

Cracks thunder through the clearing as the growths constrict, grinding bone into pulp. Blood rains down in sheets, turning the mud beneath him black and slick.

And then—

The space folds.

Closing.

The corridor he abused collapses inward on itself, compressing everything it contains. Graham's body jerks once more as pressure exceeds tolerance—

—a final, wet sound—

—and then nothing recognizable remains.

No body.

No shape.

No echo.

Just a scorched, cratered hollow where the system has removed an error.

The storm does not end immediately.

Thunder rolls again, lower this time. Wind tears through the trees one last time before slowly easing. Rain softens from violence to aftermath.

The land exhales.

Rowan drops to his knees.

Not in victory.

In shock.

His hands are shaking so hard he has to dig them into the mud to stay upright. He retches once, empty, breath coming in broken gasps.

Silas is at his side instantly, hand firm on his shoulder—not restraining, but grounding.

"It's done," Silas says hoarsely.

Rowan nods.

He doesn't look at the crater.

He doesn't need to.

The land has already moved on.

No monument remains.

No warning.

Just absence.

Justice delivered without spectacle.

Without mercy.

Without appeal.

And inside the cabin—safe, alive, breathing—Isorae does not feel the moment Graham dies.

She does not need to.

The system that violated her no longer exists.

The land has corrected itself.

And Rowan—kneeling in the mud, rain plastering his hair to his face—finally lets himself break.

Not because Graham is gone.

But because she lived.

And that has to be enough.

69
THE SHAPE OF RELIEF

The storm does not end with a victory.

It ends the way bodies end panic—slowly, unwillingly, in pieces.

Thunder recedes like something dragged backward through trees. Rain thins from sheets to needles to a quiet, lingering drip that keeps falling long after the sky has moved on. Water runs off the cabin roof in steady lines, as if the land is trying to rinse itself without knowing where the stain actually is.

Stonewake holds.

But it holds differently now.

Not gentler. Not kinder.

More awake.

Rowan stands in the yard until the last of it passes.

Not because he's waiting for something to happen—he knows it's finished.

Because his body won't accept finished as a word that means safe.

His hands tremble when the adrenaline drains. Not dramatic. Not visible at a distance. A fine vibration under the skin, like a tuning fork struck too hard and left ringing. He keeps his fingers curled, nails digging lightly into his palms to anchor himself in sensation that belongs to him.

Silas stays near without touching him.

Dax watches the tree line as if the trees might confess something.

Erin is still. Too still. Her face has the exhausted blankness of someone who has spent weeks reading patterns that never wanted to be understood—and has been proven right in the worst possible way.

No one speaks.

There is nothing clean to say.

The land does not gloat.

It doesn't feel like triumph.

It feels like a system restoring equilibrium after a contamination event.

Like a wound clenching closed.

Like a mouth finally spitting out what it could not metabolize.

Rowan hears a sound behind him—soft, uneven, deliberate.

He turns too fast.

His body is ready for another impact it will not be given.

Isorae stands at the edge of the porch, wrapped in a blanket that's too big for her. Her hair is damp and unbrushed. Her face is pale in a way that still makes his chest tighten if he looks at it too long. Her eyes are open.

Present.

Not fully.

But here.

Evan is half a step behind her, hands hovering—not restraining, not guiding—just ready. The way you stand near someone who might forget gravity without warning.

Isorae's gaze moves over the yard.

Over the soaked ground.

Over the places that used to be wrong.

Over the air itself, like she's checking whether it will behave.

Her mouth opens like she might speak.

No sound comes.

Rowan doesn't move.

He doesn't rush her with relief. Doesn't flood her with questions. Doesn't try to pull her into him like proximity can fix what proximity couldn't prevent.

He just stands there and lets her see him.

Lets his presence be simple.

Unarmed.

Unperforming.

Human.

She takes one step forward. Then another.

Not toward him.

Into the space itself.

Each step costs her something small and internal—a negotiation, a recalibration, a body deciding whether motion will be met with consequence.

Rowan watches her hands, not her face.

Her fingers are curled into the blanket edge, knuckles white—not in fear of him, but in effort, like fabric is a boundary she can trust while the rest of the world recalculates.

When she stops, she stops at a distance that is deliberate.

Not avoidance.

Not retreat.

A line she chose.

Rowan's throat tightens anyway.

He swallows it down.

"Hey," he says.

Not calling.

Not reaching.

Just placing the word in the air.

Isorae blinks once.

A long blink. Like she has to close her eyes to make the world stay where it is.

She looks at him again.

Her mouth moves.

This time, words come out—thin, careful, scraped raw by disuse.

"Is it—"

She doesn't finish.

Rowan answers the question she can't complete.

"Yes," he says. "It's done."

Isorae holds the word like it might fracture if she grips it too tightly.

Evan's voice is gentle behind her.

"You don't have to process it right now," he says. "You don't have to carry it today."

Isorae doesn't look back at him.

She's still watching Rowan.

Rowan doesn't know what she sees when she looks at him like that.

Not a savior.

Not a solution.

Just… the person who stayed in the shape he promised.

Her breath shakes once.

Not a sob.

Not release.

A physiological tremor of something that has been held in check too long.

Rowan takes one step forward—slow, announced by the creak of wet boards.

He stops there.

Close enough that she can feel the warmth of him through the rain.

Not close enough to claim.

"I'm here," he says.

Not reassurance.

Orientation.

Isorae's shoulders soften a fraction. Not collapsing—unlocking.

She nods once.

Then she takes a step.

Not rushing.

Not reaching.

Just… narrowing the space.

Her hand loosens on the blanket, fingers uncurling like they've forgotten they were braced. She exhales, long and uneven, breath shuddering as her body recalibrates around the fact that nothing is coming for her now.

She stops again.

Close enough that Rowan can see the moisture gathering in her eyes.

Not panic.

Relief—arriving late, unsure whether it's allowed.

"I didn't think it would feel like this," she says quietly.

Rowan doesn't ask how.

He just nods. "I know."

Her throat works. She swallows hard, and the tears spill—not violently, not all at once—but in slow, silent tracks down her cheeks, like something finally allowed to leak.

She doesn't wipe them away.

She steps forward again.

This time, when she stops, her forehead rests against his chest.

Not an embrace.

Contact.

Rowan doesn't move.

He doesn't wrap his arms around her yet. He lets her set the terms of gravity.

Her breath hitches once more, sharper this time, and her hands—uncertain at first—find the front of his coat, fingers curling into fabric the way they did in sleep.

That's when Rowan moves.

Carefully.

His arms come around her—not tight, not enclosing—just enough to say you're held. His hand settles between her shoulder blades, steady and warm.

Isorae exhales into him, the sound breaking now, grief and relief tangling together in a way that doesn't need sorting yet. Her body leans fully into his, weight given over in increments, like she's testing whether the ground will stay solid if she lets go.

It does.

She cries then—not hard, not loud—but thoroughly, tears soaking into his shirt as her face presses into the place she knows by heart.

Rowan lowers his chin to the crown of her head.

He doesn't speak.

He just holds.

The rain continues to fall around them, quiet and ordinary. The land hums low beneath their feet—not closing, not watching.

Continuing.

And in the middle of it, Isorae stands in Rowan's arms—not healed, not finished—but no longer bracing for the next impact.

Relief, at last.

Not joy.

Not yet.

But real.

Evan steps forward carefully. "We should go inside," he says. "Warm. Food. Water."

Isorae doesn't answer at first.

Then she says, barely audible:

"Bones."

Rowan's breath catches.

"Stay in your bones," he says. "Just stay there."

The words hold.

She turns toward the cabin.

Evan matches her pace.

Erin follows.

Dax and Silas move without discussion.

Rowan stays in the yard one beat longer.

Rain on his face.

Mud under his boots.

Stonewake humming low beneath it all—not celebrating. Not watching.

Continuing.

He looks at the tree line.

At the places that used to hide things.

Stonewake does not speak.

But Rowan feels the truth of it anyway:

The land remembers.

And memory is not the same as fixation.

He turns and follows them inside.

Not to fix.

Not to claim.

Not to erase.

To stay.

Because love does not undo harm.

It just refuses to abandon the harmed.

And for now—that is enough to keep her alive long enough to matter.

70
Muscle Memory

Stonewake comes back the way muscle memory does—uneven, stubborn, unmistakable.

The morning bell rings again without announcement. Someone missed the sound enough to bring it back. Children drift toward the stream under watchful eyes, then fewer eyes, then none at all. The fire circle is rebuilt not as a symbol, but as a place to sit and argue and pass food.

Normal returns sideways.

Nora's voice carries across the clearing one afternoon as she argues with Parker about load-bearing ratios. Parker insists it's fine. Nora insists she's wrong. Jalen listens for half a minute and reinforces the beam anyway. Sera pretends not to smile. Maelin reorganizes storage twice in one week and claims it was always meant to be that way.

Dax moves through it all like ballast—quietly steadying conversations before they tip. Erin no longer measures first; she listens, sensing where the land tightens, where it loosens, where it exhales.

Bramble resumes his patrols like nothing happened.

He is everywhere—blocking doorways, nudging calves, thumping his tail against cabin walls. When Isorae sits near the fire, he stations himself at her feet, broad head resting against her shin, eyes tracking the clearing with the patience of something that understands guardianship as instinct, not duty.

Isorae is present.

Not constantly. Not performatively. But here.

She speaks when she wants to. She eats because she's hungry now, not because someone reminds her. Some nights she stays by the fire until the last embers dim. Some nights she leaves early without explanation.

No one asks.

Rowan stays close without hovering. He no longer moves like a man afraid of breaking glass. He moves like someone who trusts the strength of what's already mended. When she flinches, he notices. When she doesn't, he doesn't invent it.

At night, sleep still comes in fragments—but they are shared fragments now, bodies familiar again, breathing syncing without effort.

Weeks pass.

Not cleanly.

But forward.

One evening, after the fire has burned down to coals and conversation has softened into murmurs, Isorae stands and looks at Rowan.

"Come with me," she says.

Not a question.

Inside the cabin, lamplight pools low and warm. Isorae closes the door behind them and leans back against it for a moment, palm flat to the wood—grounding herself, steady, deliberate. Rowan doesn't rush. He watches her the way you watch weather when you know it's about to break.

She meets his gaze, chin lifting slightly.

"I don't want careful tonight," she says.

"I want real."

Something hot loosens in Rowan's chest—relief braided with want.

"Show me," he says quietly.

She does.

She steps into him and kisses him hard—mouth sure, teeth grazing his lower lip like a dare. His hands come up instantly, confident, settling at her hips like they've been waiting there. She makes a low sound against his mouth, approving, and he answers it without restraint.

Her back hits the door again—harder this time—and the sound punches a gasp out of her before she can stop it. Rowan's body is right there, crowding her space, heat and weight and pressure pinning sensation into her skin until there's nowhere left for it to go but through her.

His forearm braces beside her head, trapping her in the narrow space between wood and muscle, and his mouth claims her throat like he's starving for it—tongue, teeth, lips dragging slow, intentional lines that make her legs weaken instantly.

She arches into him, friction lighting up her nerves, hips grinding without permission from her brain.

"That's real," she breathes, voice already shredded. "God—that's real."

Rowan's answering sound is low and rough, something feral breaking loose as his teeth sink into her shoulder harder now, enough to make her cry out. Not pain. Presence. His hands slide down her sides, gripping, spreading heat everywhere he touches, and she grabs his shirt and yanks him closer, nails biting into skin like she needs to feel him now.

Clothes are gone—pushed, dragged, forgotten. Cool air hits her skin and she shivers, but the second his body presses fully against hers again, heat floods back in fast and overwhelming.

When he lifts her, she wraps her legs around his waist without thinking, ankles locking behind him like her body already knows where this is going. He carries her to the bed and drops her onto it with just enough force to knock the breath from her lungs before he's on her again, mouth everywhere, hands roaming like he's relearning every inch.

She's already wet—slick enough that when his fingers slide between her thighs, she gasps and arches hard, knees spreading instinctively as sensation spikes hot and urgent.

"Rowan—now," she begs, hips rolling helplessly against his hand.

He doesn't tease her.

He presses into her, slow at first, deep and deliberate, making her body open wider, wetter, until her breath breaks completely and she's clutching at the sheets, whimpering his name like she can't hold it inside anymore.

"Stay with me," he murmurs against her mouth, voice wrecked. "Right here."

She is.

Gods, she is.

When he pushes into her, it's deep and full, the stretch sharp enough to tear a cry from her throat as her hands fly to his shoulders. Rowan groans into her mouth as he sinks all the way in, holding still just long enough for her body to register everything—heat, pressure, the way he fills her completely.

She clenches around him without meaning to.

"Yes," she gasps, nails digging in. "Like that—don't stop—"

He doesn't.

He starts to move—harder now, deeper—each thrust driving sensation straight through her, knocking broken sounds out of her chest as the bed creaks beneath them. His hand slides under her thigh, lifting her just enough to change the angle, and the new depth makes her body lock tight around him.

Her cry is sharp and helpless.

"Fuck," he growls, mouth at her ear. "You feel so good."

Heat coils low and fast, pleasure stacking until she can't track individual sensations anymore—just pressure and friction and the sound of skin meeting skin, of his breath breaking as he drives into her again and again.

She meets him desperately, hips rocking, chasing the friction she needs, legs tightening around his waist as her body starts to tremble.

He slows deliberately.

Not to tease.

To feel her.

The drag of it is unbearable. Her breath fractures, sound tearing loose before she can catch it, hips jolting like her body refuses to be held back. Rowan feels every reaction—how she tightens, how heat floods, how her need sharpens fast enough to hurt.

"Rowan," she warns, voice stripped raw.

He doesn't answer with words.

He answers by holding her right there—by keeping the pace agonizingly slow, by letting sensation stretch until it turns thick and dizzying, until her body starts chasing friction without permission from her mind.

She shoves at his shoulder, impatient, breath coming undone.

"Move."

He lets her.

The shift is sudden, gravity flipping, control sliding sideways. He goes down willingly, hands catching her hips as she climbs over him, skin flushed and damp, mouth parted like she's already drowning in it.

She settles above him with intention.

Not hurried.

Not unsure.

Her body rolls once—slow, deep—and Rowan's breath punches out of him like he wasn't ready for it even though he absolutely was.

"Fuck," he snarls, hands tightening, thumbs digging in hard enough to anchor. "You're—"

She moves again, cutting him off, setting the rhythm herself now—deliberate, punishing, wet heat dragging him right to the brink and holding him there.

The sound she makes when it hits right is broken and unguarded, like her body doesn't know how to keep it inside anymore.

Everything is slick.

Bodies sliding. Heat everywhere. The bed rocking under them as she takes control and doesn't give it back.

Rowan's head tips back, teeth bared, breath wrecked as sensation stacks too high to parse—pressure and heat and the wet slide of motion that refuses to let up.

His hands flex uselessly for a second before gripping her harder, not to slow her—never to slow her—but to survive the way she's riding him like she means to undo him completely.

"Look at you," he growls, voice gone rough and dark. "You're wrecking me."

She leans down, mouth at his throat now, teeth scraping just enough to make him jerk.

"Good," she breathes.

And then she moves faster.

The pace turns relentless, overwhelming, her body demanding everything, sensation flooding until Rowan can't tell where it starts or ends—only that it's too much and not enough at the same time.

Her breath shatters.

His follows.

The world narrows to heat and friction and the wet, obscene sound of skin meeting skin, of her voice breaking into his shoulder, of his name dragged from her throat like she can't stop herself.

She starts to shake—tiny tremors at first, then harder—body riding right up to the edge and staying there, eyes bright and unfocused, mouth open as sensation overwhelms her completely.

Rowan snaps.

Not explosively.

Viscerally.

A broken sound tears out of him as he drags her down against him, holding her tight while release hits like a wave that doesn't stop crashing, his body shuddering under her as he loses all restraint.

She comes undone with him—cry ripped loose, body locking tight as pleasure pours through her, too much, consuming, leaving her gasping and shaking above him.

They collapse together, tangled, slick, breathing like they just barely survived something.

For a long moment, neither of them moves.

Then Rowan rolls them slowly onto their sides, still inside her space, still holding her close, hand heavy and possessive at her back.

No reassurance.

No words.

Just heat and breath and the aftershocks fading slow and deep.

She doesn't sleep right away—not because something's wrong, but because her body is still humming too loud to shut down. Every nerve feels overused, rubbed raw in the best way. There's a dull, satisfied ache between her thighs. Her pulse keeps jumping like it expects more.

She lets it.

Her cheek rests against his chest, skin slick and cooling where they're pressed together. She can feel his heartbeat, steady and strong, the rise and fall of him under her mouth. Her fingers drag lazily over his ribs, not searching, not checking—just touching because she wants to.

Rowan doesn't move.

Not restraint.

Possession.

He's loose now, heavy with it, the edge burned out of him and replaced by that slow, animal calm. His body knows it got exactly what it wanted. He feels her breathing even out, the way her weight settles instead of holding itself up. No tension. No hesitation. Just the quiet certainty of being done and satisfied.

Her leg hooks over his hip, claiming him without effort.

That's when she smiles.

Satisfied. Real.

She stays awake a little longer, drifting in and out, riding the last ripples as they fade. Every time she almost slips under, sensation tugs her back—the warmth of him, the ache, the smell of skin and sweat and sex still thick in the room.

Eventually, sleep takes her sideways.

Not collapsing.

Not retreating.

Just easing in, breath deep and even, body loose and unguarded against his.

Rowan feels it when she goes fully still. He doesn't mark the moment. Doesn't adjust. Just lets himself sink too, muscles finally letting go now that there's nothing left to take or give.

Outside, Bramble's familiar weight presses against the door, solid and unbothered. Stonewake hums low and steady around them, not watching, not warning.

Just existing.

Not healed.

Not untouched. But fully alive.

71
SPENT

The cabin Dax and Erin use sits farther east, tucked into the trees where the land still hums quietly instead of shouting.

It's late enough that the night has settled into itself.

No alarms.

No recalibration spikes.

No Erin pacing with her tablet like the world might fall apart if she blinks.

The cabin is quiet in a way that feels earned.

Not calm.

Spent.

Erin didn't mean to fall asleep.

Dax knows that the moment he sees the tablet beside her hand, screen dimmed but still warm, data half-frozen like she planned to check it again in just a minute. She's sprawled face-down on the bed, nightshirt pushed high, one knee drawn up, back arched in an unconscious offering she would never allow herself while awake.

She looks emptied out.

And open.

Dax stops in the doorway, towel hanging low on his hips, water still tracking down his chest, and feels it hit hard and fast — heat, possession, a low pull in his gut that doesn't ask permission.

He closes the distance and sits heavily on the edge of the bed.

His hand lands on her hip — firm, claiming — sliding his fingers between her thighs, digging in just enough to wake her without mercy. Erin makes a soft, broken sound into the mattress, breath hitching before her eyes even open.

She knows that touch.

Her body reacts immediately — hips shifting, back arching, breath going shallow.

Dax leans in, mouth at her ear. "Stay."

It's not a question.

She nods once, barely there, but deliberate. Her body sinks back into the mattress instead of rolling away.

His weight comes down behind her, heavy and sure, pinning sensation into her until there's nowhere left for it to go but through her. His hand slides again, rougher now, fingers pressing in like he's testing how much she can take.

Erin exhales sharply, fingers clawing into the sheets.

"Dax," she breathes — wrecked with sleep and need.

He answers by biting her shoulder hard enough to make her gasp. Not enough to hurt. Enough to mark. She arches reflexively, pushing back into him like her body already knows what comes next.

He grips her hip and stills her.

Not cruel.

Absolute.

"Don't move," he says low.

The words land hot and heavy.

She freezes for half a breath — then melts, thighs tightening, breath breaking apart as she sinks deeper into the mattress.

"Okay," she whispers.

That single word tightens something sharp and dangerous in his chest.

He presses in slow and relentless, drawing it out until she's rocking back without thinking, mouth open, sound spilling out unchecked. Her body stays open, receptive, awake in the way that matters.

Nothing gentle.

Nothing careful.

Just friction and heat and the familiar edge of being held exactly where she wants to be held.

She reaches back for him, fingers grabbing his wrist like she needs proof. He gives it to her — grip tightening.

"You always do this," she pants. "Act like you own the space."

"And you always give it to me," he growls.

He shifts then — just enough to change the pressure — and the reaction is instant. Erin cries out, body locking tight, sound breaking loose like she didn't see it coming.

"Fuck—Dax—"

He thrusts again, harder now, rhythm set and unyielding, letting momentum take over where thought has no place. The bed creaks under the force of it. Her breathing shatters into sharp, helpless sounds as she pushes back harder, meeting every drive without hesitation.

He leans down, mouth brushing her shoulder, his weight increasing until she feels contained—like the space around her has narrowed to nothing but heat and pressure and his body pressing her deeper into the bed.

"Don't run from it," he says quietly. "Let it hit."

Her body listens before her mind can object.

The tension coils tight—too tight—until her breath starts coming apart completely. Each inhale is a struggle, each exhale a shudder, her lungs burning as sensation stacks faster than she can process.

She trembles.

"Oh—fuck—" The word fractures into breath as her body locks, muscles clenching hard enough that it borders on panic.

Dax feels it immediately.

He doesn't stop. He holds her there.

Right on the edge.

His grip firms, steady and relentless, keeping her suspended in that unbearable place where everything is too loud—heat, breath, pressure, awareness screaming all at once.

She gasps, dragging air back in, chest heaving like she's fighting gravity itself. Her fingers claw at the sheets, knuckles white, every nerve lit so bright it feels like she might shatter.

"Dax—" Her voice breaks. "I— I can't—"

"Yes," he murmurs, voice low and grounding, right against her ear. "You can."

The words land like an anchor.

Her breath hitches again, then comes rushing back in a harsh, shaky pull. Her body gives—yielding—letting sensation flood through instead of bracing against it.

The release hits her hard.

Not all at once.

In waves.

Her body shudders, breath tearing free in helpless sounds as the tension finally snaps, muscles shaking, awareness narrowing to nothing but heat and pressure and the sound of her own breathing coming undone.

She rides it there—hovering, wrecked, gasping—until her strength drains and she sags into the mattress, lungs dragging air back in like she's just surfaced.

Dax stays right where he is.

Heavy.

Present.

Her breath slowly finds a rhythm again—ragged at first, then deeper, steadier—until the shaking fades into a low, spent warmth spreading through her.

She presses back into him without thinking, chasing the weight, the containment.

He exhales once, slow and controlled, chest rising against her back.

"Good girl," he growls.

She's fully awake now.

Fully inside herself.

By the time it slows, she's loose and spent, tension burned clean out of her muscles. Dax doesn't pull away. He stays heavy behind her, arm locking around her waist, holding her exactly where he left her while the aftershocks roll through slow enough to hurt.

Erin shifts back into him automatically.

No thought.

No request.

He adjusts without thinking, anchoring her there with the quiet certainty of someone who has never planned to leave.

Outside, Stonewake hums — no longer braced, not asleep.

Just holding.

For tonight, that's enough. And so are they.

72

IN THE SPACES BETWEEN

The night does not end all at once.

Stonewake exhales in layers.

Doors close. Lamps dim. Inside one of the cabins, Ryan sits on the edge of the table, boots dangling, watching Evan rinse his hands at the basin.

"You're still counting," Ryan says.

Evan doesn't look up. "Habit."

"You don't have to," Ryan replies gently.

Evan shuts off the water and dries his hands, slower than necessary. He turns, leans back against the counter, and studies Ryan the way he always does when he's deciding whether to argue or concede.

"I know," he says. "But it helps."

Ryan nods. He understands that kind of help.

He hops down from the table and steps closer, slipping into Evan's space without ceremony. No tension. No question. Just the quiet alignment of two people who learned, a long time ago, how to be near each other without asking permission.

"You were good today," Ryan says.

Evan snorts. "I was adequate."

Ryan smiles. "You were kind. That's harder."

That earns him a look—softened at the edges, tired but real. Evan reaches out, fingers brushing Ryan's wrist, thumb resting against his pulse like he's checking it out of reflex.

"Go to bed," Evan says. "I'll be there in a minute."

Ryan leans in and kisses him—not urgent, not heated—just warm, familiar, grounding. "Don't take too long."

Evan watches him go, something steady and grateful settling into his chest.

Outside, the land hums.

It isn't loud about it.

It doesn't need to be.

The paths between cabins are dark but familiar, worn smooth by years of feet that know where they're going without light. Doors close softly across the clearing, one by one — not in retreat, but in rest. Somewhere to the east, laughter fades behind timber walls. To the west, a lamp is extinguished with a quiet click.

Stonewake settles into its separate rooms, its many small hearths, its people folding back into their own spaces.

Sleep comes the way it does when nothing is chasing it.

Uneven at first. Then deeper.

The cabins cool. The fires burn down to coals.

Somewhere in the night, Rowan shifts and Isorae shifts with him, bodies finding the same shape without waking fully. Breath syncs. The world holds.

The next morning seeps in.

Rowan feels Isorae before he sees her.

Not the pull—not the old, sharp awareness—but the simple presence of her moving through the cabin, bare feet against the floor, breath even, glow quiet and warm instead of guarded. Dawn light threads pale gold through the window, touching the edge of her shoulder, the line of her spine.

She stands at the window for a moment, watching the valley soften into morning.

"Everyone's still asleep," she says.

Rowan hums softly. "Good."

She turns then, the corner of her mouth lifting. "You didn't."

"Didn't feel like it."

That's enough.

She crosses the room without hesitation and climbs into his lap, knees bracketing his hips, hands settling on his shoulders like muscle memory. There's no carefulness in it. No testing.

Just choice.

He rests his forehead briefly against her collarbone. "How do you feel?"

She considers — actually considers — then nods. "Here."

He kisses her slowly, deeply, hands sliding up her back, fingers spreading wide, grounding without trying to fix anything. She kisses him back just as deliberately, shifting closer, heat familiar and unafraid.

"There you are," he murmurs, more observation than relief.

She smiles against his mouth. "Yeah."

They don't rush.

They don't need to.

It's not hunger this time—it's continuation. Warmth building the way it does when no one is braced for loss. When she settles more fully against him, he lets his hands roam without restraint, thumbs brushing skin that no longer flinches, mouth trailing where she leans into it.

"I like when you let me," she says quietly.

He exhales a laugh against her throat, hands tightening at her waist. "I like when you take."

They stay like that a while—kissing, touching, drifting—until the morning grows louder outside. Footsteps. A door opening. A voice carrying across the clearing.

Eventually, she curls against him again, warm and heavy and undeniably here. His arm wraps around her automatically, thumb tracing lazy circles against her hip.

Outside, Stonewake wakes.

Inside, people breathe.

Love does not erase what was done.

But it fills the space around it.

73
WHAT REMAINS

Months later, Stonewake is louder. Not in the way storms are loud. Not in the way grief once was.

In the ordinary way—voices overlapping, tools clinking, children arguing about rules that have never existed and never will.

Morning comes clean now. Not cautious. Not testing the threshold.

Smoke lifts from several chimneys at once, thin and blue against a sky that has learned how to stay open. Someone has planted winter greens where the soil burned itself sterile; they've taken, stubborn and alive. The stream runs where it always did, but the banks have been reinforced by hands that remember what happens when the land is pushed too hard.

Stonewake remembers too.

It remembers without flinching.

The fire circle is busy by midmorning. A pot simmers. Someone laughs too loudly. Nora is correcting Parker again, this time about grain storage instead of beams. Jalen pretends not to listen and fixes it anyway. Sera sits cross-legged on a stone, sharpening a blade that doesn't need it, talking to Maelin about nothing and everything.

Children run through the clearing with Bramble lumbering after them, tail a weapon of mass destruction, delighted by the chaos. He lets one small hand grab his ear. He endures it with saintly patience.

Dax and Erin cross paths near the tool shed and don't slow down—just a brush of fingers, a look exchanged like a shared joke. Later, they'll spar. Later, they'll fuck. Later still, Erin will sit barefoot on the steps and listen to the land until Dax brings her tea and pretends not to know why she went quiet.

Ryan and Evan emerge from their cabin arguing amiably about inventory. Evan is holding a clipboard. Ryan steals it, reads nothing, hands it back upside down. Evan rolls his eyes and kisses him anyway before remembering there are witnesses and pretending he meant to check a pulse instead.

Life has edges again. Not fractures.

Rowan watches all of it from the edge of the clearing, hands wrapped around a mug that's gone cold. He looks older—not worn, but settled into himself in a way that doesn't ask permission. The bridge inside him is different now. Narrower. Stronger. It doesn't reach the way it once did.

It doesn't have to.

He feels Isorae before he sees her.

She's coming down the path from the eastern ridge, hair loose, sleeves rolled up, dirt on her palms. She walks alone these days because she wants to, not because she has something to prove. Some mornings she still turns back halfway. Some mornings she finishes the circuit and sits with the land until her breath matches the world again.

Today, she comes all the way back smiling.

Not bright. Not performative. Real.

She takes the mug from his hands without asking and drinks, grimacing at the temperature.

"You're supposed to tell me when it gets cold," she says.

"You're supposed to let me keep things," he replies.

She snorts and hands it back.

Someone calls her name. Sera, waving her over to look at something half-built and probably unnecessary. Isorae hesitates only a second before going.

There are places near the outer perimeter where nothing grows yet. Scars, not wounds. No one avoids them. No one tries to fix them all at once. Children have been known to sit there and ask questions adults don't rush to answer.

Graham is not spoken of.

Not because he's forgotten.

Because Stonewake does not give names to things it has already finished with.

As afternoon turns toward evening, the fire is lit again—not because it's needed, but because someone wanted it. Food is passed. Stories grow taller. Laughter loosens into something unguarded.

Isorae returns to Rowan's side when the sky starts to bruise purple. She leans into him, solid, warm, present.

"You okay?" he asks.

She considers it. Then nods. "I am today."

He doesn't ask about tomorrow.

The bell rings at dusk. Someone remembered. Someone always will.

Stonewake settles—not into silence, but into rhythm. Doors close. Lights dim. Lives fold inward without disappearing.

Rowan and Isorae walk home together. Not careful. Not rushed.

Behind them, the village breathes.

Ahead of them, the night opens.

The land keeps what matters.

Not innocence.

Not perfection.

Survival, shared.

And the quiet, stubborn knowledge that love didn't undo the harm— but it made a life afterward possible.

That is what remains.

And for Stonewake—it is enough.

A system that requires silence to function has already failed.
Collapse is not an accident. It is an outcome.

AFTERWORD

This story does not end where the danger stops.

That is intentional.

Stories about harm often rush toward resolution—as if survival alone is proof of healing, as if love or courage or justice can rewind what was done. They cannot. And pretending otherwise only creates a second injury: the demand that the survivor perform recovery on someone else's schedule.

Isorae survives.

Rowan pays a cost.

The land remembers.

None of those truths cancel the others.

What happens to Isorae is not a metaphor. It is not a test she passes or fails. It is an experience that alters the shape of her inner world, her access to herself, and the terms under which safety can exist again. Dissociation is not weakness. It is not surrender. It is a precision instrument the nervous system deploys when no other option remains.

It kept her alive.

And it does not disappear just because the threat is gone.

Rowan's arc is not one of triumph. It is one of consent—learning when not to reach, not to pull, not to demand presence simply because absence is painful to witness. Love, here, is not a force that fixes. It is a discipline that stays.

Stonewake does not return to innocence. It returns to rhythm. That matters. Communities that survive harm do not do so by erasing what happened, but by refusing to let it define every future moment. The land holds what occurred without dramatizing it, without forgiving it, without forgetting.

Graham does not receive redemption. Systems like his do not fail because they are evil; they fail because they require silence, compliance, and extraction to function. When a system cannot tolerate refusal—when it punishes autonomy instead of adapting—it collapses under its own rigidity.

That collapse is not victory.

It is consequence.

If this book leaves you unsettled, that is not a flaw. Some stories are meant to close cleanly. Others are meant to stay with you, to resist being neatly shelved, to remind you that survival is not an aesthetic and recovery is not linear.

If you recognized yourself in Isorae's withdrawal, her quiet endurance, or her shame at finding relief in distance—know this: your nervous system is not betraying you. It is protecting what matters most. Returning to yourself is not a demand you owe anyone. It is a process that unfolds on your terms, in your time, with whatever support feels safe enough to allow it.

If you recognized yourself in Rowan—aching to help, desperate to fix, learning too late that presence is sometimes the only ethical act—you are not failing. You are learning restraint in a world that celebrates intervention without asking whom it costs.

This book does not offer closure.

It offers continuation.

A life afterward.

That is not a lesser ending.

It is the only honest one.

Thank you for reading.

— V. Charles

ACKNOWLEDGEMENTS

This book exists because certain people understood how to stay.

Not to fix.

Not to rush.

Not to demand progress where there was only endurance.

To those who offered steadiness instead of solutions—who listened without correcting, who showed up without asking to be needed, who trusted silence as much as words—thank you. You helped shape the ethical spine of this story more than you know.

To the readers who follow these characters into difficult places without looking away: this book trusts you with its quietest truths. Thank you for holding them with care.

To those who live with the long aftermath of harm—who understand dissociation, fragmentation, and the strange relief of survival strategies that don't look heroic from the outside—this story was written with you in mind. Your resilience is not performative. It does not owe anyone beauty.

To the friends who kept the world functioning in small, necessary ways while this book was being written—meals made, messages sent, patience extended—your labor mattered.

To the stories, thinkers, and voices that taught me that love is a discipline, consent is a structure, and survival is not a moral failing: I carry those lessons forward.

And finally, to the land—real and imagined—that holds memory without demanding explanation, that survives harm without losing its capacity to shelter: thank you for teaching me that healing is not erasure.

This book was not written alone.

It was held into being.

ABOUT THE AUTHOR

Victoria E. Charles is a writer and visual artist whose work lives at thresholds—between worlds, between selves, and between what survives intact and what returns altered.

Her debut novel, The Resonance Breach, introduced a living landscape shaped by relationship, consent, and consequence. This book remains inside that terrain, asking what endurance looks like after fracture, and what it costs to stay present when survival becomes ongoing rather than resolved. Her writing is shaped by a long-standing fascination with mythic structures, liminality, and consent as an ethical force—not as an abstraction, but as something enforced, violated, withdrawn, and reclaimed through consequence.

Rather than offering redemption arcs or clean resolutions, her work attends to aftermaths: dissociation, endurance, relational gravity, and the discipline required to remain when harm has already occurred. Love, in these stories, is not a cure or a spectacle—it is a practice. A weight. A choice that leaves marks.

Alongside her fiction, Victoria is an accomplished painter working primarily in large-scale symbolic and abstract forms inspired by ancient iconography, sacred geometry, and natural systems. Her visual and written work share a common language of containment, fracture, and resonance, often approaching the same questions from different angles.

She lives in the southern United States with her teenage daughter, a dog, and a cat, and keeps a largely solitary life shaped by land, routine, and attention. Her days are oriented around creative work, long walks outdoors, meditation, and practices that tend the nervous system as much as the intellect.

Deeply interested in consciousness, ancient history, and esoteric knowledge, she studies myth not as metaphor alone but as a form of inherited intelligence—particularly where it intersects with pre-flood civilizations, nonhuman entities, and older models of relationship between people, land, and power. Her spirituality is experiential rather than institutional, rooted in direct practice, ancestral memory, and personal sovereignty rather than organized religion or authority.

She writes essays on Medium alongside her fiction and painting, often exploring similar questions through different forms: how meaning survives fracture, how systems reveal themselves under pressure, and how care—of body, mind, and environment—becomes an act of resistance. She prefers quiet, nature, and walking barefoot when the weather allows, and believes that what persists without needing to perform its healing often carries the deepest intelligence.

www.ingramcontent.com/pod-product-compliance
Lightning Source LLC
Chambersburg PA
CBHW070553310726
48982CB00011B/1573/J

* 9 7 9 8 9 9 4 5 1 0 9 1 9 *